Published by Makin Books Publishing
Copyright ©2016 Bruce Henderson

ISBN 13: 978-1-945663-08-6

WHITE PAGES

BRUCE HENDERSON

To: Josh + Michael

Bruce S. Henderson

CHAPTER ONE

William Stradom, walked down the hallway. Just as he entered his office, Samantha Hawks, his petite secretary, who had a worried look on her face, called to him, "Sir this thing with the police has begun to escalate, that Sergeant at the police station now has got the FBI involved. They also are calling now. I think you need to make some type of contact with at least the guy from the FBI. Anyway, I left the recording of his latest message in your office. They have given you a deadline of 3:00 o'clock today to respond to them, that's about 20 minutes from now."

William turned with his thick fingers grasping the small cup in his hand and wire frame glasses slightly pulled down, with his soft spoken voice and said, "thank you Samantha, even after twenty years, you are still looking after me. This happens every so often. It is nothing to worry about." He turned and walked to the answering machine in his office and turned it on.

"Mr. Stradom, this is Special Agent Tom Plaiedeaux with the FBI, I work with a special unit of the FBI, I am not at liberty to share the details at this time, however, over the last several months we have repeatedly tried to contact you about a simple matter of you coming down to the office to answer a few questions. You have left us no alternative, but to launch an investigation into your activities, since you have been unwilling to cooperate. Based on what we have found out you have been living off the grid for about twenty-five years. You do not have any visible means of income, you attempt to remain veiled, yet you file a tax return and pay millions of dollars in taxes every year. If you are paying taxes on illegal income, you will not gain leniency from the courts because you pay taxes. I will have to admit I have never encountered someone engaged in criminal activities who pays taxes on them. People who live with this much secrecy usually have something to hide. You have until 3:00 o'clock Friday September 18, 2009 to contact us and arrange a meeting immediately, or we will be serving search and arrest warrants at 3:01."

William walked over to the window and looked out. He turned and walked to the door and closed it, then went to his desk and picked up the phone. "May I speak to Special Agent Plaiedeaux please?"

"This is he that you are speaking to."

"I am William Stradom. I understand that you have been trying to get in touch with me. I am a very busy man and I don't have a lot of time to waste. I understand that your agency trains you to posture yourself in a way that it appears you are always in authority and in control. However, these are unusual circumstances. I would like to invite you to come into my home, where we can sit down and talk. I will be at the front door in about twenty minutes."

"Mr. Stradom, things have progressed well beyond this petty posturing. You have about three minutes to walk out your door and surrender, or else we are coming in by force."

"Special Agent Plaiedeaux, there are reasons why I live my life the way that I do. However, all of your training tells you that something is wrong, which I know I will not be able to overcome quickly. There is something wrong, but it is not even close to what you are thinking. You really do not want to proceed by force, there are things that I can't explain, things you and your team are not going to understand. I know you have my office number, however, you can't trace this number that I am calling you from, let me give it to you, if you insist on going ahead with your plans, here's the number you can reach me at today only."

"Mr. Stradom, do you think this is some sort of game? We are the Federal Bureau of Investigations, and we have resources that no one else in the world has. If we want to serve you a warrant and arrest you, there is nothing you can do to stop us. We have all of your escape routes covered, and we have surrounded your house."

"Mr. Plaiedeaux, obviously you have made up your mind. The number I gave you will be good until 9 o'clock tonight. I looked into your background, and found that you have a very good record. My invitation stands for you only until 9 o'clock. I'm going to hang up now. Mr. Plaiedeaux. I will talk to you in a little while."

Just as he hung up, he reached into his drawer and pulled out his portable video surveillance monitor. He looked closely at the monitor as he saw the FBI began to move toward his house. "Samantha," he called, "What is on the remainder of my calendar for the rest of the afternoon?"

She replied by describing several short critical meetings. "Did you call," she asked.

"Yes, I did," he said. "Let's continue with the meetings. The FBI agent will call me later and we will get together. Do not concern yourself with this."

Special agent Plaiedeaux ordered his team to proceed with serving

the warrant and arresting Stradom. Over the hand held radio, he said, "everyone move in."

The team was compiled of 17 members. All wore armor, and were fully armed. One Team drove an all-terrain assault vehicle, which was used to batter down gates, doors, and walls that they could not get into any other way. Another team drove a utility Van, which was equipped with all of the latest technology, used to monitor, and help break into computer systems, and various technologies. It also carried a variety of heavy-duty weapons, designed to at least match, but mostly overpower the weaponry of any assailant. Mr. Stradom's property was set on about a 9-acre lot, with an electric gated entryway and security cameras. The FBI Standard Operating Procedure was to cut the power, and then move in. As the order was given, the electrical power was turned off. When Special Agent Plaiedeaux turned and looked at the gate and grounds, he could not see any notable changes that showed that the power was off. He reconfirmed, that the power had been shut off.

Agent Jones moved forward to test the fence, to see if it was safe to touch. "It's okay to move forward", he said.

They decided to break through the front gate, so they moved over, and put some chains around the gate and latched the chains to the assault vehicle. They motioned for the driver to tear down the gate. As he put the vehicle in gear, he backed up to pull the gate down. As the chain tightened, it broke from the strain that was put on it. Special Agent Plaiedeaux was frustrated, and said, someone get a real chain in here. The utility vehicle had a much heavier chain, but it took four men to carry it. They hooked it up to the fence and to the assault vehicle. They tried again to tear the fence down, including at one point hooking the chain up to several vehicles and trying them all at the same time, the smell of burning rubber was strong, as the vehicles spun their tires while trying to pull down the gate. The chain didn't break, and there was no visible damage to the gate. Okay, Okay, said Agent Plaiedeaux. Enough of this bring the torch over here and cut the gate down. By the time that they were set up they had been trying to get in for over an hour.

The welder motioned to special agent Plaiedeaux that he was ready. "Proceed," he said.

The welder lit up the torch setting it to its hottest temperature and approached the gate. He began to try to cut the hinges, so that the gate would fall to the ground.

He turned to Agent Plaiedeaux and said, "Sir it's working. One of the hinges is completely gone. I have about 11 more; there are six on each gate."

It took him about ten minutes to cut the first hinge. Special agent Plaiedeaux replied, "Let's just do one side. The one gate itself is wide enough to where we can get everything in with just one side opened. One of the Agents made a suggestion to Agent Jones and he approached Special Agent Plaiedeaux with it. "Tom, why don't we climb the fence? If we do that this could be over quickly."

"We might have to do that, but let's just wait and see what happens. He should be done in a little bit." As the welder completed his last hinge, he thought about something. How could I have cut all of the hinges on one side, and the rest of the hinges did not feel the stress of the shifting weight? After finishing the last hinge, he could clearly see that the hinges were cut and that there was nothing holding the gate in place. Although, the gate still hung there as if the hinges were still in place. He reached over to try and see if he could move the gate that seemed to be suspended in mid-air, but he couldn't. He turned to special agent Plaiedeaux and said, "I don't know. I'm done, and you can see that the gate is severed from the hinges, but it's still is not moving."

Special agent Plaiedeaux went over and examined the gate. He could see clearly that the fence appeared to be suspended in mid-air. He turned around. Put all of the chains on this one gate, we're going to pull it down. The chains were moved and they attempted to pull it down. Even though it seemed to be suspended in mid-air with nothing holding it, the gate would not move, and it showed no signs of damage. Take the AV and ram it, said special agent Plaiedeaux. The driver pulled back, and with a full head of steam, charged the gate, the AV rammed the gate, there was a loud thump like two tractor trailers colliding at high speed, but still the gate didn't move, and there were no visible signs of damage to the gate, but the AV's front end was smashed in about four inches. The welder began to scream at agent Plaiedeaux about what he was seeing at the gate.

"What is it?" Special agent Plaiedeaux asked.

"Look at the hinges on the gate." They turned to look at the hinges, all six of the hinges, were reattached to the gate, as if they had never been cut away.

"I have never seen anything like this in my life. What is this place?"

"Be quiet," said special agent Plaiedeaux. "Go check and see if they are made of metal, and tell me what kind of metal, they are

made out of."

The welder walked over to the gate and checked it. "I'm no metal expert beyond traditional metals, but it looks and feels like your everyday steel. The chains are larger in diameter than the bars in the gates. These gates should not be able to hold up under the pressure that we have put on them. Not to mention, whatever that was that just happened to the gate."

"Let's climb over the fence," said special agent Plaiedeaux. All the men said yes and charged the fence. The fence was made of all metal bars and appeared to be about eight feet tall. As one of the agents drove the utility van up to the fence, special agent Plaiedeaux climbed up on top of the truck, and reached to grab hold of the top of the fence, to step over it. However, when he reached out his hand to extend it past the fence, he touched what appeared to be an invisible obstruction. No matter where he touched, he could not reach beyond the fence. The rest of the agents climbed the fence only to run into the same obstruction. No one could climb over the fence.

"It feels cold and rigid like it has a metal surface sir, but we can't seem to get past it. Is there really such a thing as invisible metal?"

Immediately special agent Plaiedeaux picked up his radio and said, "this project has just become classified top security, you are to refer to protocol 51736.1C of the FBI codebook. This project is designated the name, Forced Entry. Bring the helicopter."

They were now over three hours into the siege, and still not having any success. The helicopter arrived with five agents aboard who were to be dropped in from above. As the helicopter moved over the property, special agent Plaiedeaux gave the order to drop the agents down from above. When the agents dropped the rope they were to repel down, they realized it had landed on the same invisible surface the other agents had encountered. The agents in the helicopter quickly decided it would be too dangerous to attempt to drop onto the invisible protective barrier and advised special agent Plaiedeaux they were aborting their breach attempt.

"Thank you. Give me a few minutes. I need to make a call." Special agent Plaiedeaux walked to his vehicle and entered it. He picked up his phone and dialed his supervisory special agents number. "Chief, I'm in over my head. Stradom offered to meet with me alone in his house, but I used SOP to try to convince him to come down to our office. He didn't refuse, but simply left his offer on the table. From my understanding our agency has had several close calls before but no one has ever actually made contact. He always has simply disappeared. Apparently this time it is different. He told me that I didn't really want to pursue serving the warrant by force, because there were things that my team and I wouldn't understand. I am not sure, but I don't think he was threatening us, he was just stating a fact. Between you and me, he was right; I don't understand what happened here. I know the SOP in this situation, not to talk about it. This project has been declared classified, using protocol 51736.1C. Honestly, we are not going to get into his place on our terms. He gave me a phone number that is good until 9:00PM. After that he disappears again behind his wall of secrecy. So, do I give in and meet with him?"

"Yes, meet with him!"

"Thank you Chief. I'll pull everyone back." He hung up the phone and returned to the scene.

Chapter Two

"Everyone, pull back, it's a scrub for this one," said special agent Plaiedeaux.

"Sir, we can get in there, we just need a little more time," said agent Jones.

"That's okay, there will be other opportunities, let's shut it down, no one talks to the media."

After his team and everything was cleared out, special agent Plaiedeaux picked up the phone and called William Stradom, "Hello Mr. Stradom, I'd like to meet with you now."

"Okay, let me give you a one-time code, so that you can get in the gate. You walk up to the pad, and if you reach toward the top of the pad, you will find a lid that you can lift up and it will fall down over the keypad. Once you do that, you just simply have to knock three times on the pad just like you are knocking on a door, and the gate will open and close behind you. Just so that you are aware, an alarm will go off and block you from proceeding forward if more than one person tries to enter the gate. Also, once you enter the gate, your cell phone will not operate and no tracking or recording devices will operate."

"Thank you. I will be there in a few minutes."

After a three-minute phone call, Tom proceeded through the gate. After entering the gate, he paused briefly and seemed to labor to breathe. Coming from a somewhat wealthy upbringing, he had seen his share of manicured landscape, however, this was nothing like he had ever seen. All around him were exotic flowers, shrubbery, and trees that you could not see from outside the gate. For a moment he wanted to just spend some time looking around, but he came back to himself and proceeded to the house. When he reached the door it was opened up to his surprise by an elderly man, dressed to resemble a doorman at a hotel.

"Come on in agent Plaiedeaux, Mr. Stradom is waiting for you. Please follow me."

"Thank you."

After walking through the garden the expectations of what he was going to see inside were raised to a whole new level. Once he entered the house, he was not disappointed. From the artwork, to the furnishings, to the rugs and flooring, and the overall interior decorating, everything was immaculate. After walking down a long hallway they turned the corner and entered a large dining room with a large chandelier in the center of the room. As he stood there he looked at the formal dining room, with a dining table that seated twenty-four, and several choices of food and desserts. From across the room at another entrance, he noticed the door swing open and a man walked through while spraying from an aerosol can. He recognized the man from the old pictures that he had viewed, as being William Stradom.

"Good evening agent Plaiedeaux, I am happy to finally meet you. You don't know this, but I have been planning this for a long time, said William. Forgive me for the inconvenience, but I do have to have P.A.W.L. check you out. P.A.W.L. come forward now and scan agent Plaiedeaux."

Special agent Plaiedeaux looked around to see if he could find the person that Mr. Stradom was talking to. Out of the corner of his eye he noticed the wall begin to move. A square from the wall detached and moved toward him.

"Hello agent Plaiedeaux, I am P.A.W.L., and this will be painless. I will just scan you. Think of it as going through airport security." P.A.W.L. moved up and down slowly all around him. "He's clean, P.A.W.L.

said, but he is wired and carrying two guns. Do you want me to seize them?"

"No P.A.W.L., just disable them for now."

"You're telling me; you can disable my guns. I'm not giving them to you."

"Their both disabled now sir." advised P.A.W.L.

"It's okay Tom, I'm sure you didn't come here to spend the night discussing tech toys. P.A.W.L. you can stand down now."

"Thank you sir," P.A.W.L. replied. P.A.W.L. returned back to the wall and reinserted itself in the wall.

"You can't even tell that it's in the wall. Okay William, you have some interesting toys and you carry your age well. When was the last time someone saw you face to face other than your servants? Nobody in their right mind would want to meet up with the FBI, especially in these circumstances. That was a nice trick you pulled on us. What would stop me from arresting you right now? You make it seem like you are a king or something and that you are above all of us little people."

"First of all, I know you expected to see bodyguards and a variety of sophisticated security technology so that you can describe it to your people. As I told you before I am very familiar with how you were trained. I am also familiar with your whole life. However, we have two choices, we can either spend the night wasting a lot of energy on hostility or we can spend the night talking like men and discuss why we are here at this point and time in our lives." William adjusted himself and leaned back in his chair. With a wry smile he stated, "By the way you can arrest me only when I allow you to."

Both of them laughed.

"Before we go forward, who lives like this? That little trick amounted to more sophisticated security than Fort Knox."

"I anticipated you'd ask about my security. The technology for the gate is called Transightal Security. I've just told you something that no one else in the world has heard of yet. Even my employees have never heard the term. One day I will describe it to you. If you look it up now you will not be able to find anything about it. As we both discussed in our first conversation, we both have things that we will have to discover about each other. Now, I waited for you so that we could have dinner. I know that you have worked up an appetite. So how about we sit down and have some dinner."

"How does this work anyway?"

"I don't normally have guests serve themselves, but I thought I might dispense with the formalities for the sake of privacy. Now,

would you tell me what you think intelligent means?"

"Is this some sort of game show? I'm not a game show contestant."

"Humor me a little. You are not breaking any laws."

Tom kind of frowned and squirmed in his seat. He took a deep breath and said, "It has to do with how much knowledge and education you have."

"I thought you might say that. So what you're saying is that you cannot demonstrate intelligence unless you have a formal education. I would like to share a secret with you that you will understand one day, but not today. Intelligence is actually a gift, whether or not you are educated has nothing to do with it. This secret has been shared for hundreds of years.

"You are right; it doesn't resonate as a significant revelation."

"Why don't we sit down and eat. What you are about to taste is going to be like nothing you have ever tasted."

"Yeah, yeah. Let's get on with it. By the way did you really expect to get away with murdering your former business partner Everett Storky without any consequences?"

"Now we are getting somewhere. They both began to eat. I wondered if you were going to bring the subject up. You really are pretty gutsy to be sitting here in my house, considering that you consider me a murderer. First of all, I did not kill or have anyone kill Everett. If I truly had committed such a crime, I would have changed my name immediately when I went underground. The fact that you are sitting here today calling me William Stradom is a public proclamation that I am innocent of the suspected charge of murder."

"You didn't even blink once with your canned response. That tells me that you either have no remorse for what you have done or you consider that killing him was justified. There is no statute of limitations on murder."

"It is neither. I have full confidence that in the next few weeks I will be exonerated of these suspicions. I know that today those words will mean nothing to you, but it means a lot to me be able to clear the name of William Stradom"

"You talk like that is not your name. Just so you know we always get our man."

"That's not necessarily a true statement; however, I won't get into that right now. You will be happy in the end because justice will be served and the "man" that committed the murder of Everett will be caught. I appreciate you allowing this meeting to be civil. I know you have noticed the electronic pad in my hand. I don't mean to be rude, but I am in the middle of some significant business transactions, so from time to time you will see me typing on the pad. Timing is crucial. I will turn the floor over to you now."

"Well Mr. Stradom, we would like to know where you get your money?"

"That is a very generic question. How about this, tell me what other crime I am being accused of. Or better yet, what evidence do you have on me that would merit the FBI trying to storm my facilities."

"You fit the profile Mr. Stradom. 99.9% of the time when we look into people who try very hard to remain invisible, with incredible amounts of money at their disposal, with no discernable records of how they access it, 99.9% of the time they have ties to organized crime or something illegal. Most of them prove to be cocky and arrogant while thinking that their resources and mental acumen are far superior to the rest of us mere mortals. While I am curious about all of the security, it appears to me that perhaps the technology is a little different, but the script is the same. We are the FBI. For Americans who are law-abiding citizens we garner a level of respect and courtesy that evidently is beyond your understanding, we would not have to take enforcement action just to get a meeting, although there is more at stake than just a meeting. If our office requested a meeting with anyone in America who is a law-abiding citizen, this would be simple."

"I get what you are saying agent Plaiedeaux, and like I said things are not as they appear. However, everything will be revealed in time."

"Again, how do you make your money?"

"You haven't said anything about your meal. I'm pretty sure; you've not had anything like it. I just want you know; I mean no disrespect by meeting with you like this. I have the highest respect for you and our government. I know that you have been sent here to get answers, but at this time I will not be answering your question other than to say that what I do is legitimate. It will take time for us to get through this process of getting to know each other. While I offer verbal assurances that there is nothing illegal going on here, I realized that there is nothing I can say or do that will either deter or cause you to turn and go a different course from the one you are already on. I will be happy to meet with you again, if you have any other questions."

"The meal was good, just like you said."

"I'm glad you liked it. Don't get me wrong; I know the difference between a fishing expedition and an arrest. Would you do me a favor and drop the bill for this operation off at the mailbox outside the fence. The mailbox was installed for you to drop off things. It will not be used for anything else."

"So I gather any questions I ask tonight will not be answered. This has been enlightening. I'll save my remaining questions for later. This is the beginning of the end for you. So we are clear, I will report that you were cordial and uncooperative. If you expect the outcome of this little get together and its pleasantries is going to cause me to have second thoughts about me doing my job, you don't know me very well. Thanks for the meal."

"You can take some of the food with you if you want. Also, I'd like to give you this gift. It looks like a quarter, but it actually is a recording of our conversation. Lay it flat on the table and knock on it three times and it will replay our conversation. It will only replay the conversation 3 times. After that it will self-destruct. If it is tampered with or if the three times are not used within 30 days, it will self-destruct as well. Also, it cannot be scanned. It is programmed to only recognize your knock, so no one else can operate it. I'll have my man here see you out. Thank you for coming."

William watched as special agent Plaiedeaux and the servant walked toward the front door. He then turned and walked out of the dining room past several rooms to his Technology room. He reached for the keyboard on the desk and logged in to the Acoustiological Software and pressed update. As he looked at the screen, a message flashed on the screen, voice and physical DNA match acquired for special agent Tom Plaiedeaux.

As special agent Plaiedeaux walked out the gate he turned to look at what seemed to be the house he had just walked out of. He realized that what he was seeing from the street did not even come close to resembling what he saw inside the gate. He turned and began to walk toward his car as he flipped open his phone. "Chief, I just left the house after meeting with Stradom. There is a lot for me to report about what I saw and what he said. If we do it his way, we are going to date a while before we have our first kiss." Can we get together in the morning for our debriefing?

"Lets get together first thing in the morning", said his SSA.

"Okay, and by the way he gave me a recording of our complete conversation."

"He did what?"

"Yes sir, he gave me a recording of our whole conversation."

"Let's just talk in the morning."

"Yes, sir. I'm going to head home and get some sleep."

Perplexed with trying to make sense of the things he had seen in the last few hours, he was looking forward to some rest and some time to think. This has been one strange day, he thought. He put the food he brought with him in the refrigerator and went over to his desk to write some notes down before going to bed.

He was so exhausted that he fell asleep immediately. When his alarm went off he thought it was a mistake. He hurriedly dressed and ate so he could get to the office and prepare for the meeting with the Chief. As he entered the office, to his surprise his SSA was walking past the entry way.

"Good morning Chief."

"Good morning Tom. Let's get down to business."

"Okay sir. Who else is going to be in this meeting this morning? I'm sorry let me retract that question. I am not going to tell you how to run this office, but maybe I would like to suggest maybe you read my report and listen to what I have to say, and then decide how you want to proceed. There are some things I am going to tell you, that may need to be classified."

"I guess you think you found a big whale."

"Honestly, Chief, I spent the night wrestling with what happened yesterday, and I don't know what kind of whale I'm dealing with. If you were to put together what I have so for and give it a litmus test, then the answer to your question would be yes. However, this guy is way too smart."

"Okay, you and I will go in and review everything, I'll be recording our meeting to review later."

"Good idea Chief."

CHAPTER THREE

At the Headquarters of Outer World Technologies at their executive meeting, Slovin Bayne (Slovie) the lead scientist heading up the technology development division, which has produced over 75% of the income of the company for the last 25 years, is delivering a very somber speech regarding the state of affairs of new technology forecast for the company.

"President James I have worked here now for 32 years. We have had a remarkable run during these years. What I am about to say will come dangerously close to bringing up a sore subject, but it has to be said. The genesis for most of our technology is dated between 25 and 30 years ago. We have had today's meeting date in our sights for many years. Now that it has arrived, it is not a welcome day. The technology that we have developed has been so advanced and proprietary, that we have not been successful at partnering, outsourcing, integrating, reproducing, or modifying it to extend its useful life."

"Are you trying to tell me that even though we have made billions of dollars, with all the technology out there, for lack of better words, we can't beg, borrow, buy or steal ideas to keep this company going?" asked President James.

"Mr. James, sir, in front of me on the table and behind me in boxes are both summarized list and detailed files of individuals and companies we have pursued over the last 10 years in an effort to diversify, adopt or expand our technology footprint, and all of our efforts have proven to be in vain," said Robert Thompson (Vice President and Chief Financial Officer). "It's as if we have hit a stone wall."

"You guys are pissing me off. What am I paying you guys millions of dollars a year for? You are forcing my hand; this is not some sort of game. If I have to I will clean house by firing all of you, and introducing some new blood, with new ideas."

Slovie raised his hand to get their attention. "President James, I don't believe in making excuses. You don't have to fire me; I will happily resign. I am not the only one that will resign. I am not arrogant, nor do I believe that I am irreplaceable. As was stated earlier by Robert, we have tried to hire skilled people unsuccessfully. On this I will speak for myself alone. I will resign today or whichever day you choose for me to resign. I will make myself available however you choose to help my replacement transition into my job. I believe everyone is avoiding saying what needs to be said, so I am going to lay it out in plain English."

"Hold up Slovie" said Robert, "let's not go there."

"Robert" said Slovie, "I understand that keeping secrets are necessary, however I am not talking about the thing that you are talking about. I have been quiet about these things for a long time. For better or worse I am not going to leave this meeting tonight without putting some things on the table."

"Slovie, what are you talking about," asked President James,

"Mr. James, this isn't the time or place to get into all of this. Can we convene in a private session tomorrow to discuss all of this, so that when the information is presented, it is presented appropriately?" said Robert.

President James stood up and took a deep breath as he looked around the large executive conference room with its unique custom interior, after glancing at the 20-member executive committee, he turned and looked out the 16th story window and remembered the middle class upbringing including the words of his father who was always encouraging him. He remembered when he was twelve years old when he made a commitment that he would do whatever it takes to succeed. He came back to himself. "We grew this company over the years to be one of the most successful companies in the world. I am proud of this company. I say whatever we need to discuss we will do it here and now. Slovie, if you have something so say then say it now. But, before you speak, I want you to know what is at stake. If you only have fables, fairy tales, or unproven conjecture, then you have cost yourself your job. If what you have to say can't be proven or confirmed, you have cost yourself your job. Do you understand what I am saying to you?"

"I understand, Mr. President. First of all, I had no intention of bringing these things up. However, based on where we have arrived tonight, I believe this is the correct course of action." He reached inside his jacket pocket and pulled out an envelope and laid it on the table. "This is my resignation. I will begin by saying some things that Robert can confirm if he chooses to. We've seen other promising technology develop in the marketplace. We have tried to hire some of the people who are developing it for as much as five times the going market rate plus stock options. Over and over again we made similar offers to purchase companies and to form partnerships. All of them unequivocally turned us down. In the cases of businesses, we have been out bid on our offers to acquire them several times. We have not been able to find people or businesses that are willing to work for us or with us. The offers that we have made have been unbelievable. Those are the facts. Our problem is that no one is willing to work with us."

"Robert, is this true?" asked Mr. James.

"Let me offer you a summary of our recruiting activities." said Robert.

"Robert, what I asked you was a yes or no question."

"Basically, yes it is true. We have tried several hiring options, and they have all failed. We even tried forming a new company, and hiring staff under the new company name."

"Why haven't I heard of this before?

"Our employee retention and benefits plans are unequaled in the industry. Basically recruiting is usually a simple function of Human Resources. When we analyze the market there are companies hiring employees related to technology all over the world. Until now, recruiting, except for key positions, has not needed executive input."

"What is being done about this mess? I don't plan on running every department in the company," said President James.

"Mr. James, in our hands, is an incentive package for our whole entire company. We have over 255,000 employees and 20,000 contractors worldwide. We have drawn up a comprehensive plan that includes re-allocating employee time, where they will allocate a portion of the day to come up with new ideas for the company. The programs offer both bonuses and royalties to the employee or employees that come up with ideas that we can use. I sent the proposal to the committee two weeks ago. This is one of the things that are on the schedule tonight. Because of the global impact and the cost, I need approval to move forward. I know from a timing perspective this is late, but we believe it still can work," said Robert.

"Slovie, is there something else that you need to say tonight?"

"Mr. President, there are other things that I need to say, but I do not have to say them tonight."

"Good, I do not accept your resignation. Robert if the proposal is approved, what are your projections for implementation and measurable impact?"

CHAPTER FOUR

William Stradom awoke to his alarm going off. He rolled over to look at his clock and saw that once again it showed 4:30AM as if it was going to be different this time. Being a creature of habit, he has been dedicating an hour and one half each morning to writing his memoirs.

William sat down with a pen and notebook. Before he began to write, he began to remember some of the history that was passed to him.

Henry the Duke of Visue of Portugal, later to be called Henry the "Navigator", settled in The Bay of Arguin. Prior to settling the Portuguese attempted to take slaves from Africa by force. They were a little arrogant in their attempts sending small squadrons thinking that they had superior firepower. Since the Africans had no written languages they considered them unintelligent. Despite being underestimated, the Africans demonstrated great intelligence while they fought back. Instead of victory the Portuguese sustained heavy losses. After this, Henry was hired to move into the community so that he could figure out how to get access to slaves. While he was there he helped build a fort. He stayed in the community for a year, during which they established a fort in 1445(even though later it was described as a factory for the slave trade). After developing relationships with the locals he came back with a recommendation of instead of taking slaves, they should purchase them. While this delayed Portugal's original plans for slaves, they implemented a strategy to begin purchasing slaves. In 1452 the slave trade really took off.

In one of the battles where Portugal was trying to take slaves by force Henry's brother Ferdinand was captured. Negotiations ensued for the release of Ferdinand. The terms were peace in exchange for Ferdinand's freedom. When the terms were presented to The

Archbishop of Braga and the Count of Arraiolos they refused to approve the terms to release him. Ferdinand died in captivity after 6 years.

William remembered the story of Zara Yaqob, although his reign was filled with brutality, he was one of the most prominent Ethiopian Kings of all time. His intellect allowed his kingdom to expand across many provinces. William also remembered how his intelligence influenced Africans in the slave trade. Probably the most significant passage was when he read that during 1444 to 1452 one of the kings taught the other kings to interview the slaves and keep those that demonstrated intelligence and let the others be sold. Many of these slaves were later sold and wherever they were shipped to, they remembered how the kings had separated them, and developed strategies to do the same wherever they were shipped.

After day dreaming for a while, William looked up and realized that he had used up his time for the morning. He put his pen and notebook away and went down to have breakfast.

CHAPTER FIVE

Ted Alexus and Frank Simms had been friends since the first Grade. Ted contacted Frank and asked him to meet with him ASAP. He selected a public but inconspicuous place to meet.

"Frank, you know that the FBI and local police are right on our heals."

"Nice meeting place Ted. None of our ancestors would have chosen to meet in a place like dis. Who would believe that we would meet in a museum dedicated to protecting Daisy's."

"That is why we are here. Now let's get on with it. I think it's time to let you in on a little secret. Your organization pulls in roughly five million dollars a year. Out of that about two million you get to keep. Everyday you have to look over your shoulder in fear for your life. Last year I made fifty million dollars, but only a little under ten million was from activities we learned growing up."

"You been holding out on me. Now you want to tell me to my face, and make me look stupid."

"No, No, No. We've been friends since we were kids. You know we have to look out for each other. You also know I always liked to read and I've been good with math and stuff. A few years back I began to look at what I was doing, and where I wanted my life to go. I know you hate it when I talk like this, but that's just who I am. I still think I can do whatever I want. There are things out there that I want to do and places that I want to go. Now, I think we were taught how to take advantage of only a portion of the business that we are in. We have been limited by the knowledge that they had on how to do business."

"What are you talkin bout man? We got it good."

"We were taught that if you make X amount of dollars then you have it good. It didn't matter that all other aspects of your life you have to sacrifice. I've found a list of people who choose to live their lives in seclusion, and choose to be invisible just like us, but they make from 20 to 100's of times more money than we make. No one is trying to kill them or arrest them and they can go and do whatever they want. These people get to make X amount of dollars and get to live their lives the way that they want to. I am going to be one of those people."

"So, what you sayin you droppin me?"

"No, I am saying that I am eighty percent there. I know how to drop off the FBI and police radar. I know how to take the next step. I would like to take you with me. I can show you how to do it, and we can do it together. I looked at the numbers. The percentage of us who makes it to retirement age is so low it rounds off to zero. These guys make more money and get to enjoy it and retire."

"If I don't want to go, does this mean we done?"

"I don't think our friendship will ever be over. However, our relationship dynamics will change."

"Speak English."

"I will have to cut off all ties to this world. No phone calls, no

meals together, no family get togethers."

"You talkin about retiring. You know what happens when you try to retire from dis business. Either you are the lion or the lamb, there ain't no in between."

"That's what we've been taught. If you are a lion and you are trying to become a lamb, it only means that you are going to be dead soon. If you are dead, aren't you invisible too?"

"I guess so unless there's somebody that can see dead people, Ha Ha."

"If it is done right, there are three options, lion, lamb, and invisible. This is what I am trying to tell you. About six years ago I found this guy from the list I told you about who is invisible. List is probably not the right word. From watching his business moves he's all about making money. I don't know who he is but I have been able to detect some of his patterns of doing business. I got close enough to what he was doing so that I could follow in his footsteps from a distance. It's the same way we learned the business. I now make more than I ever expected to with the business and I still don't know what I am doing. Here's the funny part, the money I am making by following him is legal."

"Okay, I get it. You want out. What's dis got to do with me? Hold up, I can't believe you droppin all dis on me like dis. I did notice how you were always busy, but I didn't expect dis. What do you think the guys is goin to say?"

"I'm twenty-four now and you're twenty-six. We were taught well, regarding how to run this business. We don't have to answer to anyone else mostly. Now I have deliberately been busy and not available to anyone else for years. They won't miss me at all. I need to know which way you are going to go. Here's what I propose. I can show you how to make more money than you ever dreamed, and we get out of the business, or we began a six-month transition where at the end you take over the business and increase your volume from five to fifteen million this year."

"If I choose to stay and choose not to take over your territory, what happens?'

"Nothing will happen with you, except that I still will move ahead with my plans with someone else, and our relationship will still change."

"This is like I got no choice. Either I'm down wit you, or I'm not down wit you."

"I am not going to blow smoke about it. It can be phrased a number of ways. It is what it is."

"What will it cost me to take over yo territory."

"It won't cost you a thing. I will give it to you."

"You are going to give me ten million dollars."

"I told you, I can't have anything to do with the business where I am going. Aren't you listening? I made forty million dollars last year outside this business. I need to focus on finding out as much as I can about this guy. The more I know the more money I can make. So, what is it going to be?"

"You know what you doin ain't my thang. I always knew you be different than me. I'm not goin wit you, but I will take the ten million."

"Good, I figured that would be your choice. Sorry man, I have to do this. We will begin immediately."

CHAPTER SIX

William Stradom stepped out his car while being intensely focused on getting into the office. He was startled by a familiar voice as Samantha greeted him from behind.

"Good morning Mr. Stradom. I didn't really expect to see you today with all the drama yesterday."

"I told you everything would be fine."

"I don't understand all of this. When the FBI gets involved, it generally means bad news. Should I be looking for a new job?"

"We have a lot of work to do. Why don't we move into the office? Don't worry so much. There is nothing wrong and we do not have any problems with the FBI. It may seem that way for a while, but in the end everything will be fine."

"Okay, but I can't afford to go to jail."

"You won't. Is there any follow up to the teleconference I asked you to set up this morning?"

"It'll be ready for you in fifteen minutes."

"Thank you."

"Give me about thirty minutes and then I need you to get the FBI agent on the phone, agent Plaiedeaux. Make sure you use the blue

phone system when you call."

"Yes, sir. Let me know when your conference call is finished."

"This conference call is one of the most important calls that I will participate in. You don't go into these types of calls unless you are pretty sure of the outcome. This is a culmination of years of work."

William walked into the conference room and closed the door behind him. He slowly strolled to the head of the table and glimpsed to his left to see that the phone was in the right place. He slowly pivoted and gazed out the large windows as he slid into the chair at the head of the conference table. The clock moved slowly as he took a few deep breaths before reaching over to push the conference button on phone. "Good morning gentlemen, I've been looking forward to this call for a long time. I know we have much to discuss and celebrate. We have all arrived here at the right time. It's going to be a tremendous collaborative effort to finish this phase of what we started so many years ago."

Meanwhile,

"There is a phone call for Tom sir" said Dana a new agent with the FBI.

"Whoever it is, I'll call them back," said Tom.

"It's Angie."

"I'm in a meeting. Tell her I'll call her back."

"I'm just following orders."

"Who gave you an order to interrupt official business for her?"

"I did," said supervisory special agent Smithren.

"Why did you do that?'

"Do you really want to go there?"

"Go where?'

"Okay, we tolerate her because of you. If they don't let her through, she will keep calling and berating everyone in the office until she gets to you. She's nuts. I don't know how you put up with her. It has become easier to just let her have her way, than to not."

"She is not my girlfriend and I don't want her calling here. All you are doing is enabling her. I want it to stop now. She gets no privileges here."

"You know it doesn't matter that we are the FBI to her, she just keeps calling."

"I don't care; I want it to stop."

"You put that in writing. The only way to convince her that this is serious is to put her behind bars. Now I'm willing to do that. As a matter of fact, you have one week to get this thing under control, if it doesn't happen in that time, we are going to step in. When we do, there won't be anything you can do to help her. She will be barred from ever calling here."

"I get it chief. Let me go and handle this."

"If this is the way your girlfriends are going to turn out, we might have congress pass a law that will not allow you to have relationships."

"Funny. I'll be back in a minute sir."

After Tom completed his call, he returned to the interrogation room.

Another knock at the door, " Mr. William Stradom would like to talk to you and he said it was urgent." Said Dana.

"Your second date I presume, so now you have another girlfriend." said SSA Smithren with a chuckle.

"I'm going to ignore that, if it is okay with you chief I'll have it patched through to here."

"Go ahead."

"Dana, please put the call through to me here."

"Okay Tom."

Tom reached over to put the call on speaker.

"Good morning Mr. Stradom" said Tom.

"Good morning agent Plaiedeaux. Sorry to bother you during your debriefing, but I wanted to make sure that you knew how your equipment was not functioning before you had to go back out in the field."

"What are you talking about? Is this another game to you?"

"No, no, no. Remember P.A.W.L. deactivated your guns last night. We did not reactivate them before you left."

"There are no electrical parts on the guns, and you guys never touched it, there is no way you could have deactivated them."

"Honestly, I have more important things to be doing rather than playing games with you. I suggest two things. Find some place and test your gun to see if it is working or skip the test and drive by the house and just stick the guns in the mail box in front of the house and count to 3 and then take them back out. This will reactivate them."

"Why are you calling? You are not making any sense."

"I've told you what I needed to tell you. It is on you now. I need to go, we will talk soon, good bye."

"Chief, why are you laughing?"

"He wants to be in control of you. He's inside your head. He set you up in a no win situation. If you go check out your gun, he is in control. If you don't you're not going to be able to use it with any confidence. You're right, he is smart. I'm going to let you off the hook. I order you to go and check out your gun. I will go with you. I want to see if this criminal can deactivate a gun."

"Are you telling me that you believe him?"

"No, I am saying that there are too many lives at stake to take a chance. So, let's go. By the way, I know he is innocent until proven guilty . So, technically we can't call him a criminal. However, if he walks, looks, smells, and sounds like a duck, then he is a duck."

"Okay sir."

"It will only take a couple of minutes; let's just head down to the range."

"You do know that there is no way that he or anybody can deactivate a gun, without touching it don't you?"

"Listen Tom, be reasonable. We have worked together awhile. You have already described a couple of things from last night that would seem to be almost impossible. Yet, you and your team have described what you saw exactly the same. So, at this point we have to make sure."

When Tom reached the range, he put the protective glasses and earmuffs on. He checked to see if his gun was loaded. Then a thought came to mind. He emptied all of the bullets out of the gun and went over and reloaded with new bullets from stock off the shelf.

He turned and looked at SSA Smithren and walked back to the firing line.

"Are you sure you want me to do this?"

"Stop stalling and get it done."

Tom aimed and pulled the trigger, but nothing happened. Over and over again he pulled the trigger, with the same result. The double action of his gun didn't even draw the hammer back.

He asked SSA Smithren to try with his own gun.

SSA Smithren stepped up and fired his gun with no problem.

Tom took a couple of bullets from his gun and a couple of bullets from the ones he took out of his gun and put them in the SSA's gun and asked him to fire the gun again. Again the gun fired with no problem.

"So, what now chief."

"To settle this, you need to go over to the mailbox and do what he said with only one of them, then return and test that one again. I presume you had your backup. We need to know if there is someone capable of deactivating a gun. Put only one in the mail box and leave the other one in the safe here. Come back and test it afterward. Either way you are going to have to pick up two new guns."

"What about the debriefing."

"We'll pick up where we left off when you get back. If the gun works when you get back you will need to turn it and the other one into me, and we will reissue you two more. Now get going."

"Yes sir".

"Take Dana with you, she will ask fewer questions. Make sure she stays in the car when you go to the mailbox."

After returning from the trip and testing the gun Tom walked into the Smithrens office and turned his gun in. No words were spoken, but the SSA Smithren reached into his desk and handed Tom two identical guns.

"Tom, you were right from the beginning this morning. Good call. This case and investigation will be classified from now on. I will assemble a team and let you know who has clearance and who does not while we proceed. Now that you know where he lives, you need to keep that house under surveillance."

"Honestly chief, this one is going to be a long drawn out investigation. It will probably take years. He showed up on our radar by accident. An electricity outage caused a transformer to go out in the area where his house is. When a new electrician tried to resolve the issue, it turned out to be associated with a connection to the house that he was unfamiliar with. After looking at the usage for the house it seemed kind of strange that a house with that much acreage and square footage actually had a credit every month. He is getting paid by the city, rather than him having to pay for electricity. When he tried to gain access to the house for the electrical easement, he discovered that all of the electrical easements were outside of the security fences. He mentioned it to a friend of mine, who mentioned it to me. The electrician's name was Greg Bolden.

We took a cursory look at the blueprints of the house and could not make heads or tails of what we were seeing. After this we decided to check out who owns the house. It took us a while to work through a maze of companies to track down the person that is staying there was Mr. William Stradom. We have not established ownership yet. We tracked down Mr. Stradom's tax returns and it only made matters worse. Last year he paid 1.4 billion dollars on his personal taxes. On his return, he filled out his return address as a P.O. box, however, he had no W-2's, no schedule A's, C's or anything. His return had the PO box and the amount he owed only. He didn't even sign it. It was stamped with some weird cymbal that we have not been able to figure out yet. We looked back on several of his returns and they all had the same information except each year the PO box changed. I'm not sure that you can even file a return like this, but we don't show that he owes any taxes either. I'm finished after this one. We tried to find out who filed the return and where it was filed and have not been able to find anything at all. We tried to trace where the money came from to pay the taxes and could not trace that either. What drug dealer can pull all of this off? I'm not asking for answers right now, but something stinks. I've never heard of a criminal willing to pay those kinds of taxes, or any taxes at all."

"Tom, when did all of this take place?"

"All this has been in my reports I've been submitting to you."

"I haven't received any reports."

"I gave you hard copies and emailed you with attachments."

"I swear to you Tom; I have not seen either."

"I had been wondering why you had been so quiet regarding the case."

"How many reports have you given or sent to me?"

"I would estimate at least 10."

"We have a problem. We need to get to the bottom of this."

CHAPTER SEVEN

Ted was sitting in his office thinking about his conversation with Frank. He realized that he not only had to sever all ties, but that he needed to move his office, home, and bank accounts, plus everything he owned. He would begin immediately. He also realized that he needed to remake himself and his image. He stood up, walked to his second story window and looked out. He started to turn when he caught a glimpse of an SUV parked across the street from his office. The SUV looked familiar to him. He thought he had seen it this morning on his way to his office. This is not good, he thought. I am so close. He walked over to his briefcase and pulled out his emergency cell phone then walked back to the window. The SUV was still sitting there. He pressed 4 to speed dial the number he needed.

When the call was answered he said, "Hello, Alpha 1 the message is fade." and then he hung up.

Fade was a code word that had been put in place to protect him and his organization. To the public it would look like he had a string of bad luck. His business, home life and personal holdings would all seem to begin to disintegrate. He would spend less time at the office and with his current business associates. At the end of the day, it would look like he had lost everything, but in reality he would not have.

He called his secretary and let her know he would be leaving for the day. As he walked out the door, he went out the back of the building so that he could get to his car quicker. He pulled his car out where he could be seen from the SUV. Before entering traffic, he moved an empty bag from inside the car to the trunk, to make sure whoever was in the SUV would see him. He wanted to be sure that he was being followed. As he pulled into traffic turning left as if he was heading to his house, he looked in the rear view mirror to see that the SUV also had pulled out.

He dialed Franks number and Frank answered, "Who is this?"

"Frank, this is Ted."

"I didn't recognize your digits."

"I know, but this is necessary."

"So, what's up."

"I know it has been only three weeks since we started the transition, but something happened today and we are going to have to move everything up."

"What chu mean man?'

"Today is the last time that you will hear from me, instead of six months."

"Hey Ted, this is way too fast. I don't think the guys are going like this."

"Trust me Frank. You will be receiving instructions from me in the next couple of days on how to complete the transition. It will work as long as you do what I tell you."

"Ted this is wack."

"Frank, come on. I'm giving you ten million dollars, and you and I have

been friends most of our lives. You know me. What I am sending you will work. Now I've got to go."

"Ok, Ted. Yes, I do know. And you always been good at dis planin stuff. I guess dis is it. See ya around."

CHAPTER EIGHT

Just as William hung up the phone, he turned to see a familiar alarm on the wall to the left of his desk had been triggered.

Immediately Daniel Frazier, his long time IT Tech called. "Mr. Stradom, it's him again. This is the fifth time he has tried to break through our firewall."

"He is nothing if not persistent."

"That's for sure."

"It's time we took it at least a step further. Obviously, he is not getting the message. Employ our Viral Genealogy program. It's about time we stretch its legs."

"Sir, we can launch our Drone Virus program, and we will be done with him."

"Not so fast Daniel. You never want to pick a fight unless you know you can win. A key element in winning battles is knowing your enemy's strengths and weaknesses. In this case you really need to know who is trying to hack through our firewall. If this guy is a loaner, then this is no big deal. However, if he is with an organization, you really need to have a strategic plan to address the whole organization, rather than just the individual. Now, a third possibility is if he or she is contracted to provide the service on behalf of a third party. Remember you really don't want to fight battles until it is clearly defined what you will gain from them. We gain nothing if we simply launch the Drone Virus program. We gain great intel if we launch the Viral Genealogy program."

"Okay, Sir. It will probably run about 2 hours."

"Let me know when the process is completed."

"I will contact you as soon as it's done."

Samantha walked into the room. "William, there appears to be some mail left in the mail box in front of the house."

"It's not mail. It's correspondence from agent Plaiedeaux, he's realized that he can't reach me any other way. He was probably a little perturbed that he needed to come back out to the house today. It's okay, I will pick it up in a couple of days."

"Sir, I can go and get it now."

"No, Samantha, everything is fine. It will work out better if I wait a couple of days before I pick it up."

CHAPTER NINE

Back at Outer World Technologies, Richard looked out his office door and saw Slovie moving past him. "Slovie," he yelled. "Come in here."

Slovie moved through the door.

"Close the door behind you," he said.

As Slovie reached for the door, he asked, "what is it"?

"I just received a hostile takeover bid for our company. It really makes no sense. Our stock is at its lowest point and everyone in the marketplace knows our situation regarding the lifespan of our software. It's about to be rendered obsolete. The company that submitted the bid is ROWT Industries. I am looking now and can't seem to find anything on it, yet it has been cleared by the US Securities and Exchange Commission to begin the process of the hostile takeover. There is also a Corporate Bylaw amendment that basically freezes the assets of the company and appoints a temporary executive committee to oversee the daily operations of the business. I've never heard of this."

"I've never heard of this either." said Slovie. "Is this some kind of joke?"

Richard picked up the phone and called Mr. James. "I have Slovie in my office and I am calling you about a legal document that I received earlier this afternoon. I uh"

"Hold on." Cut in President James. "I just got off the phone with our attorneys and I cannot discuss this with you. It is out of my hands. I'm a lame duck now. I have a title but no power and no authority. There is a lot at stake here. The new executive committee will be contacting us before the day is over. This is all that I can say. I will talk to you later. Good bye."

"So far we have not been given any restraints regarding our conversations. So either we take the opportunity now or just wait? What do you think Slovie?"

"I'm not sure what needs to be said, but I'm open to taking advantage of this time."

"Okay, then. I have not told you the half of this take over. It would seem that this proposal would be illegal, but it has already been approved by the Security and Exchange Commission."

"First of all this is a dual purchase. The offer is to purchase the company from its existing ownership and to take it private all on the same day. It is an all cash transaction. Who has an extra 40 Billion Dollars lying around to pull this off? According to the filing the company will be debt free from day one. Nobody in their right minds would acquire a company this way. Now, you know that most of us own preferred stock. This normally means that we would be paid quite handsomely. Somehow they found a legal loophole in which allows them to isolate stock ownership and offer a varying prices to preferred stockholders. This truly is a hostile takeover. The core group of us which have been around for all these years will get 7 million dollars each regardless of how much stock we own. The remaining preferred stock ownership will receive $.50 per share above market rates. Now here's the kicker, all common shares will convert to preferred stock with no penalties and will be tagged converted shares and be paid $.75 per share above market rates for the sake of sales valuation at the time of the sale. This basically means that the common stockholders will end up making more off of their stocks than the current preferred stock ownership. Also, the stocks convert temporarily only for the sake of voting rights when the board meets to decide on the sale, but during this time there is a zero-dollar valuation impact. If the board delays beyond a certain day, there is an implied consent to sale clause which kicks end. It means that if they give no answer by this time the no answer means yes we are consenting to the sale of the company. The converted stock holders will have a Put in place to protect them from any market losses of valuation and a cap for any gains. The result of this will be that at the time of the vote all stockholders will end up having equal voting rights. Since there are more common stockholders than preferred stock holders, with the money to be made off of this deal, it's a shoe in to pass. All stockholders should be receiving letters today. Do you know what all of this means Slovie?"

"I do understand how much money we stand to lose on this deal. I guess if you are talking about something besides that I don't understand."

"Slovie, this is history we are talking about. This is the stuff of legends. This will be taught in every college in the world. There will be movies, books, lectures, people will go on and on about this. This will define hostile takeovers. There has never been a takeover like this, and probably, there never will be again. I guarantee you that whatever loopholes that they were able to take advantage of to pull this off will be closed. It will be the first and the last of its kind."

"Richard, since you know so much about this, were you involved in it?"

"No, no, no, absolutely no. Don't get me wrong, I hate this. I stand to lose probably close to 1 billion dollars off of this deal. I feel sick right now. This deal forces us to voluntarily take this loss, so since we have to volunteer the billion dollars' loss that's not tax deductible. It is absolutely insane. The way this thing came down. Somebody went after us and it appears that they are going to get us. All of the core group who built this company are being penalized for something."

"Do you know that any legal action by anyone regarding the sale triggers a penalty phase which will result in all of the core group losing

100% of the seven million dollars that they would receive for their preferred stock?"

"I stand to lose about the same amount that you do. I still don't understand how this is possible. I imagine that if there was anything that we could do we'd be well behind the curve now."

"It appears so."

"This was a concise, well thought out and executed plan. We're sitting here like we are locked up in jail."

The phone rang and they both turned and looked at it in silence. It rang again and again. Finally, Richard reached over to his desk and picked up the phone. "Hello"

"Richard, this is Stanley Watson, I am the new executive committee leader. If you and Slovie have a few minutes I would like you to come down to the conference room on the 17th floor now so that we can talk and kind of get on the same page. I know that by now you have probably had time to review the buyout proposal."

CHAPTER TEN

"Sir, the Genealogy program has run. What has been found is almost unbelievable," said Daniel.

"I will be down to your office in a minute. Wait for me there."

"Yes, sir."

"Samantha, will you come into to my office for a minute."

"Yes sir, I'll be right there."

"I have a package I need you to have overnighted. Please get this sent out as soon as possible. I have to go downtown for a meeting this afternoon. I'll check in with you as soon as I get back."

"Sir, you almost never go out to meetings, especially in that area of town. With everything that's going on, are you sure this is something that you want to do today?"

"I'm sure, it is necessary today that I do this. I will be fine."

"This is what the FBI wants you to do. You know they are going to be looking for you."

"Regardless of what happens today. You have your protocols if anything goes wrong. We all have a job to do. As long as we stay focused and do our jobs everything will be fine."

William opened the door and Samantha walked out. He followed her and headed down to Daniel's office. "Daniel, let's take a look at the results."

"Here you go, sir."

"Okay, I see what you mean. The nice thing about this is it tells us exactly what we need to know. He's a for hire hacker who's been contracted to attack us. That's why he is so persistent. Usually they get paid a small fee for their services and a large bonus only if they complete their project. They are highly motivated. Now that we can see who hired him and how long he has been trying to penetrate our network. He is really good. run the Drone program with a level 2 modification and level 3 message."

"Sir, I've never thought of putting together the combinations you just requested. May I ask how the three of them will work together?"

"Yes it's okay to ask Daniel. The combination of the three will actually identify his signature hacking style, the computer he is using, plus any and all backup systems that he may be using. Since he is working with the FBI, he will need to be sent a strong message. The three of them combined will wipe his drive and backups now and every time he tries to hack us. He also will not be able to use any passwords that he has ever used before on the computer he's using. He will have to buy a new computer every time he tries to hack us. He will not be able to reformat, restore, or use the computers ever again. When the drone attacks it will be untraceable. Just so you know, the attack is isolated to the hacker only. If we wanted to we can actually allow the Drone to go after all of his conspirators as well. We're not going to do that today. Anyway, thank you Daniel."

"Isn't this a little severe for someone basically trying to break in an empty house?"

"No its not, they will forever think that they have gotten close, which is where you want them to be. Believe me, all we are doing is telling them they can't use this hacker. They have gathered enough information to pass it on to another contract hacker. As long as they are hacking an empty house as you call it, they will not be hacking any of our real sites."

"Thank you sir. I get it now."

"Hold on a second." As William picked up his phone Samantha walked into Daniel's office. He dialed Juan Carlos, who was in charge of automotive maintenance. "Juan would you fire up the Jetson, I am going to take her for a spin."

"I'm sorry sir, are you saying to load it up?"

"No, start up. I am going to drive her downtown."

"Wait a minute William," Samantha said, "you are going to stick out like a sore thumb. They will be able to see you plainly even from space. Is that thing street legal anyway?"

"Juan, I know this is unusual, but like I said fire her up."

"Okay, Mister William."

"Do you need something, Samantha?"

"I just need your signature, and then I will be on my way." She walked over to William and he signed the paper.

"Daniel, go ahead and take care of our little project. I will catch up with you tomorrow."

"Yes sir."

William stopped by his office to pick up his briefcase and then headed to the garage.

"Juan Carlos, seems like it has been a while."

"It's been a few months, but you definitely keep me busy."

"Thank you for your help today. I do appreciate your work. By the way, did you run an analysis to make sure that everything works?"

"Yes, sir mister William everything works."

William walked over and got into the car and drove away. As he drove off he turned on bluetooth and called agent Plaiedeaux on his cell phone.

"Hello agent Plaiedeaux."

"Who is this," asked agent Plaiedeaux.

"This is William Stradom. I thought I would give you a call. We still need to spend some time getting to know each other. I'm sorry about how our previous meeting went down. I know that this is not customary for you. Please understand that I meant no disrespect to the FBI or you. Things just are not as they seem to be. I imagine by now you have had time to look up some of my tax returns and it has only created more suspicion."

"What do you want Mr. Stradom?"

"I just would like us to perhaps begin meeting on a regular basis so that we can get to know each other. I think that this will be a more civilized approach rather than us always having to meet with all this hostility."

"If you're asking me if the FBI still wants you for questioning. The answer is yes. You don't get to dictate how and when and how much time we have to question you."

"You think I don't know that you have had to make your investigation classified because of what you have seen."

"I don't know how you get your information about what is going on in our office, and frankly I don't care. When you do the things that you are doing, you are disrespecting the government of the United States of America."

"I am trying to simply work out how we can begin dialoguing. I am giving you another number today to avoid the situation like we had last time. This number will be good until 9:00PM. If you want to meet again today, I will be available until 7:00PM."

"Okay, so what is it that you are not telling me? Why today? Why not tomorrow or next week?"

"I know how you work. I know you are strategizing behind the scenes to change the way that things are working. It's not necessary, but you are going to do it anyway."

"Who are you to decide what is necessary or not necessary?"

"You can never say that I am not trying. I will see you tonight."

"I will see you when we are ready to see you, not when you decide."

"Thanks for the conversation. Good-bye."

William pulled up to the building where the meeting was scheduled and parked at the corner where no one could block him in. As he got out of the car a pedestrian walked up to him and asked him what kind of car he was driving.

"It is a homemade car," he said with a chuckle.

"That is a bad car. It really looks cool, futuristic even."

"Thank you. I couldn't afford to be in a regular car so some friends and I got together and sort of pieced one together."

William turned and walked into the building, where he was known as David Starnes.

When he entered the building, he pressed the button for the intercom and was greeted by Francis. "Good afternoon Mr. Starnes. It has been a long time since you have been to the office."

"Yes, it has been a while."

"Yes," Francis said. "The conference is set and will start in about 2 minutes. It is set for 30 minutes."

"Thank you, Francis. Let me get settled in the conference room."

He walked in the empty room and closed the door behind. As he walked over to the conference table and turned to view the video conference screen. He looked at his watch and then walked over to the window to check on his car. Just as he looked out the window he heard a voice as the conference screen video display opened up.

"Good afternoon David, I mean Mr. Starnes. You did it. I can't believe it. I have to be honest. I never thought this day would come."

"Good to see you Patrice, we still have a lot to do. This is a great day, but it isn't finished yet. I'm sure that everybody will be joining us in a minute."

"David, I'm so proud of you."

Little by little the rest of the team joined the conference and they put finishing touches on their project.

After about 45 minutes the meeting was concluded. William walked over to the window to check on his car again. As he looked out the window, he saw what he was expecting. "It's time to have some fun," said William to himself. He packed up his briefcase and slipped out the side door. He knew he had to get to the car quickly.

As he reached the car, he had already opened the doors remotely. He slid into the car and started it. Just as he started the car, someone tried to open the door. When they found that the door was locked, they knocked on the window. William ignored the knock on the window and pulled out slowly making sure that no one was harmed. They began to yell at him but he continued to drive off. As he looked in his rear view mirror he saw several black SUV's pull out. He turned the corner and began to accelerate as he noticed that the vehicles were following him. He intentionally drove away from where he needed to go, so that they would follow him. He had a place in mind where he would pull up and stop for the final confrontation.

Just as he reached his destination, his phone rang. "Hello agent Plaiedeaux."

"Hello again William. I trust this is what you had in mind. This time you do not have your fortress of solitude. We have you surrounded. Make it easy on yourself and give up."

"Agent Plaiedeaux, I'm not trying to make it hard on anyone. Like a told you before I will see you this evening.

"By the way, if nothing else we can get you on having illegal tags on your car. Your license plates show that they belong to a Pacer. I'm not sure what kind of car that is but I'm pretty sure it's not a Pacer."

"Like I told you before, things are not as they appear. You really don't want to do this right now. I have no weapons and I am unarmed, just meet with me this evening and call this whole thing off."

"Talk about a control freak. Even now you are still being obstinate. You give up and we will get this over with quickly."

"I've got an important business call coming in; I will talk to you later."

With his car being surrounded, he continued his conversation as the FBI began to move closer. They could see him talking on the phone as if nothing was going on. As they moved within 10 feet of the car William reached down and pushed a button on the dash board. The car began to vibrate and what appeared to be smoke began to come from the car on all sides. Everyone began to back up because they didn't know if there was anything dangerous coming out of the car. After about 3 minutes you could no longer see the car. As the smoke spread you could not see the car from 10 feet away and up to 20 feet high. Agent Plaiedeaux told everyone to hold their positions.

He said, "No matter how much smoke he generates, he still has no room to drive out of here. When the smoke clears he will still have to try to get the car out of here." After about 15 minutes they saw that the smoke began to clear up. As the smoke finally cleared the FBI agents standing in the circle were in total surprise. William and his car were gone. There appeared to be no way out of the circle, but yet he found a way out. As it became evident that William had slipped through his fingers again, agent Plaiedeaux told everyone to stand down. "I shouldn't have to remind you that everything that happened tonight is classified." He hated what came next. He called SSA Smithren and told him what happened knowing that he was going to be told to make the call.

"Chief, I know you don't want to hear this, but we had him surrounded and he pulled a Houdini on us. His car was there and out came a cloud of smoke and then it disappeared. There was no way that he could get the car past us, but apparently he did."

"Tom, you know you need to make the call again. I know how much you hate this, but it has to be done. Obviously this is not standard operating procedure, but these guys who think they are smarter than us usually always make a mistake. We just have to keep him talking and he will eventually give us something to hang him. "

"Should I arrest him?"

"I think you know that he's smart enough to where he won't resist arrest, but he also won't let you arrest him. Either way, unless I'm wrong, we really have nothing to hold him on. Most of the time, the early arrest is designed to be an irritant and cause concern for the suspect. I don't think that this tactic is going to work on him. You run the risk of cutting off communication with him all together. For now, I would suggest talking to him, but ignoring everything that happened this evening as if it didn't happen. Force him to bring it up. When he does, let him talk about it. Do not add anything to the conversation."

"Yes sir."

Agent Plaiedeaux dialed the number that William had given him earlier. "Good evening William," said agent Plaiedeaux.

"Good evening agent Plaiedeaux. I trust that we will be getting together for dinner."

"Is the password the same as last time?"

"No, nice try though. Just stand in front of the gate and count out loud 1, 2, 3 and the gate will open. The same rules apply as before, no one can come in but you. I will see you in a few minutes."

Agent Plaiedeaux arrived at the gate and entered just as he was told to. As he walked through the gate he remembered seeing the flowers and landscaping how impressive they were. All of a sudden he stopped and looked toward the house. This was not the same house that he saw and entered before. This house was a two story structure which was totally different than the one story he had seen before. "There is no way you can build a house like this in a couple of weeks. You can't actually add a second floor in that time either. This is crazy." He reached up and knocked at the door.

The door opened and P.A.W.L. the computer answered the door.

"Hello P.A.W.L.", said agent Plaiedeaux.

"Hello agent Plaiedeaux," said P.A.W.L.

"How does this work?"

"You step inside and I lead you to the room where you will meet with Mr. Stradom."

"A computer with a sense of humor. No, how do I talk to you?'

"Are we not talking?"

"Forget it. Just tell me or show me which way to go."

"Follow me. Mr. Stradom is waiting for you."

"Is this the same house as the last time I came here?'

"Is it not the same address as before?"

"Yes, but how can the exterior and interior be so different? I would say I have never been here before except for the address.

"Perhaps you should talk to Mr. Stradom about your questions."

"I'm good. Even the furniture and art is totally different than before. The room configuration is different as well."

"We have arrived at our destination."

"Thank you P.A.W.L."

"Welcome agent Plaiedeaux," said William.

"Good evening William."

"P.A.W.L. told me that the serial number on your gun is different than the one you had last time. I figure you had to change it out so that they can try to find out how it was deactivated."

"Something like that. By the way if I tried to use it now would it work?"

"No, it wouldn't. I get it, you don't give me anything and I don't give you anything. It is a classic stand-off. I hope one day we can get past it. Do you ever get an opportunity to accomplish any of your major goals or dreams?"

"I'm an FBI agent. I can't say that this was a dream job or anything like that. However, the job kind of precludes you, no, it kind of causes you to postpone thinking about dreams and personal goals. Let me rephrase that. I think your priorities change, and you become so busy, it's like you forget to have personal dreams and goals."

"Sorry to hear it. That's lamentable."

"It's not like I have regrets, nor do I need to be pitied."

"I'm going to tell you something. Today I completed one of the biggest goals that I've had in my life. You know even though this happened today, I will keep things in perspective. Don't get me wrong, I definitely will enjoy it. I just know that it is not going to define me."

"Why did you choose a life of crime?"

"I can see how you would come to that conclusion. If I were in your shoes I would think logically, and that would be the conclusion I would have at this point also. Just remember that there are things that you do not know yet. Unfortunately, I'm not the one that can tell you."

"Tell me how it is that you can pay 1.5 billion dollars in taxes. I confirmed that it was paid, but I can't confirm how it was paid, or where the money came from to pay it."

"I am a law abiding citizen. I pay my taxes just like anybody else. I'm curious how you came up with that number."

"I will have to disagree. I looked at your tax return. I don't know of anybody that would be allowed to file a tax return like that and get

away with it."

"I'm not sure what you are talking about. I owed taxes and I paid them."

"Where did you get the money?"

"Are you racist or something? I'm sure that there are plenty of other people who have money, but you are not asking them these questions."

"You of all people are playing the race card."

"I thought that was what we were doing playing games. Hold on a second. Dinner is ready. Let's continue the game in the dining room."

"The last time I was here, the house I entered was a one story home. Now, the house is a two story home. How do you explain that?"

"I'm not sure where you are going with this. But remodeling is done all the time. By the way, I took the liberty of choosing your meal and your drink; I hope you don't mind."

"I don't mind. So why did you ask me to come? You have not answered any of my questions."

"I am waiting on you."

"What does that mean?"

"I told you from the beginning, you and I will need to get to know each other. You still come in here with a lot of hostility and preconceived ideas about who I am. I am not the bad guy that your years of experience tell you that I am. How many bad guys have you encountered that will invite you into their home, knowing who you are and who you represent. I know you probably think I'm arrogant because of how I'm approaching building a relationship with you. I also understand that you do not expect us to develop a relationship at all, because you do not develop relationships with criminal elements. I would hope that at the least you will concede that this investigation is unique in the way that it is proceeding. If you can do that, then perhaps you will concede that there are some new things that you can learn and see. You have integrity, that's important in your position. I appreciate that about you. Again I mean no disrespect."

"I'm doing my job. My job is to protect the people of this country from being preyed upon by parasites. Typical parasites produce all of this off the books income through a variety of illegal ways, and will kill, steal, and destroy anyone that gets in their way."

"I guess I know what you think of me."

"So you expect me to come over to the dark side just because you say the sun is shining over there."

"You're right. I can't say in one breath we need to get to know each other and then in the next breath impose on you to act as if we already know each other. It is going to take time for us to build trust."

"Since you are so enlightened, are you asking or telling me to drop my investigation of you? How does an FBI agent become best friends with a suspect he is investigating after the investigation has begun?"

"Nice try. Do what you feel like you have to do. But once you're done, call me. By the way this may not be the best example because both were criminals, but haven't you seen White Collar, or the movie with Leonardo DiCaprio and Tom Hanks. Apparently it happens all the time. Of course you know I'm kidding. I'm not going to be able to solve all of your problems for you. Thank you for the civility. I think this is a good place for us to start."

"I will admit that I have not had a suspect that would stand toe to toe with me and look me in the eye as if to say that there is nothing I can do, because they are too smart for me and my whole organization. It might be considered gutsy by some, but I think it is arrogant and idiotic."

"I can see if I were in your shoes, and I was armed with the limited information that you possess, how I would probably conclude the same thing. However, there is more to the story."

"So, not only are you implying that the FBI has limited information, but also that we are ill-equipped to investigate you."

"That would be arrogant even if it were true. I will let you evaluate all of those things yourself. I'm not in this for ego or anything."

"Sounds like you are saying that you chose to be investigated."

"I think we are getting a little off track here."

"Okay okay. Why do you insist on not answering any of my questions?"

"I am not refusing to answer your questions. I know it seems that way to you. However, just so you know you are not really asking the right questions. I will not expand upon this at this time, but do you think that we have been put together just by chance? There are no accidents."

"So are you trying to indicate that the universe has aligned, and some cosmic force beyond our control has brought us together?"

"Like I said, I will not expand upon this at this time."

"By the way, last time I was here, P.A.W.L. scanned me and supposedly deactivated my gun. I didn't see him do that this time. So how could he know the serial numbers have changed if he didn't scan me this time?"

"Thank you. Now that was a good question. P.A.W.L. did scan you last time and he deactivated your gun. He didn't have to this time. The password you used to get in the gate had a protocol that required you to be scanned as you walked through the gate. The system relays the results to P.A.W.L., who then relays the information to me. Just so you know, there is no radiation used, so the scans are not harmful. The system creates a history of how it scans you and it uses a lot of variables so that no two scans are alike. You are assigned a security threat level and based on your level you're assigned entry and exit protocols. You will never actually see what happens, but the system is pretty thorough. By the way you don't have to remind me to reactivate your gun this time; it is done automatically when you exit the property.

There is a lot more to it than what I described, but I wanted you to know some basics."

"Why would you give me information about your security system, while I'm treating you as a suspect and you are still being investigated? You are still wanted for questioning and we are still going to take you in for questioning when we get the opportunity. I get it. You gave me something and nothing all at the same time. What you described I would never be able to use to penetrate your fortress of solitude. One of my original questions was something along the lines of why so much security?"

"That was good also. You answered your first question yourself. The second answer is I really like my privacy, and I've found it necessary over the years to enhance it and the results of the enhancements are where we are today."

"If your security is so good, why aren't you selling it on the open market?"

"Have you not heard of many people who have incredible skills, but have elected not to use them? Just because something has value doesn't mean it needs to be sold."

"Most people do not have those types of options. If they have something of value, they either have to sell it to survive or realize that there is value in working to sell it. Not everybody gets to live your life of privilege, we don't have to get into that right now. How can you be living in a totally different house than before, even though it appears to be the same address?"

"We will save that one for another day. If you want to schedule another visit, we can do that at this time."

"How can I get in contact with you when I need to get back with you?"

"The mailbox is set up for that purpose."

"Are you telling me, that I can't call, email or text you, but I can drive by and drop a note in your mailbox."

"Yes, that is how we will communicate."

"I thought we were trying to develop a relationship."

"We are, but remember you guys decided to investigate me; I'm not going to make things easy for you. Besides, it will give you something to do other than eating donuts."

"Funny, I'll get back to you."

"Just so you know, I will not discuss what happened earlier today until you bring it up. I know you have been instructed not to bring the subject up. If you ask me I will answer the questions plainly so that you can understand me."

"On the one hand that sounds a little like you finally want to cooperate about something, however, on the other hand it seems to imply again that I'm a simpleton and need to be talked to on an elementary level so that I can understand things. If you want to volunteer information about today, I will listen."

"Eventually, we will be able to talk without all of the gamesmanship. So, are you here for a reason?"

"I'm here to take you in for questioning."

"Now we are getting somewhere. The pressure must be on you to find a way to close this case."

"Will you go voluntarily?"

"Are you going to attempt to arrest me if I do not go voluntarily?"

"I'm asking the questions here. You did not answer my question. Will you go voluntarily?"

"I can't answer that question."

"Why can't you answer the question?"

"It's a standard trap question. If I say no, then I would be resisting arrest. If I say yes, then I will have to go with you and waste all of my time."

"Then since you refuse to answer my question, I will have to arrest you."

"Just for the record from a legal standpoint; I am not refusing to answer your questions, nor am I delaying answering your question. What I am doing is called selective blocking."

"What does that mean?"

"You never asked me a question or made a statement."

"That doesn't work."

"If you were able to forcefully arrest me at this time, and I got off because of this; how would you look among your peers, especially if you already knew about the selective blocking? Don't you want to call somebody?"

"You think you are so smart. Even if you were smart, guys like you always have a tell. You are usually motivated by greed and eventually show your hand."

"As I said before and keeping reminding you, there is more to all of this than you know right now. I guess we are done then. I have some things to do. P.A.W.L. will see you out."

CHAPTER ELEVEN

When Ted hung up from talking to Frank; he made one more call. His home was located about 10 minutes from where he was raised, but about 40 minutes from his Office. After completing his conversation, he smiled as he hung up the phone. He thought if I can only make it home, everything will be alright. He took extra caution to assure he would make it home safely as the SUV continued to follow him. The mid afternoon traffic was light this day. Ted constantly watched as the SUV continued to follow him. I've worked so hard for this to be happening to me now, he thought. I just need to get to the house and everything will be fine. After looking at his watch he realized he was almost home. As he turned onto his street, he began to see some familiar vehicles. The last call he had made was to a friend to tell him that he needed to implement the plan he had put in place. The plan involved him having a flash give away of everything in his house. He had told his friends that he was going to be closing a big business deal and he was going to purchase everything new. The catch was that he would call them at a moment's notice and they had to get there quickly and completely empty his house. There were over thirty cars and trucks parked on the street waiting for him when he arrived. As he looked back, he could see the SUV pull up and stop at the corner. He stepped out of his Mercedes and began to walk toward the door. As he opened the door he turned and motioned to everyone to come on in.

Albert, was the first to reach the door. "Are you sure about this man?" he asked.

"Yes Albert, I'm sure."

"You know this is crazy, you got some nice stuff in there."

"It's okay, I'm glad I'm able to do it."

"You could be making some good money off of this stuff; maybe we ought to at least get a list of who got what?"

"Let's go Albert, I don't have a lot of time, and no I do not need a list."

"Okay, Ted. Thanks man."

Albert turned to the crowd and said, "Alright let's do this. Do not leave anything in the house."

Ted went out back and grabbed a lawn chair and sat down. He wanted to be away from the front door when all the stuff was being moved out. As he sat down, he realized it would probably be better if he was out front where he could be seen, so he picked up the chair and moved outside by the front door and sat down. As he sat down he looked and saw two men in black standing by the SUV. They looked and saw him and then they got back into the SUV.

The scene began to resemble a mad house as so many people were in and out and scattered up and down the street loading furniture and things. The quick and drastic transition from his home to an empty house happened in a span of 30 minutes. As the last piece was carried out the door, Albert walked over to Ted and said, "That's it man, we got it all. Thanks again."

"Thanks Albert and thank you all for your help. I hope you enjoy the stuff; I know I will enjoy my new stuff when it arrives."

Everyone walked by to shake his hand and to express appreciation for the gifts before leaving.

Ted turned and looked as the last vehicle drove off. The street returned to the quiet neighborhood that he had grown so accustomed to. He turned and looked at his car still parked on the street, and his door to the house standing open. Slowly he walked into the empty house and closed the door behind him. He knew he needed to finish his plan because the time was short. As he opened the interior door to walk down the stairs, he heard the doorbell ring. He closed the door behind him and continued down the stairs. The doorbell rang once again. He heard a man's voice yell out.

"I know you are in there, this is the FBI, open the door."

Ted hesitated at the bottom of the stairs, and then he turned and looked back and smiled, and continued to a hidden door and room, opened the door and closed it behind him.

CHAPTER TWELVE

Stanley stood and said, "Welcome and good to meet you Slovie and Richard. I know that these circumstances aren't how you would prefer to meet your new leadership. I wouldn't expect that a change in leadership is a surprise to you. You two have been here for a while. Before we begin, do either of you have anything to say?"

"Yes," Richard said. "You are right about the expectation of change, maybe even knowing that the change is necessary. This looks more like a made for the movies take over. I've never seen anything like this before. I'm not even sure that it's legal. Okay, I've said it. So what is this about anyway?"

"Slovie, do you have any questions?"

"Of course I do. However, I prefer to spend my time more constructively. Getting to the bottom of things are more important to me."

"I see. Do you also want to get to the bottom of things Richard?"

"Yes, I do. What is this?"

"Well guys, first I want to put you at ease. After reviewing your work and your efforts over the years, we would like you to stay with the company. You are going to be asked to do something extraordinary. Nothing will change regarding your existing stock transition as it has been stated, but you will be put in a position to earn it all back."

"Even if what you just said was true, no one in their right mind would voluntarily give up a billion dollars with no real explanation. Besides I am a little too old to think I can invest another 30 years to do it again," said Slovie.

"This is good. You speak as though time sets a limitation on how much money you can earn and how fast. This has been the way you have been taught. The education system is based on past experiences when it comes to earning money. Your business processes and modules are antiquated. The new market place doesn't have the same constraints as the market place you grew up in."

"What are you talking about? We have been the leadership of one of the most profitable companies in history. The money this company has made for the investors is nothing to sneeze at," quipped Richard.

"That's the problem, you look at what the company is doing and you make decisions based on a model and the history that is all about you. I'm not foolish enough to think that in one sitting I'm going to change your mind. Let's talk briefly about something that is familiar to you. You know this company inside and out financially. However, you know absolutely nothing about me. Before today you have not even heard my name. On the desk in front of you is a package that you need to review. It tells you about me and my work history. You may want to find a quiet place with no one around because it's going to cause you to wet your pants."

"You little arrogant piece of. Okay, it's going to be games and ego now," said Richard

"I apologize if that is the impression that I have given you. You will find that I am not arrogant, but that I am very good at what I do. This is my way of saying that we have a lot of work to do, and that we must move quickly to accomplish the plan that has been laid out for us."

"So, who are you then? Do you own the company? Do you work for someone else?" asked Slovie.

"Just as I have stated I will be working the plan that has been provided for me. This is not meant to be hostile. I believe that you have been looking for this opportunity for years. Today it has landed on your doorstep. Just so you know, what I am giving you in the packages, will begin to degrade after tomorrow. It will last two days."

"If you were in our shoes and this all was presented to you just as it has been to us; how would you respond?" asked Slovie.

"I would be the very definition of skeptical, just as you are. However, at some point I would realize that I live my life by making good decisions based on the things that I can decide on. In the scenario, there are things that I used to be able to make decisions about and there are things that I can make decisions about now. Once I arrive at that point, I will then make the decisions on the things that I can make decisions on. This may not be scientific or deep, but it gets me through. I suggest that you take some reading time now and when you're finished we will get back together. You have been relieved of your duties until then. The only work assignment that you have is to read the document before you. I have set up a meeting for us to get back together at 10:00AM tomorrow."

"At least for me," said Richard, "I am going to need to consult my attorney about all of this. It's going to take me some time to work through all of this. So, tomorrow morning's meeting is too quick for me."

"Thank you for your honesty Richard. However, the offer is good only if you are working on our time table. If you can't meet tomorrow, then you have worked your last day at the company today and there will be no need for you to take the package. I suggest that you convene with your attorneys and or advisors through the night and therefore keep your options open. You will not have to say anything to me, but when you leave and I see that the package is either there or not, I will know what decision you have made."

"Slovie, do you have any questions?"

"No, I think I'm good for now. Just to let you know I was fully prepared to walk away from this company. I'm not worried whether I stay here are not. I'm not going to be intimidated by anyone. I'll choose to stay or go because I want to, not because of anything you are doing."

"Thank you then. I will see you gentleman tomorrow."

CHAPTER THIRTEEN

After another day of meetings late into the night, William sat in his office at his house and noticed the archive book that was protruding out from his bookshelf. He walked over and grabbed it and sat back down. He opened to a familiar passage which he often read over and over again. He looked at the top of the page and read Chapter 14 the need for a better education.

It was August 18, 1840. The White Council, which consisted of the top black educators in the community, was meeting with some of the students in the community. "We know that our books and materials are sorely lacking in comparison to what the white students are getting. We are not legally allowed to even purchase the books that they have," said Walter Jones, the Dean of the local college.

"I think we all know what we are up against," said Nellie Evans, the English department head at the college.

"So, why are we meeting, if we know that we can't change anything," asked Bradford Adams, editor of the local black newspaper?

"We are here to brainstorm about how we can improve or enhance our educational opportunities. While we have stated the obvious about some obstacles we have faced in trying to improve our educational system, I can't help but believe that there is something that we are missing," said Walter. "Does anybody have any ideas?"

In the back of the room Theodore Wexell stood up and waved his hand toward the podium. "I know I'm only 12 years old, but I think we may be looking at this wrong. What if we stopped looking at what we don't have, and start looking at how we can get the slave owners to provide us the same education that they provide to their own children."

Bradford stood up and said, "I don't know what he is talking about, but what he said is exactly why I have been against having these kids at these meetings. He just wasted our time by talking about something that he knows nothing about."

"Hold on,' said Nellie. "Let's hear what he has to say. No one else has any thoughts."

"Send me back to the plantation. I know how to get them to provide at least me with the same education that they provide to their children," said Theodore.

"You are one of the brightest students that we have. We do not want to risk losing you. There has to be another way," said Walter.

"What I'm proposing can be duplicated. If I can do it then we can teach others to do it as well. It is not going to be easy, but it will work," said Theodore.

"They don't even allow slaves to read or write. They specifically consider that to be illegal. So you expect them to go from that position to voluntarily teaching you," said Bradford.

"Yes, I do. They have a dilemma. They plainly say we are not only ignorant, but we do not have the capacity to learn on one hand, and on the other hand they have rules to keep us from any materials that would allow us to learn. Why both? If we truly do not have the capacity to learn, then they would have no reason to keep the materials away from us? My proposal is simple. We are forced into slavery. Whether we like it are not we have to do whatever they tell us to do. They think up all of this stuff and we have to do it. What if we used that against them?" asked Theodore.

"What do you mean?" asked Nellie.

"I will come right out and say it. I believe that we can give them some ideas and they will require that we do and think that it was their idea all along. I saw one time on the plantation when an old slave was showing one of the white men how to get rid of some bugs that were killing the crops. The white man did what he said and later took credit for the idea. The reason I want to go back to the plantation is because the master is an attorney. He has a son that is about my age. I believe that I can come away with a legal education there provided by my master. All I have to do is convince his son that it is not right for him to have to carry his books. If I can convince him of that, he will let me carry his books for him the rest of his educational life. Wherever he goes to school I will be there also. He will require me to sit in class so he does not have to carry his books. I will learn everything he learns. If this works, it will have to be the right person, because they cannot know that you are learning, but we can do this everywhere there is an opportunity. Now, send me back to the plantation," said Theodore.

"I don't like this either. It's a good idea. He just might be the one that can pull this off. There is definitely risk involved, but if he can pull it off, the opportunities would be tremendous," said Walter. "Theodore, you know we have high hopes for you. You are at the top of your class. Since we've not tried anything like this before, it might make sense for us to form a committee to figure out who we would want to send."

"I do not mean any disrespect, but you just said that I am the best student, and that you thought I could pull this off. To me either it is a great opportunity and we need to send our best or it is not worthwhile and we're just wasting our time. I want to do this. I am supposed to do this. This is the reason I was born. We take risk every day. Just being here and having these discussions we're taking our lives in our own hands."

"Theodore is right Walter. I think you know he's the one that needs to go. It is a good idea and too important to be left up to chance. I agree he is important to us, but this could be why he was sent to us," said Nellie.

"Bradford, you are very quiet. Do you have something to say?" asked Walter.

No, uh Theodore, sorry for what I said earlier. I know that you are different than the average kid. It's a lot to put on a kid. I don't see how an adult could pull it off. Actually, I don't see how anybody can pull it off. We will be putting your life on the line."

"So, I guess it is settled, we've reached a consensus, I'm going," said Theodore.

"Yes, I believe so," said Nellie.

"I reluctantly agree as well," said Bradford.

"Well then, let's plan his return," said Nellie.

William smiled and closed the book. "I never get tired of reading this story. This kid was amazing. Now he's one person I wish I could have seen pulling this off. I guess I'd better get some rest."

CHAPTER FOURTEEN

It had been six months since Ted walked through the passageway from his house to a new life. Relocation and setting up his life again had seemed to go very well. He thought he could understand the stark contrast of his life style between his now two lives; only to realize that he didn't even have a clue. His days while filled with activity seemed to last forever. His nights had become uninspiring. He realized that he had never had an opportunity to not be on guard, because it would have cost him his life. It became more obvious as each day passed that he needed something from this life that he didn't know he would miss from his past life. Every day you had to wonder whether you were going to live or die. Now, he just had to learn how to live and keep the edge that he has always had.

As Ted looked to finish off another Friday and head into the weekend, he decided to grab some dinner at one of his favorite Mediterranean restaurants which in the past he had rarely visited. As the waiter placed his food on the table, he noticed out of the corner of his eye a group of people assembled at the front of the restaurant. He began to eat his meal when he felt someone staring at him. He looked backed at the front door again to see the group still standing there. As he looked he saw a familiar face. Without a doubt it was Big Thug, a member of a previous rival gang. His cover had been blown. Big Thug had recognized him and had begun to make his way toward him. Ted jumped up from the table and headed away from Big Thug to find another path to get out the door. As he hurried he looked back to see Big Thug in hot pursuit. He pushed over a table as he headed for the door. He figured if he could just make it out the door he could get away safely. He pushed through the people standing at the door and made it outside to fresh air. Just as he began to reach full stride he heard a loud noise and then a very painful burning sensation emanating from his back. He had been shot. He continued to run toward his car and just as he reached it he looked back to see Big Thug lying on the ground with several people holding him down. He jumped in his car and drove off. The pain was intense beyond what he could imagine, but he knew he couldn't go to a doctor. He headed back to his place, while trying to think of who he could call for help. He had to cover himself as he entered the high-rise where he lived. He made it inside the door and closed it as he stumbled and fell to the floor. He reached up to an inside door knob in an attempt to get up, but passed out instead.

William turned on the television in his bedroom, just as a news story came on about a shooting at a restaurant. He turned to look at the television just as his cell phone rang.

"He's been shot, the man on the other side of the phone explained. He knows he can't go to any medical care facility, so he went back to his place. It's bad sir, he will not make it through the night."

"Calm down, I'll get someone to go to his place as soon as possible and see what can be done." William hung up the phone and made a call to get him help. After, making the call William laid down to get some rest.

CHAPTER FIFTEEN

Richard looked over at his clock and saw that it was 9:30AM. He picked up the phone and dialed Slovie's number. "Good morning Slovie."

"Good morning Richard."

"Are you going to the meeting this morning?"

"Yes, I plan to attend. After reading that entire file, I feel compelled to go."

"I will admit to you, but not to Stanley, that I feel the same way. Truly where else can we go with the expectation of getting our money back? By, the way have you ever seen a resume like that before. I mean I have seen my share of resumes, but this one, honestly I couldn't even comprehend half of what was on it."

"I too struggled with it. I think we're supposed to be impressed. I won't say that I am not impressed, but maybe intrigued. Never in my wildest dreams would I have imagined I would be in this situation in my lifetime, but here we are."

"Yes, here we are. You have been a good friend, Slovie. I know we don't always agree on things, but I respect and trust you."

"Enough of this, let's get to the meeting. I'll see you in a couple of minutes."

A few minutes later, Slovie greeted Richard outside of Stanley's office as the secretary called to let Stanley know that they had arrived.

"Send them in." Stanley said to his secretary Bethleen.

"Gentleman, he is ready for you."

Stanley watched as they both came in. "Good morning gentlemen. Does anyone have any comments or questions before we get started?"

Richard spoke up first. "I'm not sure how it is possible to complete a transaction so completely and quickly and at some point I would like to know how it all was done. I'm not so sure if this is the time or place right now. You have to know that this will haunt me."

"Yes, we are aware that it is something you will want to reconcile, and we will save that for another time, if at all. You are actually asking me for trade secrets whether you know it or not."

"When we left yesterday, your office was clean and neat and everything in place. What's with the 15 stacks of papers on the table over there?"

"Let's not get ahead of ourselves gentleman. Slovie you actually don't have one single question or comment?"

"No, I do not have any questions."

"Honestly, I expected something different from you. Okay then are you all in or out?"

"I'm in," said Richard.

"I'm in also," said Slovie.

Stanley walked from behind his desk and shook both of their hands.

"We have a couple of choices right now. We can spend a lot of time getting to know each other or we can get right to work. I think for the sake of setting aside the suspense, let's get to work."

"You know about our initiative to come up with ideas to expand the company?" Richard asked.

"Yes, I know of them. Before you go there how about you both read this first." Stanley handed them both a packet with two sheets of paper.

As Slovie and Richard began to read, Richard walked to the chair next to Slovie and sat down.

"Is this for real?" asked Richard

"Yes it is. It will take about 6 months to complete the software migration, but when it is complete, it will propel the company to the forefront again in the industry. The modifications are a result of 10 years of programming. The cost is about 2 billion dollars and will enable us to quadruple our revenue in the next four years."

"This type of presentation kind of discredits you and all of your credentials. Why don't you present us with something that is believable?" replied Richard.

"You have to admit, that it is rather lofty and seemingly unrealistic. We have seen more than our share of get rich quick schemes," stated Slovie.

"You guys are making this so much fun. I probably couldn't have scripted this to go any better. I told you I am good at what I do. If you take a look at the cover page I handed you it indicates that it is a packet one of 15. Please go over and skim the summary pages of the other 14 packets."

Richard and Slovie looked at each other and moved over to the table.

In the meantime, Stanley turned and walked back to his desk to sit down.

"Slovie kind of laughed out loud. We did something like 43 billion dollars last year, which is down from previous years, but still 43 billion dollars. Are these really legitimate contracts?"

"Look at when they were executed," said Stanley.

"They were all executed yesterday. I assume that there is a plan. From what I know, of where we were yesterday, we are nowhere near to being in position to fulfill these contracts."

"Richard, what do you have to say now? Before you answer, the contracts are legitimate."

"I think I'm going to have to hold my tongue. Those contracts are for at least 43 billion dollars a year. It was you who stopped us from growing all this time. You said this is the result of 10 years planning. It was you."

"It would be nice if I could take credit for this, but I can't. I have been involved for 10 years, and my job was to complete a portion of the plan. Yes, it is 43 billion dollars per year in contracts, and again yes they are legitimate. I know you have been up all night. Sorry for the time crunch. Why don't you two take the rest of the day to rest up and let's get a fresh start in the morning. There is much to do."

"Thank you, I will," said Slovie.

"I concur," said Richard.

"See you tomorrow."

CHAPTER SIXTEEN

The alarm going off the next morning while intrusive appeared to be amplified as well.

William turned over to see that he had forgotten to turn the television off. As he reached for the remote, he heard some startling words. An FBI agent had been shot and killed at a downtown office building while investigating a major criminal conspiracy. The conspiracy is projected to be one of the largest in US history. Due to the fact that this is an ongoing investigation, no other details were provided at this time.

William jumped out of bed and reached for his phone. Before he could pick it up, it began to ring. "Morning Doc, how did everything go?"

"It was touch and go, but he is going to make it. He was out on the floor when I got here, I had to fund a break in to get in. Do you want more details?"

"No, I'm good for now. Thank you. I just need you to do me one favor. I need you to leave a message for him when he wakes up. Oh, and make sure you do not leave any contact information, and send the bill to me. Also, include reimbursement for the funding as well."

"Will do. Whatever happened to that thing that you were working on? Did you finally complete it?"

"Yes, I did, but we will talk about that another time. I've got to run."

"Okay. You are always so methodical. Congratulations. I'm always here for you."

William picked up his other phone and dialed agent Plaiedeaux's phone.

"Hello," said agent Plaiedeaux.

"Good morning agent Plaiedeaux, I just heard the news. I'm very sorry to hear what happened."

"Are you kidding me? You're calling me now."

"What's that suppose to mean?"

"He was killed while investigating you. Now, I suppose you are going to tell me that you are innocent."

"I am innocent. You are blaming the wrong guy."

"He was killed at 37216 Broadway, on the 5th floor. I suppose that you are going to tell me that the location has nothing to do with you as well."

"No, the location does have something to do with me, but not the death of this agent."

"Well, unfortunately this changes everything; this ratchets things up to a whole new level. I need you to come down to my office right now and make a statement."

"Like I said; I did not do this and I am not involved in whatever this is. I will be back in touch with you."

"William, this is more heat than you can imagine. It's time to stop the games and come clean. This is a life and death situation now. Don't you get that?"

"I get how serious this is."

"William, William, you don't want to do this now." Agent Plaiedeaux kept speaking but he soon realized that William was no longer on the line. He tried redial, but he received a message that the phone was disconnected.

William walked to his security room in the lower backroom of his house. As he entered the room he once again noticed the cold nature of the room being filled with electronics up and down all the walls except one. He sat down and checked the streets around his offices and houses that he knew the FBI was aware of. As expected, every area was surrounded with FBI Agents. He turned to see the time was 7:05am. He sat down in front of the computer and sent out a message to all of his employees in the affected area, at this time we will be implementing emergency protocol 1. The protocol closed down the offices where they were working and moves the work to another building with no pay interruption and it implements Transightal Security for all of the buildings. No one could enter the buildings without a security check.

"P.A.W.L., open up the security wing," William said.

The door opened up and William walked into the inner room and closed the door behind him. The room was dimly lit with low level lighting and an overhead chandelier in the middle of the room. There were three computers in the room with one main printer. The main terminal sat in the middle of the room on a high end executive desk with a red phone sitting next to it. It would have rivaled any spy movie secret room. William walked over to the main computer and sat down at the desk. Here we go, he thought. He typed in the security password and then sat back to watch as the system booted up. Once the system was booted up he typed a request for, Aerial and Voice DNA analysis of 37216 Broadway, on the 5th floor and cross reference gunshot residue and chronological time stamp the output for yesterday June 13th and send it to the Level S1 printer. Use public format 6 for the output report and route it to secure fax SF17 while holding the fax in spool for user interface. After about 30 seconds, the analysis was printing. The report showed that at 9:32 PM and 34 seconds that gunshot residue appeared in the lobby of the fifth floor and that there were two FBI agents present in the building, Sarah Snenkle and Bradley Jamison. However, Sarah was not in the lobby, but Larry

Janklin an employee was in the lobby at that time. There were no other people found in the lobby at that time. The report also showed that most of the gunshot residue emanated from the direction of Larry Janklin and dissipated nearer to agent Jamison. William turned and typed in Larry Janklins name and requested a financial back ground check and designated the search to be across secure and unsecure networks including public, private, and government networks. Once this report is complete, forward it to the previous printer used and merge this report to the existing spooled fax adding the report after the last page of the fax using public format 6 as well. William used public format 6 because it actually is used to present evidence to law enforcement in legal terms that they can use in a court of law. Since Aerial and Voice DNA systems are not known to law enforcement yet, they are dropped from the report.

After reviewing the report, William realized that Larry had been depositing six times the amount of money that he made from the company. He had been up to something illegal. He probably thought they were on to him.

He reached over and picked up the chameleon phone that he had been using and called agent Plaiedeaux.

"Hello, this is agent Plaiedeaux."

"Good morning again Tom."

"You hung up on me."

"Yes I did. I was finished with our conversation and we were wasting valuable time."

"If you are innocent, why is that you are not allowing anyone to get into any of the buildings. No one lives with that much security for no reason."

"That only means that I have a reason, but you don't know what it is yet."

"You think we can't trace your phone and pin point where you are at?"

"Now that's one of the smartest things you have tried yet. If I say yes, then it gives you some direction to go in order to find out how to trace my calls. If I say no, then you will think I'm arrogant and you will keep coming. I'm going to give it to you. No, you can't trace my phone. You sure make it difficult to help you. Before you speak again, I know that you are at 1712 Welden right now and that you are sitting outside in your car. I need to send you a fax and you will want to read it ASAP. If I tried to talk to you about it, you would waste hours with questions that you can ask me later. I am sending the fax to you on your laptop computer which is on the seat next to you. I will talk to you later."

"William, William, he did it again," agent Plaiedeaux said.

Agent Plaiedeaux listened for the fax machine to ring. He then opened up his computer and read the fax. He slammed the computer shut and just sat there. What am I supposed to do with this? He picked up the phone and called his boss.

"Chief, you won't believe what I have sitting on my computer. I am absolutely beside myself."

"Calm down Tom and tell me what is going on."

"Stradom called me this morning either pretending or not knowing that he was a prime suspect in the murder of Bradley last night. We went at each other and he claimed that he was innocent. I didn't give him any details of the crime or the crime scene other than the building address where the shooting took place. I requested that he turn himself in immediately. Of course he ignored the request. Thirty minutes later he calls me back and sends me a fax that includes conclusive evidence of who was there, the exact time that shots were fired down to the second, the name of the agents who were in the building, who was killed and who the shooter was. He provided the motive for the murder as well as the murderers' email address, phone number, fax numbers, parents and siblings addresses, known hang outs, and the murderer's' wife and kids names and birthdates and the make model and license plate of the car he drives. One other thing, he gave me the exact location of the car and murderer. He told me that the fax is a living fax and that wherever the suspect moves for the next three hours the fax will change to show us his exact location. He also created the report on an official looking FBI form with my name on it as if I was the one that completed the investigation. I can send it to you now."

"Hold up Tom. Don't do anything. Don't send it to anyone. I want to say that there is no such thing as a living fax. Get to my office as quickly as possible with your computer. Don't worry about how we got the information right now; it's more important right now that we solve this case. If the case can be solved this quickly it will make criminals, ah never mind, just get here ASAP."

"Yes sir, chief. I should be able to get there in about twenty minutes."

Agent Plaiedeaux headed toward the office. He remembered that he was supposed to meet someone at the location he had just left. He made a quick call to the agent and explained that he had been called back to the office immediately by SSA Smithren.

When he finally arrived at the office SSA Smithren was waiting in the lobby for him. He immediately ushered him into a secure meeting room, and closed the door behind him.

"Tom, I'm not sure about this Stradom guy. Let me see it."

"Tom opened up his computer and showed him the fax. I can print it out on the printer in the corner."

"Go ahead."

Tom sent the fax to the printer and walked over and picked it up when it was finished printing. He walked back and laid it on the table in front of them. As he sat down, he noticed that the address on the fax where the murderer was located was changing as he looked at the paper.

"Did you see that chief?"

"Yes, I did unfortunately. So that's what a living fax looks like. I'll be honest with you Tom; this is crazy science fiction stuff. We can't report how we got the information, but we can use the information. If it's true that the living fax is only "alive" for three hours, we can probably use it after three hours, but I don't know for sure. If you ever tell anyone about how we got this information it will end both of our careers. Do you get that?"

"Yes, I know. Let's see, the primary suspect of an FBI agent's' murder, provided the FBI with leads and or evidence that leads to the arrest and possible conviction of the murderer, while still being invested for conspiracy in one of the largest FBI cases in United States History. That should go over very well."

"Smoke and mirrors. This is what this is."

"What do you mean?"

"We have a simple directive. Arrest bad guys and protect the people from them. If we simply focus on that we don't even have to discuss anything else. An FBI agent was murdered; we have compelling evidence as to who actually committed the crime. Let's confirm the information, and if we come to the conclusion that the evidence is true then let's go arrest the bad guy. It's that simple. We should be able to do this in time to know exactly where the bad guy is, if this living fax really works. How about that?"

"You do not actually believe that there is something called a living fax?"

"I'm not endorsing it, but if it ends up helping catch the bad guy or guys, what does it matter. Honestly who can we tell about this anyway? I've seen the ink on the paper change right before my eyes, and I still don't believe it. We have a plan, let's just go with it for now, and see what happens."

"Okay, chief, I'll follow your lead."

CHAPTER SEVENTEEN

Ted rolled over in his bed, thinking that he had awakened from a really bad dream. He quickly came back to reality when he felt the pain emanating from his back. He looked around to find solace in the fact that he was in his home with familiar surroundings. He reached for a glass on the nightstand next to the bed, but missed and knocked it over. When it hit the floor, the nurse hurried into the room to see what was happening.

"Who are you?"

"I'm the nurse, and I am here to take care of you during your healing process."

"Who sent you?"

"It's okay. I am instructed to make sure that you are okay."

"What's your name?"

"I can't tell you my name. That's kind of how this works. You were shot, we removed the bullet and have been taking care of you."

"Again, who sent you?"

"Hey man, there won't be no bills for you, everything is paid for, does anything else matter? I mean you were almost dead."

"Don't get me wrong, I appreciate the fact that you guys saved my life. I just know that nothing's free. I can imagine that someone is going to show up one day and say you owe me. I'm not interested in being in debt to anyone."

"They don't tell me enough for me to answer all of your questions. I can say I don't think that they work the way you are thinking. I will keep my job if I monitor your recovery and nurse you back to health. I know you are not going to get the answers that you want from me, and I would be surprised if you get answers at all. They have really done a great thing here in saving your life. Of course, they kept the police out of it. I don't know what you did to get shot, but they must think a lot of you to do this without the police. I prefer that whatever happens you do not ever tell me what happened or anything about you. Okay."

"You're okay with living like this. Is this really how you want to make a living?"

"I could ask the same of you. I get paid good, have benefits, safer environments, and I get to spend time with my family. I know of others who work traditional nursing jobs and are always having to sacrifice family to keep their job. Personally I think I got the best of both worlds. Anyway, I think you should rest up. I will check back with you later."

"Would you do me a favor and let them know that I really appreciate everything that they have done. Since I don't know who did this I am going to trust that it was a friend."

"Okay then. See ya. I'll check on you in a couple of days."

After a few days Ted decided to turn on the television to watch the news. He walked to the kitchen to get a sandwich when he heard that a car had exploded near where he was staying. He dropped everything and hurried back into the living room, to see if he could see what type of car it was. He had a feeling that it was his car. After the news reporter described the vehicle, he was convinced that it was his. Trying to put everything together he realized that Big Thug probably saw his car the night he shot him. He knew he needed to shut down again and move one more time. After stopping for a moment to look around and take everything in, he made the decision, that it was time to go. This time he was moving a little farther away than the last time.

CHAPTER EIGHTEEN

"Chief, I just received the last confirmation regarding the information that we have collected. It appears that the data has been confirmed as credible. What do you want to do?"

"Let's see if this thing works. We will pick up the warrant on the way out."

"Chief, if it works, what about William?"

"Tom, we have work to do now."

"Okay, Okay. I'll get geared up and assemble the team to meet you out front. According to the fax he's about 15 minutes away."

"Let's go then."

Tom picked up the warrant and met SSA Smithren in front of the building with a team that included six cars and twelve agents. They had pulled up to the front of their fifteen story office building in their vehicles and parked alongside the curb.

SSA Smithren spoke into the radio to the team. "The suspect is expected to be armed and extremely dangerous. I know that we lost a good man and friend in Bradley. I don't want anybody taking any unnecessary risks today. We are going to do this by the book. The suspect is mobile and has been spotted about 18 minutes from here headed north on Valley. If he continues in that direction, I believe we can cut him off at Valley and Fourth, which is an ideal location to minimize any risk to the public. If we split up into three teams we should be able to surround him and immobilize his vehicle. Our ideal situation is to take him by the book without incident. Everyone understand?"

"Yes sir," said the agents one by one.

"Let's go, I will continue to monitor his location as we approach."

"Sir, forgive me this is agent Matthis, how can we be monitoring his location?"

"We know what he drives, he will be driving a green 2007 Ford Taurus license plate 764-D22. We are picking him up by satellite GPS."

"That's good chief. You didn't lie, I don't think," said agent Plaiedeaux. "That was actually the truth."

"I have been doing this for a little while. Okay guys I show that he has stopped right at the corner of Fourth and Valley, exactly where we wanted him to be. Now team three I want you to approach from the north bound side of Valley heading south from north of Fourth street. Team two I want you to approach from the west bound right lane of Fourth street on the east side of Valley. We will approach heading north on Valley toward Fourth street. We want to make sure that the suspect is in his car before we move in. Since Fourth street terminates at Valley, we should be able to surround him and minimize pedestrian risk." He released the talk button on the radio and said to agent Plaiedeaux, "he is walking toward his car. As soon as he closes his door everyone move in."

All of the agents moved in and blocked Franklins ability to move. They jumped out of the vehicles and ran up to the car before Franklin could react. Franklin raised his hands and was pulled out of the car and placed face down on the sidewalk. He was read his rights and put into agent Matthis back seat.

"Good Job everyone. Let's head back to the office. Make sure that we have the car picked up and taken in as well."

"That could not have gone any better. Less than 24 hours after an FBI agent was killed the suspected killer is caught and arrested without incident. I believe we have enough evidence for him to spend the rest of his life in prison. Let's get back to headquarters and make sure that everything is done properly. I will talk to you about everything else later. Apparently Stradom's technology works. I said it first. He just became an unknown quantity."

As they were driving SSA Smithren called the head of the FBI Director Hart to inform him that they had a suspect in custody. Before, he could finish his call agent Matthis called. He asked Director Hart to hold on.

"Sir, Franklin started talking while we were driving. We did not ask him any questions. He confessed to killing Bradley. He confirmed details that we had not released as well as time of death. He keeps confessing over and over. We are recording every word including this conversation with you. He won't shut up."

"You are doing the right thing. Hold on and we will see you in a couple of minutes at headquarters. I will talk to you then. Director Hart, the suspect confessed in route. We also have DNA evidence. We've got him."

"How do you have DNA evidence so quickly?"

"That's a long story. Can I get back to you with that?"

"Yes, just make sure that everything is done by the book. Setup a press conference and let my secretary know the time. I will be there. Perhaps you may want to withhold the DNA information until we can discuss it."

"Yes, sir."

As they arrived back at headquarters, they could see agent Matthis and his partner as they pulled Franklin out the vehicle. As they pulled up behind Matthis, three shots rang out. They jumped out squatting down beside their car, and then they looked back at Matthis. Matthis, his partner, and Franklin were down. Just as they started to move toward agent Matthis, the vehicle that they arrived in exploded. The blast caused everyone to fall backward. After gathering themselves they looked around and ran over to Matthis to see if they could help him. They were all dead.

"Secure the scene Plaiedeaux," said SSA Smithren.

"Director Hart, Franklin and two more agents are dead. When they stepped out of the vehicle to head into the office someone shot them and blew up their vehicle. It was a pro. Three head shots."

"What is going on down there? They actually were willing to kill FBI agents in front of FBI headquarters. What else do you know?"

"Sir it has only been about 3 minutes. Obviously I will share any and all information as we gather it. There is something going on that we apparently do not know yet. We will get whoever is responsible for this. You can count on this. They were willing to kill their own as well as FBI agents. I don't believe that they are terrorists, but I do believe that they believe that what they have done is acceptable to protect the interest of their organization. Somebody is willing to fight a war with the FBI and I believe they think they can win."

"Smithren I do not have to tell you that you have the full weight of this office and the US Government at your disposal. Go get whoever is responsible for this. Make sure that you keep me informed. There is going to be a lot of heat for this one. Three agents dead in less than 24 hours."

"Yes, sir."

SSA Smithren, hung up and turned to look for agent Plaiedeaux. When he stepped out of the vehicle he could see him as he stepped up on the curb by the burning vehicle.

"Plaiedeaux, how many people knew that we were going after Franklin this morning?"

"Chief, just about the whole office at least, if not more."

"I want every phone call, email, text, and any other forms of communication checked, immediately."

"Chief, if we are going to leave no stone unturned, we still have to consider people who knew outside the agency. There can be more, but at least William Stradom knew as well. I still haven't figured him out yet. Also, the people could have been following Franklin as well."

"You know what this means, you need to get him down here for questioning immediately. I don't care if you have to camp outside his place for days, you need to find a way to get him down here. No excuses or details of how you can't get through his little mouse trap this time."

"Yes, sir. We know where he resides, so that's a start. I will head over there now."

"Do what you have to do."

"Yes, sir."

As agent Plaiedeaux jumped in his car, he called the tactical team and told them they needed to assemble at the address where they tried to raid before. He instructed them to bring with them the tech team who specializes in getting into high security areas.

"This project is a continuation of Project Forced Entry which is classified." He informed them that they may be there awhile. "We all need to meet at the address in about 20 minutes. Everyone stop a block out and I will go in first. As soon as I give the word you will move in."

Agent Plaiedeaux pulled around the corner, and pulled up to the curb that he had grown familiar with. As he stepped out of his car, he turned to look at the gates that they had had so much difficulty with before. He reached to wipe his eyes, before turning to look around. He was absolutely shocked as he looked and then walked over to where the mail box had been a couple of days before. There were no gates, no signs of a house, no flowers, but just an empty field. He walked over to where the gate and house had been and touched the grass. It looked like nothing had ever been there.

"How am I going to explain this?" asked agent Plaiedeaux to himself. "Stand down everyone," he said after mashing the button on his radio.

"Agent Plaiedeaux, we believe we can get in this time. Give us a shot, sir. We are here as long as it takes, just as you said. Let us come over and get setup."

Since he knew he wouldn't be able to deter them or explain to anyone why he pulled back, he told them to advance to the location. As they all converged on the location, many of them who had been there for the original encounter stood in silence. "I know we all have questions, but we need to move on right now. I need two of you to rope off this site, we need to thoroughly investigate this site. In the mean time let's head back to the office. This is a bust right now."

When agent Plaiedeaux stepped back into his car; he dreaded the call he had to make to his boss.

He picked up his phone and dialed SSA Smithren.

"What is it now Plaiedeaux?"

"We've got nothing chief."

"What do you mean? I told you no excuses."

"I understand sir. I agreed with you on that. This is not an excuse but a cold hard fact."

"What is it?"

"The address where I have been meeting with Stradom and where we tried to get in last time is no longer there. There are no fences and gates, no house, no mailbox, nothing but an empty field."

"What are you talking about? You were there three days ago."

"There is not even an indication that there was a house there, chief. I don't know what else to say."

"So now you are telling me we are dealing with Houdini?"

"No sir, I left a couple people there to try to figure out some things, but I'd like to keep moving forward. I would like to follow up on Franklin, by checking out any family and or known associates, if that's okay with you, after all he appears to have a big family here. We will get back to Stradom at some point. We currently have no way to contact him and no leads to determine where he is at."

"Continue with what you plan to do."

"Thank you sir. You know he knew exactly where I was and where my computer was, and even my fax number. None of these things are necessarily known, except at the office."

"I know, I know, I will leave those things alone for now. I have already left a message at the office for them to start reviewing all communication for the last twenty-four hours."

CHAPTER NINETEEN

After sending the fax, William turned on the television to watch the news. As he walked through his office he went to his computer lab to turn on the Active DNA communications monitor. He turned on the news station to monitor it as well. As he turned to sit down he saw the news flash about the shooting in front of FBI headquarters. He immediately invoked a Transition 3 shutdown. He knew that at some point agent Plaiedeaux would have looked at who knew about Franklin's arrest and that he would have to go by FBI protocol which would include him as a suspect. I have some time, they are going to be busy for a while, he thought, because if I contact him now they will waste precious time looking in the wrong direction.

William sat down and reached over and pulled out the Archive book. After turning to his marker, he began to read again. He has always felt like the book was not complete because it did not include what happened to Theodore. It simply picks up after he had accomplished his objective.

As he opened the book, he began to read Theodore as a slave had been able to get the free education that he had worked toward, including law school. He succeeded beyond anyone's wildest expectations. The first communication with him left everyone surprised. He announced that he had learned a great deal more than he expected. By the time he was 20 years old he had been able to form a few companies and had purchased 24 banknotes from a variety of Southern Banks. He only purchased the notes that the banks were having trouble with. He found out that the banks really didn't care who was purchasing them especially if it was a company purchasing the notes. He was able to purchase the notes with no money. He had an employee through his company negotiate with the banks to get the bad notes off their books by rolling them up into one note at a discounted purchase price under a new company and borrowed the money from the banks to pay his expenses including salaries. He was able to reduce the payments on each of the notes to the borrower and also pay the bank more than they normally received from a bad note and still able to make money from the interest on the notes. When he attended law school he learned how to leverage the notes that he owned to acquire more notes. By the time he finished attending the college courses he had acquired an additional 250 notes, 16 commercial office buildings, and some major company stocks. He learned how to structure things legally through a maze of shell companies. He realized that being black and a slave, any and all that he had acquired was always going to be in jeopardy. If anyone found out that he owned any of his notes, properties, or stocks, they could be taken legally. He had to come up with a way to protect them two fold. He needed to buy notes from people and companies who would have something to lose if anything came out publicly about a slave owning their notes. He began to read and study about companies and people who supported slavery, radical groups, racial segregationist, and any other anti-government groups. He followed and tracked them and looked for any opportunity to buy notes, real estate, and even businesses when they got in trouble. He bought all of the properties and notes through companies from the South and moved ownership to companies he owned in the North. With him still being a slave, he knew he could not ever show that he had any income, so he continued to reinvest 100% of his income after taxes. Eventually, he knew he had to pay taxes, but he couldn't declare his income because he would have to reveal how he made it. He came up with a way to pay taxes but not disclose how he made his money.

William wanted to refresh his memory of what Theodore went through so he reached down to pick up the supplemental book that listed the details that Theodore had written about how he received a free education. Theodore arrived back at the plantation at night time a week before his thirteenth birthday. He was met at three o'clock in the morning just as planned. The exchange went without incident and he was accepted back in the family of his real parents. They didn't understand why he was back.

"Good to see you mom and dad", he said. "Just as you know when I left, you could not be told of anything about me. This is no different. Anything that you are told will put you and many others at risk. I love you and I appreciate what you did for me. I do understand why you did it, and I have benefited greatly from the time away from you. This is all I am going to say on the matter. For everyone here, tomorrow is just another day."

"Son, the way you be talkin, it will be trouble. You can't be talkin like dem, they will kill you and us too."

"You be right Dad. They don't be wantin no slave to be talkin much of anythin, I will be talkin the way that my massa wants me to talk."

"Good son, we be glads and sad to see you."

"I know Mom. Let's get some rest, we have a big day. The kid that left told me how he was working, and the names of the kids. He was about my size and color, this was great."

Theodore knew he had to take some time to get acquainted with the environment. So he spent the first month just getting to know all the people being careful to not stick out. He was finally able to see Johnny Joe, the son of the plantation owner.

Now everything is set. He thought.

He just had to work his way into working with him. For weeks he had been observing him, while he worked around the yard. Theodore, was short and thin for his age, which made him useless in the field for now. He didn't have any scarring, even though the kid he replaced has some slight scarring

He continued to see Johnny Joe around the house, but had not been put in a situation where he could work with him. One day he noticed that one of the slaves was carrying some wood into the house. He went over and grabbed some of the wood and followed him into the house. He knew that this was taking a risk because he was not a house slave. Slaves were chosen to go in the house, but they could not go in on their own. The slave that he followed did not notice that he was being followed. As he reached the door, he saw Johnny Joe walking by. He walked into the house with the wood in hand. Johnny Joe looked at him. "What's your name boy?"

"It be Theodore, massa Johnny."

"Boy, who told you that you can come into the house? I don't remember you being in the house before."

"Massa Johnny, I sorry I just be bringin in wood. I don't be knowing what you be saying. I just be bringin in wood. Ize don't want no trouble, I just be workin."

"You go on and get, I haven't decided if I'm going to tell my Pa yet, but you go on and get." he said.

"Thank you massa Johnny." He didn't get to take the wood in the house, so he headed back outside with the wood to put it back in the wood pile. As he was walking out the door, Johnny said, "I owe you a beatin for this."

"Yes, massa Johnny."

Theodore, was excited that he got an opportunity to make an impression on Johnny. He was the only one that he needed to concentrate on. As he began to walk home it began to rain hard, it continued to rain throughout the night.

The next morning the area around the house had became really muddy. Normally this is no big deal for the slaves. The weather conditions didn't matter for the slaves. However, this morning, the ground conditions became Theodore's asset.

As Theodore was working outside the window, he heard a knock on the window. He turned to see his massa Johnny knocking on the window.

"Go around and meet me at the front door." he said.

"Yes, massa Johnny."

Theodore walked around to the front of the house.

"Remember I told you I owed you a beatin. Well it's time." Johnny flashed a whip that he had in his hand. "Come on up here and get your beatin. I told my Pa and he said it's about time I started handling things myself, but that I could not let another day go by without givin you that beatin."

"Yes, massa."

'Take off your shirt and turn around."

"Yes, massa."

Johnny raised his hand and began to whip Theodore. He had decided to give him 20 lashes. But after he broke Theodore's' skin and he began to bleed, he reduced it to 10 lashes.

Theodore, thought he was prepared for the beating, but he had not expected the type of pain he was experiencing. He fell down from the beating. After Johnny quit beating him he stood up. There was a moment of silence as he stood waiting for Johnnie's next move. Johnny was kind of dazed and just stood there looking at him.

Finally, Johnny said for him to put his shirt back on.

Theodore gently put his shirt back on then turned and looked at Johnny.

"Stop looking at me," he said.

Theodore turned his gaze to the porch. "Yes, massa."

"You see those shoes over there. They are muddy from the yard today. Clean my shoes boy. If you do a good job, you just might get to do them all the time. Have you ever cleaned shoes before?"

"Yes, massa Johnny. I do shoes good."

Just like my Pa said, "beat an animal and it will try harder to please you."

William thought about something that he read in the other book, so he put a bookmark in the page where he had ended and turned back to the main book. As he picked up the book he began to read where he had left off. He decided that he had to document all that he accomplished and put in place a succession plan. After much consideration, he decided that the whole process will be named White Pages. He remembered how the college had named their counsel the white counsel to be hidden in plain sight and he figured no one would ever look at the cover and think that it will be a historical reference forever tied to slavery.

So the stage was set for Theodore, he never was able to escape the bonds of slavery regarding how he made his money, but he was able to die of natural causes at an estimated age of 78. By then, he had found a successor and passed all of the documented history to him.

William closed the book and put it back on the shelf. It had always been an affirmation for him to read the precious words of White Pages.

He sat down and turned the television on again to watch the news. There were still news reports regarding the possibility of where the shots could have been fired. He thought of how he could get down there to look at the scene, but decided that that would not be a wise choice. The phone rang just as the news reporter completed his story before going to a commercial break.

"Mr. Stradom, will you be coming in today? I have already canceled a couple of meetings," asked Samantha.

"Yes, I will be in about 25 minutes. I didn't get a chance to look at my schedule yet, but see if you can adjust my calendar to accommodate the rest of my meetings today. I would like to not have to cancel any more of them. I will try to clean up any loose ends when I get there regarding the meetings that I missed."

"Yes, sir. I will make the necessary adjustments. Is everything okay? There doesn't seem to be a right time for this, but just so you know I am open to having dinner again."

"Yes, Samantha, everything is fine. I will see you soon and you know that the other dinner was a mistake."

"William, the term mistake is your word, not mine. I enjoyed it and I offer no apology for it, nor do I agree with any part of it being a mistake."

"Okay, Samantha. Let's talk about this some another time."

"Yes, sir."

By the time William reached the office the news station was reporting additional agents had been killed in the line of duty across several states. When William walked in he could see that everyone was glued to the television sets. They began to tell him of what the news station was reporting.

"Hold it, hold it. I know that there is lot going on right now, however it is necessary that we get back to work. We have a busy day with some unforgiving deadlines. Samantha, I need about 15 minutes, see if you can adjust my schedule again. Also get Devin on the phone, I need to speak with him now."

"Devin, does he even work for the company now? I haven't heard you mention him in a few years."

William turned and looked at Samantha.

"Okay, I will get him."

William walked into his office and closed the door.

As he walked toward his desk, the phone rang. He reached over and pressed the speaker button. "Yes."

Samantha said, "I have Devin on the phone for you."

"Patch him through. Hello Devin."

"Hello Mr Stradom, how are you doing and how is your family?"

"Everyone and everything is fine. Thank you for asking. And your family, how are they?"

"They are fine as well. Thank you for the gift to help with my son's surgery. I really appreciate that."

"You are welcome."

"So, do you need something Mr. Stradom?"

"Devin, are you sitting down?"

"No, but I will. Go ahead."

"It's time. Time to wake up the warehouse."

"Is this a joke? I have been working on the warehouse for over 15 years?"

"No it's not a joke. Here is the catch I need her fully operational in no more than 48 hours; sooner if possible."

"We had discussed different phases of mobilization."

"I know. Things have happened very quickly, and therefore it is necessary to move as quickly as possible."

"With the right people, I can have her up in 24. However, either way it is going to be expensive."

"What is the number?"

"For 24 hours, it will be maybe $150,000."

"Let's do it. You know this is not a test. Once she goes operational there is no turning back."

"I wasn't sure, but I am now."

"Is there anything about her that is not ready for this? By the way, contact Samantha and she will coordinate any payments needing to be made."

"No, sir. Part of our testing included fully operational testing. That was the only way for us to be sure."

"Are you up on all of the protocols that we established including our Doomsday ones?"

"Yes, sir. This is why you hired me. I've been preparing for this it seems like my whole life. We are ready sir."

"You know that going fully operational there are always going to be some kinks, new technologies, contingencies that we cannot account for. The warehouse will forever be adapting and learning to deal with new threats, which means that we will have a few glitches."

"Yes, sir."

"Keep me informed."

"Yes, sir."

"We have never worked before on this level. There will be a few bumps, but we will get through them."

"Yes, sir we will."

"From now on we communicate through our own network of Sectional Transitional Phones."

"Yes, sir. All of the team will be informed as well."

"I need to go, Devin I am excited as well, there is nothing like this in the world. Let me know when it's up. I will let you know when we will add our target interface."

CHAPTER TWENTY

Slovie woke up in the middle of the night thinking, what about the rest of the team, and the board? This has been so crazy, I haven't thought about whom we are going to be working with, or who all decided to stay or go. He lay back down and went back to sleep. He hurried to work with the thought fresh on his mind; however, he did not pay attention to the clock. He arrived and hour early for work. As he entered the office, he realized he didn't even know if his office was going to be in the same location. He grabbed a cup of coffee and headed toward Stanley's office. He could see that the light was on and that his door was partly open. He pushed open the door and said, "Good morning Stanley."

Stanley replied, "Good morning Slovie. I was told that you liked to be called Slovie. Is that okay with you?"

"Yes it is fine."

"You are eager to get started I see?"

"I always like to be on time."

"You're a little over an hour early."

"Oops, I'm sorry, I didn't pay attention to the clock this morning."

"I will come back."

"No, no, no, there must be something on your mind. Come on in, let's talk about it."

"You've kept us busy the last couple of days. We haven't had a chance to look up. What about the rest of the team, that helped build this company? I mean, there had to be a reason that everything went down the way that it did. So, what is the flip side?"

"That's a good question Slovie. I will shoot straight with you, because this is business. Not everyone is making the trip and or even being given the opportunity to choose. That's just the nature of the beast. The analysis clearly defined who would and who would not be able to make the transition with us."

"Okay, then this whole thing is for real. Are some of the ones not going with us really going to lose millions and billions of dollars?"

"In some cases, yes."

"How are we supposed to live with that? Strike that. How are we supposed to be able to trust that at some point that you won't do the same to us?"

"First of all, thank you for asking the hard questions. You and Richard will be among a select few who will have the privilege to attend a meeting in 30 days that will answer these questions specifically. I am not going to be the face of the company, and it has not been given to me to answer these questions. The people that put this together will be gathering in 30 days to answer any questions about how the new teams will come together and even why some people were not invited to come along. If for any reason you encounter any problems with previous employees or legal problems regarding your continued employment with this company, the company will defend you and cover all costs. This is not as sinister as it seems. I do realize almost nothing I say to you at this time will instill trust, but not too many companies would be a direct cause of you losing close to a billion dollars and then help you to get it all back."

"You did say that you were direct. If you had said that to Richard, he would already be gone. My guess is you already knew that as well. Ten years, Is there anything that you don't know about us?"

"If we didn't do our homework then we would be in the wrong business. Surely, if you take a look at the enormity of this project and think about what you would have done, you would know everything about the people that you would choose to work with as well."

"Why me? I don't need anyone giving hand outs or feeling sorry for me. You don't know me and you haven't asked one question about me being in a wheelchair."

"You know better than I the policies around addressing and speaking to employees who have disabilities."

"Yes, I do, but to completely ignore the fact that I am disabled is just as bad."

"I'm glad you came in early this morning. I would have never had this conversation in a group setting. I just don't feel it would have been right. So, since we are putting all of our cards on the table. Let's talk about it."

"Thank you. I really need to know that this isn't some sort of charity cause."

"Slovie, I told you we did our research regarding all of you. When you had the accident that caused the nerve damage that put you in your chair, the work you produced for the company improved one thousand percent. Probably nobody has ever told you that. It was like you had something to prove."

"No, they haven't."

"That percentage unfortunately is not our words, but it was recovered from a company executive evaluation done long before this buyout started. For some reason, after the wheelchair you put out better work by far than what you had ever done before. It took you a few months to gain some traction, but when you did, it was incredible."

"So, this isn't about me being a charity case?"

"No, not at all. It is about you being a valuable asset to the team."

"Okay, I will give you that. So I guess I will have to try not to reconcile this in my head until the meeting in 30 days. Thank you for your honesty."

"Thank you, Slovie."

"Stanley, this has been interesting. I say let's go to work. By the way, where am I supposed to work now?"

"You can keep the same office, because your team with its new members will be located around you. Richard will have to move his office, but it will be no big deal. Now when you get to your office there will be some instructions on your desk. Your job will change a little but you will find it to be a better fit for you now. Oh, by the way, you didn't even notice that our stacks grew a little bit since yesterday."

"No, I didn't. I hope you know that I am just a little bit skeptical about all of this. After all, you can count on one hand the number of companies in the world that could take on this many projects seemingly so diverse at one time. I really hope that this isn't some cruel joke."

"Nothing but time will help you overcome your skepticism and you will. Richard will be here soon, and then we can get together."

Slovie just missed Richard as he went into his office and closed the door, Richard walked past his office, not seeing him. He walked directly to Stanley's office and tapped on the door, "May I come in?"

Stanley responded, "Sure come on in."

"Richard looked around the office before sitting down. There seems to be more stacks today, or am I seeing things?"

"No, you are not, there are 3 additional contracts that we picked up. Good eye."

"I've been here for over 25 years and I have not seen anything like this. That's not why I'm here. Currently, we have not had a board meeting, and you are the only person we have been allowed to meet with. Are you really the person that orchestrated all of this?"

"I am glad that you are feeling comfortable enough to ask that question. No, absolutely not. I am not the head of this transition, and no I am not the head of the company. Also, I will not be the face of this company to the public or to the employees."

"So, at what point will we be permitted to communicate with the rest of the leadership of the company. This seems a little strange to me."

"I understand. Your job will be much the same as you had before. You are well suited for it. On your desk in your new office you will find a package that includes a list of all the department heads, their titles, and all of their contact information."

"Hold on, you said my new office. What about all of my stuff?"

"We thought it necessary to move you. Your staff has grown by about 30%. We had to strategically place you to help create an accessible work environment. The office is quite a bit larger than your other office, but I think you will be able to manage it. After viewing your office if you feel like you do not like the decorations, furniture, or its arrangement, we can accommodate any changes that you would like to make. What is not up for discussion is the location of your office. Do you have any more questions?"

"Not really."

"Okay then, let me tell you a couple of things. Perhaps answer some questions that you should have asked. Some of your friends didn't make the cut for the new company. They lost everything, and we did not invite them to continue with us. As a company we want every person here to be concerned about more than themselves. The work environment we want to foster is comparable to true family. There will be training and gatherings where we will create opportunities for all employees to embrace these concepts. It is going to be imperative that all senior management embrace these concepts because you will have to lead the way."

"Secondly, you are invited to a meeting in 30 days that will explain this whole transition. You will be introduced to the new leadership of the company including new staff and board members. In that meeting it will be explained to you, why we chose to keep you and what will be fully expected of you. There will also be a forecasted vision of the company as a whole. On the desk in front of you is an envelope, which tells you where all of your stuff is in your new office. I will give you about 30 minutes to get acquainted with your new office then you, I, and Slovie will meet back here."

"Yes, sir." Richard was glad to have a little time, because he was offended by the way that Stanley spoke to him. He stood up, turned and looked at Stanley once more and then walked out the door.

CHAPTER TWENTY-ONE

"Samantha, see if you can reach Thayor our PR genius. He is about to get the job of a lifetime. I need to speak with him," said William.

"From my understanding you have never met him. Is that accurate?"

"Yes, that is true."

"How do you want to me to proceed then, if you still want to remain anonymous?"

"He has worked with me for about 12 years and has done a wonderful job for us. However, it is time for us take our relationship to a new level. Please set up a meeting for 10:00 AM, on Thursday in the red office."

"The red office. As long as I have been here, you have never used this office."

"It was established for this day. Security is already in place, you just need to have IT and maintenance set up a few things for Thursday. The list is in your inbox."

"Okay. By the way, did you catch the news this morning?"

"Yes, I did. It is tragic."

"No, No, No. After I got off the phone with you two more agents were killed in a separate shooting."

"Are you talking about in the last hour?"

"Yes sir. It happened again."

"My goodness. Samantha, clear my calendar for the next hour."

"Sir, may I speak to you in private?"

"Yes, Samantha, but not now, I need to have some time."

William, went in his office and closed the door behind him. He picked up his Sectional Transitional Phone and dialed agent Plaiedeaux.

"Hello, this agent Plaiedeaux."

"Can we talk?"

"Who is this?"

"This is William."

"The only way that we are going to talk is if you turn yourself in."

"I am sorry to hear what happened today. But, I don't think you get what is going on."

"So are you finally admitting that you are involved?"

"Do you understand that they have openly declared war on the FBI. This thing isn't over, it is only going to escalate from here."

"What are you talking about?"

"You think this is over now that they have killed a few of you? This is only the beginning. No one in their right mind would do this unless somehow they live under the delusion that they could finish their objective."

"William, I am done discussing this with you. You know the terms I just laid out to you. Are you willing to turn yourself in right now?"

"You are going to need to get some answers very quickly, to save lives. You've seen some of the technology that is available to me and how quickly you were able to gather information on the one murder. I am offering my help to stop this."

"You arrogant cuss. You are talking to the FBI as if you are superior to us. This is not a game. You are putting the nails in your own coffin."

"This is a sectional transitional phone. You won't know what that means, but you can now reach me at any time, since time is of the essence. Since you are going to take this stand, the number you dial to get me is 911. You will be calling. By the way you need to dial the number from your cell phone; otherwise you will get the 911 operator."

"William, WILLIAM, WILLLLIAM. You stupid jerk."

Agent Plaiedeaux dialed his supervisors number.

"I'm assuming that you have something."

"I hate what I am about to say in the middle of all of this, but you said you wanted to be kept in the loop. I just got a call from William."

"You What?"

"Yes sir."

"Okay, what is it now?"

"First I told him he needs to turn himself in. Then he said that this was only the beginning and that things were going to escalate from here."

"Are you telling me he is admitting he is involved in killing federal agents?"

"No, sir, even though I asked him the same thing. He said basically that no one in their right mind would have declared war on the FBI unless they thought they could accomplish their objective. I think he was calling, well no, he said he was calling to offer his help."

"His help to do what?"

"He gave me a telephone number where I can reach him at any time, and said he was offering his help to solve this problem, to find out who was doing this."

"Who the heck does he think he is? This is the FBI he is talking to. Whatever you are saying to him, he is getting the wrong impression of us. He acts like he is superior to us or something. I can't wait until we nail him to the wall."

"Chief, I think we are spending way too much time talking about this. With everyone on high alert, we are basically bringing everything to a halt here in the city."

"My gut tells me that this is exactly where the perpetrators want us to be, which is not good. Get back to the office as quick as you can. By the way, you will be assigned a partner until this is over with. If you have a number for him, we should be able get him?"

"You know it's not that simple. It is apparently a sectional transitional phone, whatever that means. My guess is that we can't track it, trace it, or anything."

"You do know what you just said. You are acknowledging that he's been able get inside our heads with technology that is different than we have. While William is definitely an irritant, he is too close to everything to leave him out of the mix. Somehow he is involved. I don't know his end game. What is the likelihood of him showing up with his superior attitude, thinking that he is smarter and perhaps more technologically advanced than us? Then while we are pursuing him some other group shows up thinking the same thing and decides that they can declare war on us with expectations to win."

"I hadn't thought about it like that. He is such a pain. I hate that smug face sitting their talking to me like we are going to be friends, when he should be sitting somewhere in prison. How else can you explain all this façade? He thinks this is some sort of game. I can't wait to nail him to the wall. I want to see the look on his face then. I get it chief. I will do whatever you want me to do."

"This is not personal. The people who are doing these evil things are cold, calculating, unfeeling, and basically terrorist. We have an obligation to protect the people of this great nation. We will leave no stone unturned until we finish this, wherever it leads."

"This seems like it's a home grown kind of a power play. I should be back in about 15 minutes chief."

"We will set up a conference call with the other offices. I am walking into the office now. The call will be set up in about 25 minutes."

When SSA Smithren walked into the office, Sarah approached him frantically at the door.

"Chief, it happened again."

"What happened again?"

"We just got a call that in three other states; there have been six more agents killed, two in each state. Before, you say anything the President wants you to call him on a secure line. They said he did not want to contact you on your cell phone."

"Get everyone together in the boardroom. Set up an interoffice satellite video conference for 20 minutes. I will be there as soon as I can."

After his conversation with the President, he hurried into the boardroom. As he opened the door Tom walked in beside him.

Before they could speak Dana walked up and handed SSA Smithren a note.

He stopped and read the note, took a deep breath, and walked into the room.

"I think we need to go back to the beginning, which was the murder of Bradley Jamison, he said to all that were listening."

Everyone started talking at once.

"Hold it, hold it, let's get a hold of ourselves. In the last 20 minutes, there have been 18 Agents murdered. Immediately, we need to implement project rebirth, throughout the agency. We have been trained for this even though we never expected to have to take this drastic of measures. I just got off the phone with the President."

"Sarah raised her hand, I'm sorry but what is project Rebirth?"

"Effective immediately after this meeting everyone will be moved into shadow mode. All active cases will be suspended and handed off to the United States Bureau of Investigation. All FBI personnel will be reassigned to Federal Bureau Security. Every form of communication at work and at home, our transportation, our homes, will all be swept. All of the equipment will be destroyed and replaced." Just as he began to speak, the door opened and a man in plain clothes walked through the door with a team of special forces soldiers escorting him.

Everyone jumped to their feet and pulled out their weapons.

They were blocked from approaching SSA Smithren.

"SSA Smithren, my name is John Alfred. I have been sent by the President of the United States. I can't tell you the division of government that I work in, but I can give you some information that we have obtained. I don't exist on paper. This is a sealed envelope that is for you. You can share the information however you deem necessary, but first you have to read it."

"This is rather dramatic isn't it?"

"We are all working toward a swift and resolute response to these acts of terror."

SSA Smithren motioned to Dana to bring him the envelope.

Once the envelope reached his hand, John Alfred and his men backed out the door and left.

After he opened the envelope, he sat down in a chair by the podium. He looked up at the screen and out into the room. He stood back up and walked back to the podium. The room was silent. "All of the series of murders tie together neatly into the major drug case that we are pursuing, said SSA Smithren. In the case of the last eighteen murders; nine of the agents were involved in the case. The other nine were killed because of the fact that we required them to partner up, due to the murders. The whole thing is one big hit that was put out on FBI Agents. The going rate is $500,000.00 per head, dead. The hit was posted on some obscure website, after the first hits. They wanted us to know that it was a hit."

"Tom spoke up, sir what agency has this information and how and why would they have it and not us?"

"That is a good question Tom; I will get back to it later."

"As I was saying, every household, car, all electronics, clothes, will be swept. No stone will be left unturned. Everyone's families will be moved to mandatory secure locations to stay and live temporarily, until we sort this out. This is an unprecedented departure from agency policy, but we felt that we had to get ahead of this thing and stem the tide of needless deaths. Shadow mode means that you become invisible to the public. You do nothing and go nowhere that is customary to you. Also, everyone will be issued tracking devices. Everyone in the agency will be issued a packet with instructions specific to your roll in the agency. The package will include everything you need to get through this transition. You all have your orders. Now let's move."

CHAPTER TWENTY-TWO

As Ted completed his second move by hanging his last picture, he realized how different his life had become. He had misjudged the emotional impact of moving away from all of his family and friends. He realized that meeting new people was not a problem, but trusting them with intimate parts of your life was something else. He was having success in his business ventures, but failing at building friendships. The value of childhood friendships became more significant to him. The loneliness began to become a distraction. "What good is it to have the whole world if you have no one to share your life with," he said.

One day he contacted his business office to ask his secretary to do a couple of things. "Hello, may I speak to Mary," he asked.

"I'm sorry sir but Mary no longer works here. May I help you?"

"Who am I speaking to?"

"I am new here sir. My name is Mareelynd, Mareelynd Hawks."

"Okay, my name is Ted, oh uh I'm sorry, my name is"

"That's funny sir, you must have a lot on your mind, since you can't remember your own name. Oops I did it again. I interrupted you. I'm sorry about that sir."

"It's okay; I am James Thorne the owner of the business where you are now employed. I'm not sure that you can help me, but I will leave a message for Chad to call me when he gets out of his meeting."

"I will do that sir, however if you give me a chance maybe I can help you with your original questions. Again I'm sorry for interrupting you."

"This is how it's going to be with you. I need to review contract #NY126347, it needs to be set up on my remote teleprompter. My laptop is being replaced right now, so below the contract will you please add my calendar schedule for the week. Now if you can get this done, then you can disregard having Chad call me."

"Yes sir. If you would check your teleprompter now, you will see that the contract and your schedule are there. Is there anything else that I can do for you?

"No, not at this time. Where did you come from?"

"I'm not sure what you are asking me. Are you asking me where I was born and raised or possibly where I went to school?"

"Never mind for now. I will speak to you later."

"Sir, I will be happy to answer any questions you have."

"Trust me, I know that Mareelynd. I need to go now. I will be back in touch."

When Ted hung up the phone, he reminisced about how his life had changed in the last year. He thought his life was over when he had gotten shot. After he realized that he was going to survive, he desperately wanted to reach out to someone, only to realize that he couldn't. "I don't understand," he thought. "How can I be feeling this way when I'm starting to live my dreams?"

Ted began to talk out loud as if he was talking to someone. "Okay, now I get it. You've been trying to tell me something, but not with words. I get it now. I have been selfish. I admit that this new direction is way out my comfort zone. All of my life I have been trying to be clever and figure things out on my own. I am self reliant. Initially I thought that this new transition would be more of the same. My life is not my own. This doesn't help me unless I know who my life belongs to. I am use to trying to control things. There is nothing about this life that allows me to be in control. What am I supposed to do about that? What am I supposed to do now?"

"Nothing. That's just great. Somehow you convinced me to come here and I came, but now you are silent. I know you hear me. There is no way that I would be alive if somehow you are not watching over me. You are elusive to say the least. I told you I know that I messed up and I apologized for that. I know that there is no going back. So how do I go forward from here?"

CHAPTER TWENTY-THREE

"Good morning Thayor."

"Good morning Mr. Stradom. I hope everything is going well for you. Scratch that. I would say that to someone whom I haven't communicated with in a while. Good to talk to you. Do you want me to report on the project?"

"No, just submit the report through the usual channels. Are you done with the project?"

"Yes, sir I am done."

"Thayor you have been with us for a little over twelve years. I wanted to commend you for the work you have done with us; it has been exemplary."

"Thank you. Usually when someone starts off a conversation the way that you are someone is getting fired. So if that's the case then let's just say it and be done with it."

"No, no, no, that is not the case. Not too many people would have lasted as long as you have when you are working outside the government or military. We have never met and I'm your boss. You have worked for me twelve years and you have never asked to see me. You kept your head down and really have done some remarkable work. You have been trustworthy and dependable. The nature of your work has required our relationship to remain status quo. Today, I wanted to let you know that things have changed. In about three minutes my driver will be at your office to pick you up. He will bring you to a meeting place where we will meet for the first time. We have much to discuss."

"Sir, I'm not sure what to say."

"You don't have to say anything. It will take you about 15 minutes to get there. I look forward to meeting you."

"Thank you sir."

"I will see you in a few minutes."

William hung up and called Devin. "Good afternoon, Devin."

"Good afternoon, sir."

"Samantha processed the payments. I see that there was little bit of a cost overrun."

"Yes sir. I explained it in my paperwork that I submitted. A couple of the guys were going to have to pay a performance penalty in order to postpone their current jobs, so we had to absorb the penalties."

"No problem. Since we are up, are we having any problems?"

"No sir, everything is online."

"Good. Did you reach the scaling and production of the Preemptive Anti Weapons Limiter?"

"Yes sir. However, you know that we have received the delivery of all kinds of equipment like this, but we have no clue what any of it is, or rather what it does."

"I know Devin. Yesterday a manual was delivered to you. Check your safe. It will give you an overview of what the system does. You are going to have your work cut out. Remember you will not have to be the expert; you will just need to be familiar with the different kinds. It will be called P.A.W.L. There are several systems besides P.A.W.L. that you will be handling. No matter what anyone tells you, none of this equipment will ever be for sale. Each one has a tracking device that only we can track. Do you understand?"

"Yes sir. I know that I am the head of logistics and deployment which includes mobilization of all equipment. I'm sorry sir, but I can see that you may have concerns about this all working. We have trained for this sir, and we are ready."

"Okay, Devin. I will get back to you when we are ready to go with P.A.W.L."

"Come on in Thayor. I am William Stradom. It is good to finally meet you face to face."

"It is good to meet you as well Mr. Stradom. I am still kind of in the dark about all of this. I guess I do have to ask the why question now."

"First all the room is clean. That means it has been swept by security to insure that we have absolute privacy. I will start at the end to help you be at ease, and then work from the beginning. This is a job offer for you to continue to work with me. When we hired you, you already had invested quite a bit of money into your education. Based on our contract with you, we agreed to reimburse you over a thirty-year period monthly, all of the expenses you had incurred for your education, pay off your education loans, limit you to working no more than thirty hours per week for us, and ten hours per week to continue your education, while we paid 100 % of your additional education, and starting at $200,000.00 per year salary. We believed in you. Obviously there were some pretty specific restrictions that you had to adhere to; and if you failed them, then you would get nothing. You passed them all. Now first of all after twelve years I know that your salary is now $300,000 per year. The job I'm am offering you will pay you $10,000,000.00 per year. Before I go any farther, does this sound like something you would be interested in?

"Mr. Stradom."

"Hold it. Please call me William."

"William, this is a set up. Nobody on planet earth would listen to that presentation and then say no I'm not interested. Secondly, I do not think that you would reveal yourself to me before you presented this to me. I am honored and yes I am interested, but please do not hold it against me if I wait for the details."

"I have monitored you and how well you have done with your continued education. You seem to excel at learning. You allowed us to redirect your education and career track without knowing what was at the end of the tunnel. We have groomed you for a specific job. We have built a company that now needs a public face. I can't be the public face of the company. I am asking you to become the public face of the company."

"I don't understand. Are you talking about CFO, CEO, COO or something like that?"

"No, your title will be Company Representative. My anonymity needs to remain intact. If you would, walk over to the table and pick up the paper that is laying on it. It contains details regarding the job description. Take a moment and review it."

Thayor sat down and began to read the brief one-page document. As he finished, he looked up and leaned back in his chair. "You're telling me that you are going to pay me that kind of money to do this. You can easily pay a fraction of that to get the work you are talking about done."

"Before we go any further, I need to ask you a question. Thayor, do you believe that what we do as a business is legal. At any time have you considered the possibility that we may be covering up illegal activities amongst all of the secrecy?"

"Ah, I'm not sure how to answer that."

"We are men and we are talking. Before you lay the greatest opportunity of your life. If there is ever a time to come clean is now."

"Okay, yes I have had thoughts of that being a possibility. I have always wondered, why so much secrecy and security."

"Thank you. You just took a big risk. I needed you to do that. In this country even today, there are things that cannot be discussed publicly. Today I am going to tell you straight up, there is nothing that we do here that is illegal. However, in order for us to continue to exist and thrive we have to take some drastic steps. This job will not be easy. We are going to force our way into the political arena, not because we have aspirations but because it is a necessity to allow the company to grow and prosper. When you are in the public eye, they are going to want to know all of your dirty laundry. You will have the unenviable position of not knowing all of the secrets, which means that you will not be able to tell them even if you wanted to. You may be dragged into court, possibly jailed, but none of the secrets will be traded to get you out. You can never use my name, and I will never be available for any court cases, trials, or anything like that. You will learn a lot about the company, but you also will learn nothing. You will have one of the toughest jobs on earth. People will not want to talk to you, but they will also have no choice. There are things that are coming and have already arrived that we are preparing to deal with. There are going to be days when you are going to wish you had never been born. There are also going to be days where you are going to be confident that the things that happened on that day, were why you were born."

"I woke up this morning thinking, I'm going to get another project today. Let me ask you a question. When my little brother got in trouble with the drugs, my dad called me and told me that he was in trouble but begged me to not come. He said he had everything under control. Was that you? When my father got laid off and my mother got sick, he ended up not needing any money, and from the medical care my mom got she is okay now. Was that you too?

"Yes, it was. We take care of our own. We have a philosophy of working with families to help their children achieve success. Particularly if there is a perceived purpose for the child being here. In simpler terms we understand that odds are almost always against a child born in the ghetto with no familial support system toward education, and no examples of success. We simply developed the system that protects the child's potential by becoming familial support to the entire family. This diminishes the things that would prevent a person from becoming successful."

"Why haven't you told me about this before?"

"Typically every time we've tried that it has failed. In most cases the child and family members have changed and began to live with a sense of entitlement, which caused them to break the rules and so on. The biggest issue usually forms because of the employee. They begin to think that they should be able to direct the care and support that we give to their families and they figure the cost doesn't matter."

"I get it. How long do I have to decide this?

"Until you walk out that door today."

"You know you usually give me nothing when we have our conversations. This is obviously a drastic change. When would I start?"

"Counting the last hour, you have already been on the job an hour."

"I couldn't imagine with the classes that I was taking, what you had in mind for me. I did research, but never got close to this. I will basically have no power but I will be one of the most powerful company representatives in the world."

"Yes, that is exactly it. You and I will work closely together, but you will be in the public eye and I will remain anonymous."

"I will take the job. By the way also, thank you for helping my family. I won't say that I understand how all of this came about, but I am at this point fully convinced that whatever this is based on your word, it is not illegal."

"Good. Welcome aboard. Now that you have made your decision it's time to go to work. By the way in addition to the raise that you are getting, for calculations purposes the company will go back to when you completed your fifth year of employment to calculate a bonus to be paid out over the next eighteen years. The bonus will be the difference between what you were getting paid and your current pay based on your new rate for the last seven years spread out over the next 18 years."

"I am not sure what you just said."

We will be paying an additional almost $68,000,000 on top of the $10,000,000 spread out over the next eighteen years. However, if you quit, break company policy, and or fired, you will forfeit all of this."

"That's crazy. How is that possible?"

One of the things you are going to learn is that you have only represented a portion of our companies. As a conglomerate we are a much larger company than you could imagine. Now, not all of our companies are going to be known to you or the public. Many you will never represent. However, there are some that you are going to need to get familiar with for a board meeting we will be having in about a week and a half. I am going to present you there as a representative. This will be the only board meeting that I will attend. It is necessary."

"Why take the risk?"

"Like I said, it is necessary."

"So, yesterday I was working for you but not in the inner circle. Today I leave and I am in the inner circle. What is the company name that I will be working for?"

"You will actually be subcontracted through one of my companies that only serve as an employment agency."

"How will I be able to explain this to anyone?"

"They won't believe you. You will find it easier probably to just continue working and concentrating on work rather than sharing the news about your new promotion."

"So, I'm not going to be able to tell anybody about my new job either?"

"You're going to realize how beneficial it is to not have to involuntarily deal with the fallout of family and friends knowing that you are making fourteen million dollars a year. You are never going to own stock in any of the companies. The world is going to want to know everything about you. They can't learn anything other than what we allow them to learn. If you own stock, there has to be a trail of the stock and the earnings. Your tax returns will start out fairly simple. You will be able to invest and do whatever you want to do with your money, just as long as it doesn't violate any covenants with us, and as long as it doesn't compromise the job that you are going to be doing with the company. You can never get in financial trouble, not even once. You have learned a lot over the years, and have done well with your income. Here take this card. Jonathan Mays, whose name is on the card will be able to assist you with some financial strategies. You will have to cover the cost of his services yourself. Just say to him when you call him, I'm a first time private member and he will take it from there. I will never meet your family or attend public gatherings. Just as before, you are not to bring up my name to anyone. Many will not like it. Trust me we are not giving you money; you will earn every penny. Out of respect for you I will now give you one more opportunity to back out. Are you still willing to accept the job?"

"Yes, I am still in, you just added intrigue. I will say this; it is obvious that you have been planning this for a long time. It appears that you haven't left anything up to chance. I will assume that you have a package for me to read and sign?"

"Yes, I do. Congratulations. When you go out to your vehicle, the rest of the package will be in your briefcase. By the way, you have a lot to learn. You and I will be joined at the hip from now own."

"I was waiting for that. I am in 100%."

"Before the board meeting there will be at least three news conferences you will be attending. The speeches are already written and ready for you to get familiar with. You can change them to reflect your personality; however, I would like to review your final take. Once this starts, you will begin to receive invitations to talk shows and news stations all of which you will turn down. I think this is enough for now. The card attached to the job description has the number where you can reach me at all times. Obviously, the number is only to be used by you. Memorize it and then destroy the card."

Chapter Twenty-Four

As William returned to his office, he shut the door behind him. He sat down at his desk and logged in to the acoustiology software in order to retrieve the new telephone number for agent Plaiedeaux. He dialed the number.

"Agent Plaiedeaux speaking."

"Hello, Tom. Did I catch you at a bad time?"

"Mr. Stradom. How did you get this number?"

"Is that what you really want to ask me?"

"Yes, it is."

"Let's just say it is good to have technology that helps you through the day."

"As usual, that is not an answer. Do you know the laws you are breaking by hacking into the FBI's systems like this? These numbers are only for the use by the agency."

"I did not hack into your system, and have broken no laws. By the way this is agency business. When are you going to get it? I helped you catch the guy that started all of this by killing your agent. He knew nothing and was just a pawn. He didn't have any information that would help you stop this. Your own prejudices are clouding your judgments."

"You really think that you can play this game claiming that you are innocent and that you can simply do and say anything you want because you are above the law. We are going to bring you down off your high horse. It doesn't matter how smart you are, you will eventually slip up, and when you do I will be right there waiting for you. I do not believe in coincidences and it just so happens that all of this started happening around the same time we began to close in on you. Whether you are a co-conspirator, or the leader, you are involved, which makes you public enemy number one."

"Information interpreting is often tainted because of flawed or damaged receptacles. Everyone has the opportunity to deal with issues, but it is their own past that will skew or influence the interpretation tailored to their experiences. If you take five different people and have them interpret the same data without either influencing the other, you will end up with five different views. You do have your perspective but you don't know everything."

"You know that you have been on the phone for a while, so we know where you are."

"You cannot trace my phone. I called you because your old phone that they took from you was the only way that you could reach me. I am giving you my information again."

"It appears to you that the most powerful nation in the world has a problem, which I believe to be manufactured by you, now needs help, because they can't solve a problem without you. Don't expect a call from me except to say I got you.

"You only know what I have permitted you to know. I keep trying to tell you that you don't know even as much as you think you know. You don't even know my name."

"What are you talking about?"

"I gave you the name William Stradom. That is not my real name."

"I, oh, I, oh."

"That's what I thought. You are putting lives at risk because of your ignorance. You are supposed to be operating in the best interest of the people of America, not just the agency where you work. I can no longer stand by idly and watch as innocent people die. Mark this day, Tom. For today is the beginning of our new friendship. Today things have forever changed."

"I know what they told you Tom. All of your case loads and all of your contacts are rerouted to someone else. Isn't it ironic, how you refuse to believe almost anything that I say because of my secrecy, and things about me that are not public knowledge, but the agency you now report to is not the agency you've known, and you know nothing about them either. How is it that you trust them implicitly even though you don't know any of them and you can't even acknowledge that they exist? As I told you from the beginning, I will only be working with you. I will not have a single conversation with anyone else. Now it's your turn to be in the hot seat. If you tell them about this call, then they are going to think that you are disobeying orders. How do you explain to them how I got your number, when there is no one else in the agency that has had their number compromised? It will be worse if you change your number and I get it again. If you don't tell them, you are withholding information and that can cost you your job. At some point their training will kick in and they will begin to ask the same questions that you have been asking me, and they will come to the same conclusion that you have. You will be inside the agency, but they will not be able to trust you anymore. You are going to have to make a choice. No one will trust you and you will trust no one. That is a recipe for disaster for you. You are no good on your own exclusively. I am going to help you. They are going to have to trust you."

"Let's say that all of that is true. I knew the risk when I joined the agency. I have done nothing wrong. I will stand by my record. I didn't ask for nor do I need your help."

"Obviously you know your agency handbook well. Everything that you said is right out of it. There is one small problem with that. What if less people die because you are alive, rather than when you are dead? What if by you living, millions will live instead of dying at an early age?"

"You are never going to get me to come over to the dark side; no matter how logical or seemingly reasonable your arguments. By the way, again you have not denied or acknowledged any accusations that I laid before you. I will not hide from any of this."

"Since you have worked in the agency haven't you ever been propositioned before? Those who want you to come over to the dark side as you call it do not give a choice as I have given you a choice. They will leverage something in your life like a family member or something important to you and then give you a death or submit option. Perhaps you need to read your own story and experiences. I have not asked you to do anything for me. I know you study behavior sciences as a way to understand and capture criminals. There are stages of recognition that help you in your pursuit of criminals. Where do I fit in your categorization?"

"William is what I will continue to call you. William, I am done with this conversation."

"Just remember there is no turning back for you now. You are in this to the end."

CHAPTER TWENTY-FIVE

"Chief, William called again."

"How is that possible Tom? We just received the new phones."

"I don't know sir. He told me it basically doesn't matter how many times I switch phones; he still will only talk to me. He also knew about the new agency take over. Sir, I know that it was breaking protocol to come to you first, but I just wanted someone else to know because this can't end well for me. How can I tell them that someone called me that possibly is the cause of all this, but that I can call him anytime I want to, but no one else can? Also, the person can only be called from my phone and is willing to only speak to me and no one else. How can I tell them that I have seen this person face to face and had dinner with him, but did not arrest or interrogate him and that he lives in a house which is where I have had dinner, that sometimes it is a two story house, sometimes a one story house and sometimes doesn't exist at all? The latest is that William Stradom apparently is not his real name. He claims that he gave us the name but it isn't his real name."

"Tom, the problem is that all of that is true. However, he has been clever because the only person who had seen the house close enough that it changed from a two story house to a one story house is you. By the way, because everyone was focused on getting in the gate, you don't have any witnesses that will actually say that they have seen a house at all. They will acknowledge that they saw a fence and a gate and that it appeared to disappear and come back after a welder cut it with a torch, but even they would say that they don't know what they actually saw. Tom, I know I am your boss, but I am also your friend. I will admit to you if you came to me and told me all of that you would have to first go for a psych evaluation. Even if you passed the evaluation, I would not be able to put my full confidence in you. Any agent required to work with you would probably refuse. This could not have come at a worse time."

"So, what do you suggest I do?"

"I know you know there are no options. Protocol dictates full disclosure and therefore full disclosure is what we are going to do."

"William told me it was going to be like this. Chief, I will be honest with you, I am not a politician. I am a simple servant. I have never been interested in playing with words as a means of accomplishing what I want. When I signed up, I could have never imagined losing everything because of words and protocols. I have not done anything wrong, yet it appears the writing's on the wall when it comes to my career."

"This thing isn't over. Don't give up on everything yet. I will do whatever I can to help you. I know you know that. There is going be some rough times, but somehow I believe we will get through it together. At least the killing has stopped for a while. Take a few minutes and gather yourself. Then I suggest you go do it."

"Thank you chief. I don't need to wait. I will go in now."

Tom turned and walked down the hall to Special Agent in Charge Johnson's office. "SAC Johnson, I have something to share with you that happened to me today. I also need to share with you about a case that I had been working on that won't leave me alone and I have not yet been able to solve. I can only say that the facts are bizarre but they may or may not be a part of what is going on. It might take a while. Do you have time now?"

"How much of this is in the case file?"

"Most of it. There are two files regarding the case. The one you currently have contains the information that I thought I could explain.

The other one has the total records of the case whether we can explain it or not."

"I have some time. How long have you been with the agency? Tom isn't it?"

"Yes sir, it is Tom. I have been here a long time sir."

"What made you come in today?"

"I didn't know how to transition with the new team in place. Initially with being removed from all my cases and contacts I thought okay, everything is good. But today, somehow the suspect who I am talking about called my new number. That seemed impossible, but it happened."

"So does this suspect have a name?"

"Yes, sir. The suspects name that he goes by is William Stradom. He called me today."

"You said that he goes by. Is that not his real name?"

"I don't know sir."

"How long has this case been open?"

"As you can see in the file, it has been about 10 months."

"Did your SSA know of the second file, and if so was he aware of the contents of the second file?"

"SAC, I am familiar with the protocols of case files. I respectfully defer that question so it can be answered by the SSA himself."

"Agent I order you to answer the question."

"Sir, I again respectfully decline to answer the question."

"I know you know what this means."

"Yes sir, I do."

SAC Johnson reached over to his phone and pushed a button to call agent Lyles, "come in and arrest Mr. Plaiedeaux and hold him until we gather more information."

"May I say something sir."

"No, you may not."

Agent Lyles, walked out of SAC Johnson's door and started toward the elevator with two guards escorting Tom toward the elevator. As they walked toward the elevator agent Lyles grabbed his head as if something was wrong. He motioned to the two guards and then he fell to the floor. His two guards fell immediately after he fell. There was no one else in the hallway. Tom turned with his hands cuffed behind his back and walked back into SAC Johnson's office.

"Sir, I know you didn't want me to say anything, but you have three men down in the hallway and they need help."

SAC Johnson jumped up and drew his weapon.

Tom dropped to his knees, and said, "I didn't do anything. They just fell down."

"Don't come near me stay exactly where you are." SAC Johnson reached down and pushed an alarm on his desk and called out code Orange with officers down on the 26th floor. He looked out the door to see the three men lying on the floor. "If they are dead not only is your career over but your life as well."

"Do you realize that I didn't have to come back in here? I could have left. Nobody would have stopped me. I chose to stay and try to get help for them. I'm not very dangerous with my hands cuffed behind my back. I could have gotten the keys and unlocked the cuffs and been on my way. No matter what happens I believe in what the FBI stands for and I will go through whatever is necessary to prove that I have done nothing wrong. I don't know what is going on out there and I didn't have anything to do with it."

"You are still under arrest," the SAC said as agents were headed to the floor. "I imagine hazmat will want everyone to stay off the floor and they will probably quarantine the building when they arrive." As they arrived they began scanning the complete building and everyone in it. When they reached the 26th floor all three men began to awaken on the floor. They tested them and couldn't come up with anything hazardous in the air or on the men. After the testing they sent them to the hospital for additional testing and to be precautious. During this time Tom was held at gunpoint in the Chiefs office until they determined that it was safe to move him. SAC Johnson added six additional men to escort him to his holding location. As they approached the elevator all nine of the men fell to the floor, the same as before with the other three men.

This time Tom went to SSA Smithren's office.

"What are you doing in handcuffs?"

"It's a long story. I have been arrested and they are attempting to take me to a holding cell. How could you miss all of the commotion on this floor?"

"Tom, I was on the phone. More agents have been killed. Three more to be exact."

"I'm sorry I didn't know. I need to get back to SAC Johnson's office. I don't know what is going to happen next."

"Sir"

"What are you doing here?"

"Again, I could have left. All nine of them are laid out on the floor."

"Code Red, Code Red." He screamed into the telephone. The building was put on lockdown. As he said that his phone rang and he continued with his earlier conversation about deploying resources to help with the investigation of the three FBI agents that were killed in Maryland with three separate incidents within 30 minutes of each other.

As he was still on the phone, hazmat walked back into his office. They had been in touch with the hospital and EMS and nothing had been found other than the fact that all of their oxygen levels were slightly off.

"I don't know what you're trying to pull Plaiedeaux, but it's not going to work. We don't have time to play these little games. People are dying and you are wasting our time with these little games. Your career is over Mr."

"I didn't do this sir."

"I've been listening to your conversation SAC Johnson, and I know agent Plaiedeaux, he has always been one of the most honest agents that I have ever met. Integrity has always been his strength," said SSA Smithren.

"So, how do you explain what just happened here Smithren?"

"This may sound weird, but I actually think that someone does not want him locked up."

"What kind of organization are you running? You actually believe this crap he's spewing."

"Do you have a better explanation? He had an opportunity to run twice, and both times he stayed. I don't know what to believe, but I do believe Tom. I know this puts me at risk as well, but we actually really can't explain a lot of this case."

"You are temporarily suspended with pay. Turn in your badge and gun. Keep your phone. I'm not having anymore agents laid out in the hallway. You are not to talk to anyone about this."

"What am I supposed to do? How long is the suspension?"

"You will be off for a week. In the meantime, we need to get on with the rest of this situation. We need to get ahead of this."

"SAC Johnson, do you want me to head out to Maryland?" Asked SSA Smithren.

"No Smithren, I need you here. You are going to be responsible for all of the mess with Tom. I've got a feeling that this is only the beginning."

Before they could leave his office agent Langley walked into the office. "Sir, these are the names of the three agents that were killed. One of them was a good friend. We came into the agency together."

"Do you know his family?"

"Yes sir. I met most of them before I was transferred here."

"I need you to go and take agent Moore to do the notifications of the families."

"Yes sir. I am leaving now. I will notify the agents at the site."

"Did they give any more details?"

"They only said that so far the scene has yielded the same amount of information as the other sights, which by absence of evidence make them look like it was the same perpetrator."

"Go, let me know when the notifications are complete."

"Sir, were the three agents that were killed underground?" asked Tom.

"Yes they were."

"Then we know a lot more than what we think. How is it possible that they were found by the same people if everyone followed protocol? There has to be someone on the inside if agents are still getting killed or they were being followed before the protocols were put into play."

"Hold on Tom," said SAC Johnson. "You can't just go on a witch hunt and turn against each other. Let's just tread lightly because either way we need to get to the bottom of this."

"Sir, I was sitting here thinking the same thing. With all of our intelligence strategically placed throughout the nation yielding nothing concrete, we have to consider everything."

"I have already begun to assemble a team," said SAC Johnson. "There are a few that I know that I can trust with my life."

"Why are you telling me this?" asked Tom. "I'm suspended."

"Yes, you still are. That may work in our favor. Now are you ready to go to work? I want you to be a part of my team. I have reviewed your service records. You both have excellent track records with the agency, and have done exemplary work. You both have a variety of commendations for your efforts including ethics. Tom, you seem to thrive more when you are dealing with difficult cases. This is going to be as difficult as they come. We read your case files. We know about your nemesis Stradom. We think that he may be involved. Some way he is fixated on you. We hope to use that to our advantage. If the hallway is any indication, he is tied into every aspect of your life. We believe that he did this little hallway trick. He is protecting you and using you at the same time. He really is arrogant if he believes that he is so smart that he can do this to the FBI."

"Let me get this straight. A number of agents have died, and this whole thing including the FBI going underground is a ruse to get at Stradom?" asked SSA Smithren. "I am supervising this case and you didn't feel it was necessary to include me in the details."

"You and your office have been experiencing security breaches. You yourself had to initiate a building shut down on more than one occasion. We don't know how far and deep this goes, but we couldn't take the chance that they are somehow listening in on your conversations. Even now the conversation that we are having is tempered because of the possibility that someone is listening. We have swept the room and everyone in it. We are activating a three stage communications link, including a non verbal, non electronic and coded electronic transmission that will allow us to communicate with each other. The combination of this threefold process may make for a little slower communication, but it will also be less likely that anyone trying to listen in will be able to make heads or tails of what we are saying. Tom where are you at?"

"You set me up."

"Sort of, yes. If you take time to think about it. You will end up realizing with everything currently at stake, you would have done the same thing."

"You're right I would have."

"Do you have any idea why he is fixated on you?"

"No sir I don't."

"What kind of knowledge about you has he demonstrated?"

"He has indicated that he knows almost everything about me."

"Did he drop any specific details?"

"I will have to think about that one."

"Has he given you any indication of people or anyone else that he is working with? Have you met anyone else that he is working with? Or has anyone else been present when you spoke with him?"

"The first question. No question number 2, yes. The day I first met with him he had an older butler that answered the door. I don't believe I can give an adequate description of him, but I can of William. Question number 3, I'm not sure how to answer this one."

"What do you mean?"

"There were no other humans present, but there was a shape shifting flying computer."

"Okay, this is one of those things that you left out of the original reports."

"Yes sir. The computer didn't speak to me but it did speak to him. The computer's name is Paul."

"On your original transcript it appeared that there was someone named Paul who appeared to be performing security checks."

"Yes, but that wasn't someone, that was a computer."

"It didn't sound like a computer."

"I had never seen a part of a wall change into a computer, then the part that changed separated itself from the wall flew over and supposedly scanned me and then returned back to the wall to reconnect itself to the wall and then turn back into just a regular wall before either."

"Okay, I get it. It didn't even sound like a computer generated voice. This explained why the pitch on every word and syllable were so perfect. What do you think his next move is?"

"I've no idea."

"Do you think he will contact you again?"

"I'm pretty sure he will. Although, we have switched phone numbers to an interagency phone, we had to switch mine a second time because he has already called my first interagency phone."

"We can give you back the phone that you had."

"No, that would not be the wisest thing to do." He would already know that my phone has been changed out. We just need to wait. If I know him, it won't be long. I don't know yet who he really is. He gave us a name to use. This guy is really smart and a very good strategist. He appears to have almost unlimited resources, which makes him dangerous."

"You expect him to hack our interagency network again?"

"Yes and no. He appears to have some kind of phone network that we can't trace but he can do whatever he wants. I actually don't think he even considers it hacking or illegal. Let me be more accurate. How ever he is doing this, he claims that he is not hacking our network or breaking the law."

"By the way, you two are the last of the team that we are assembling. Smithren, you and Tom have worked closely together. You know a lot about this as well. You know how interagency investigations can get. Both of you know that this could come down to friends and family turning out to be enemies. So are you up for the task?"

"Yes, I am" said Tom.

"Yes sir we are," said SSA Smithren.

"Even though I am suspended, am I going to be permitted to participate? If so, then there is something that you are not telling me."

"If you are willing to permit me to tell you when it is the right time and the right communication network, we will go into more detail."

"Yes sir."

CHAPTER TWENTY-SIX

Stanley reached over to the intercom and told his secretary to call Slovie and Richard in for a meeting.

Richard arrived first and Slovie entered the office shortly after him.

"Good morning gentlemen."

"Good morning Stanley," they both said.

"Okay, then who wants to go first. Reports first."

"I'll go," said Richard. "The new divisions that we have established, maybe that is the wrong word, all the new divisions have received and are ramping up the production as requested. They expect to be at full production in two weeks. Usually these types of changes require years of planning to resolve issues like personnel, inventory, infrastructure, cash requirements and availability and so on, but apparently that is an obsolete or dated methodology for doing business."

"Richard, Richard, before all of those decisions were totally within your control. They are not outdated concepts; you are just in a different position in the supply chain. The company that you are working for now is one thousand percent nimbler than the company that you ran. You are going to learn new ways of doing business, and production will be more than 50% more efficient than you can ever imagine. If we had left you in that position without you understanding the changes, everything would have come to a screeching halt. Trust me there is no lack of planning."

"Why didn't you tell me that from the beginning?"

"We all have our jobs to do. You have a job and an opportunity to recover your substantial losses. I don't report to you Richard; you report to me. It is not necessary for me to tell you everything that we are doing. Look, I know I'm having to be a little hard on you, but in the end you will thank me. Now Slovie your turn."

"Stanley, we have completed the merger of the software, which updated our old software which we thought was useless. Some of the options are so radical, they are just amazing. The fact that we have enhanced capabilities now that synchronize our software to facilitate manufacturing products borders on revolutionary."

"Slovie, you do understand that these enhancements are why we have all of the contracts. Before the takeover ninety-two percent of the revenue of this company was tied to software development. We have increased revenue in the software division by more than eighty percent, but the revenue for the software division will now be only thirty percent of the overall company revenue while sixty-two percent will come from manufacturing."

"Okay, we are not a manufacturing company. We are a software company," said Richard.

"Actually to be accurate Richard, the company was primarily a software company. Now, today we are primarily a world solutions company. The branding identity change was necessary for the company to become relevant and viable in today's economy."

"Stanley, currently we had one small setback. We had a glitch in two of the semiconductor manufacturing plants. It caused about a week delay. However, that delay will not delay our production schedule. We were more than a week and a half ahead of schedule on production," said Slovie.

"My turn. Now that you know that we are in manufacturing. I gather we have been keeping you all busy. That's not a bad thing. Richard the work that has come across your desk doesn't include any manufacturing. There is a different division handling that. I will be introducing you to them as a resource, but you will need to requisition information from that department to get familiar with how they work. Slovie the software merger that you have overseen is impacting the whole company. Your division builds the software infrastructure while a separate division deploys it after testing. Now what you both did not know about the contracts is that they were originally for six months. We had to complete some legal hurdles before the long term contract came into effect. We simply had to show evidence that we completed the transaction with no legal hurdles that would hinder the company. We did complete that phase and now we have 14 contracts with 40 year terms. We are going to be around for awhile."

"Each contract is 40 years?"

"Yes Richard, each is 40 years."

"Okay, okay, no more questions. I just have never seen anything like this. I do not have knowledge of any companies willing to sign a contract for that length of time. I'm not asking for a comment; I guess I just needed to say something."

"Guys, all of these contracts are for manufacturing products of another company. Our ramping up production gives us production at full capacity for eight hours a day. We still are not manufacturing our own products. We have twelve locations but only 8 are in production. We are going to triple our production in the next five years without having to add any capacity. The way we manufacture because of our software enhancements allow us to produce products thirty percent less expensive than our competitors. I trust you are getting the picture now. There is one question that has not been asked yet. Richard, why don't you ask me."

"Like I said, I don't have any questions."

"Because of the tool and die, I have seen the schematics of some of the stuff we are manufacturing. I saw them, but I did not know what they were. I guess if I was going to ask, I would ask what are we manufacturing and why is it in such demand? Oh and are there minimum order quantities that require so much per month to protect our revenue streams, and provide security for the employees," asked Slovie.

"That's the question. We are manufacturing mostly no moving parts. There are some that are moving, but mostly non-moving parts. Yes, there are monthly production minimums. The parts are unique for this one company."

"Thank you for your hard work. Richard, someone will be calling you from the manufacturing division."

"By the way you have not mentioned the board meeting since it took place. Is it something that we can't talk about?"

"Richard, we can definitely talk about it."

"After seeing and hearing how all of this came about, for the first time in my life I was kind of speechless. It was obvious to me at least that he was intent on retribution regarding this company. I wasn't here for the startup, but I was here for a while when he was here. I'm not making any excuses or claiming that I was involved, it is still beyond my comprehension to see how all of this ended up."

"As he stated when he left that he became so despondent regarding how everything went down that he could either remain broken or get up and take back what was rightfully his. By the way you are here because he determined that you were not the architects of the separation before. He understood that both of you were used. He also determined that both of you would want to become successful the right way once you knew all the facts."

"We only knew about his software development skills. We never knew the man and his potential for business. How ignorant the company looks now knowing that at some point, possibly its greatest asset was run off all because of being short sighted?"

"Slovie, actually, both of you; we are headed in the right direction. The board meeting was kind of like windshield wipers. The way the acquisition began, the windows were a little muddy, but you could still see enough to drive, though your vision was restricted some. You turn on the wipers and now you can see clearly with no restrictions. It wasn't meant to impact anyone any other way except to provide clarity of sight so that our progression and ability to move ahead will not be impeded. Nothing more, nothing less."

CHAPTER TWENTY-SEVEN

"Thayor, you have a few months under your belt now. Do you regret making the decision?" Asked William.

"No sir, William. However, it is a bit more intense than what I expected. That board meeting was both awe inspiring and transformational for me. Based on the subject matter, I could not imagine any other possible way that it could have been handled so skillfully. Frankly it was a little intimidating. The history really helped me to get rooted in this thing. I am beginning to see how you work. You have planned and directed me for twelve years. That is a long time to train and educate someone for a job. How is it even possible to plan that far ahead to know that you have chosen the right person to train. I do believe in planning, but I think that what you do is beyond that. At first your job description didn't quite do it for me. Now I see why it is right on target and necessary. The press conference last week was pretty much gloves off. They acted like I was some sort of criminal."

"That's because they are taught to not trust anyone. They feel that you have a sort of angle that you are hiding. You are not going to be able to overcome that, but they will eventually at best try to blend the news and research into who you are. No matter what you tell them, they are not going to believe you. It will get worse before it gets better. Help is on the way. Now, make sure your shoes are laced because you have just scratched the surface. All of the meetings you have had so far are to build a platform for you. In about six months the platform will be complete. Over the next few months you are going to start to meet some very high ranking people. At times it is going to feel like you are working for them, rather than for me. They are going to influence your speeches and sometimes set the protocols regarding your speeches and media interaction. You and I will work through these transitions together. None of this is a bad thing. It's actually a natural progression to where we are going."

"Again, I am at a loss. It is pretty clear that you have a lot of business going on. I don't necessarily have to completely understand, but I don't have a clue where we are going with this. As you said before you have no aspirations for politics or becoming a public figure."

"Let's just say in these next six months' things will become a lot clearer to you. If I told you everything right now, it would put you at risk. Some things still need to develop first and then you will be able to see everything more clearly. I don't mean to make things seem to be so clandestine. There are going to be some very strong positions taken and some very tough decisions that are made as a result of them. A lot of people are going to be upset. You may be away from your family for a few days without the ability to contact them."

"You basically trained me how to stay out of trouble from my youth. Now it is going to be my job to get into trouble with no way out."

"Exactly. The word trouble is misleading. If the company protocols dictate that you take a stand in some fashion that is contrary to some higher authority's opinion even though there is a threat of incarceration, then yes you are going to voluntarily get in trouble. Realize that since you are not a decision maker, and you often times will have no known foreknowledge of decisions being made the only thing they will constantly threaten you with are conspiracies, which can't be upheld in a court of law."

"You have obviously been in this mode for a long time. You just gave me something and nothing at the same time. You did tell me it would come to this. For now, I will say that I am ready, however, I know that since this is all new to me, I don't know if I'm truly ready are not. I have my resolve and I will get use to the rest."

"Thayor, you are right, most of my communication with people has had to be this way because there is a lot at risk. We all have a purpose and things that we are responsible for. I am thankful for the opportunities that I have been given and plan to remain faithful to complete every task given to me while I am on the earth. Now our relationship will evolve as we move forward, but there's always going to be things that you and I will never talk about because it will put you and all of your family at risk."

"I've implemented all of the security measures for my family that were suggested."

"I know, but I'm not sure you understand me yet. Take a deep breath. You remember when I told you that we adopted and became familial support to all of your family."

"Yes, I do."

"We do that because all of your family will eventually be at risk, not just your wife and kids. When some get desperate they will do whatever it takes to get to you and to me. It is truly all of your family."

"My god. Why didn't you tell me this before?"

"I did. Thayor, the work you are going to do, will save thousands of lives. You are talking about the difference between doing a job for money and fulfilling your destiny. You are very well educated; I do not have to tell you the difference between the two. By the way, Jonathan told me you and he have worked things out. Why do you think his plan required you to have so much cash available to you? I know you know enough about finances to know that is not normal."

Thayor, got up and walked around the room running his hands through his hair. "For the sake of discussion between me and you; what if I want out?"

"If you want out, just say the word and you are out."

"What does that mean?"

"I know you probably have heard the saying there is no going back to Egypt. When you are out you are out. The only place we need you is in the position where you are at. There are no other positions here for you."

"How can I live with taking a job that will put all of my family at risk?"

"How can you live with not taking a job that will give you the opportunity to rewrite and reroute your family heritage and save thousands of lives. There is no reward without a risk. The path to significance is flooded with risk. You do this job and you will become the patriarch of your family for all of its history."

"All or nothing?"

"Yes, all or nothing. Don't you know that's how destiny works? Your date with destiny will always be accompanied by a requirement for you to go all in."

"Yes, but no one has defined it in the way you have today. I do feel like I belong here, but my god. It just sits on me like a ton of bricks."

"That's called a Destiny Jacket. You have to learn to wear it. First you have to recognize where you are in life, then you have to wear it, after that you get use to it, and you get to the place where you don't even realize you are wearing it. It becomes natural to you."

"I get it."

"So, are we still ready to go?"

"I know you have given me and my family opportunities beyond our most ambitious imagination, and since I have started something here I'm committed, I need to finish what I started. No, more surprises?"

"Not today." Chuckled William.

CHAPTER TWENTY-EIGHT

William picked up the phone and called Devin.

"Devin, I need you to get the package I ordered to the jet in the next thirty minutes."

"Yes sir, it will be ready including all of the tracking."

"Good. I will be in touch." He hung up and placed a call to Samantha. "Samantha, call Larry and have him fire up the jet I need to leave in an hour. Tell him we will be headed to Baltimore, Maryland. He will know what to do."

"How long will you be gone?"

"At the most forty-eight hours. Do you need anything?"

"You know we need to talk. You deal with everything else. Why can't we just deal with this as well? Devin called; he needs you to transfer some more money."

"Check and see if he can wait till I get back. Let me know, otherwise I will call him. You're not going to leave this thing alone are you?"

"You give me no choice. Apparently I must go to war to see justice done."

"War, my my, what a peculiar choice of words for the subject matter. Let's just get through these next few days."

"You know you have that media event tomorrow and I will hold you to that timeline."

"Thayor will handle it. Follow up with him and the speech writers. Have him contact me if he needs help. I need to run."

"Okay, sir. There sure is a lot going on."

As he hung up the phone, he knew he had a few minutes so he decided to make a call to agent Plaiedeaux. "Good afternoon Tom, or do prefer agent Plaiedeaux."

"I prefer you only call when you are ready to confess your involvement and you are surrendering. Obviously, that's not happening yet is it?"

"You are such a comedian. You said you were not going to call and you haven't. You actually kept your word. I'm impressed. You see two can play that game. Now let's get serious. No, it's not time to talk about your new phone number and how I got it. I will tell you this; your suspension doesn't hold water."

"What are you talking about?"

"You can play dumb if you want, but I'm not going to play the game with you. I know that now I am supposed to be facing the A team rather than the B team. It is not that simple. I still, will only be talking to you. Since they have suspended you they took away your laptop. You are going to need it, because I am going to be sending you some information in the next two days."

"I don't know how you are doing all this. What is this all about? Why did you choose me?"

"It's going to be a lot of information."

"So you are still not answering questions. You still think that you are above all of us?"

"You are starting to repeat yourself. You think that the new assignment they gave you is going help you capture me. I heard about the additional deaths. I would think that you being the FBI and all that you would be concentrating on putting a stop to this madness."

"I'm not going to sit here and listen to this. You got something to say, then say it. We are never going to be friends."

"I told you that you have forced my hand. I have helped you and you know it. You are just too confused to admit it. That's okay. I'm going to help you all. I told you that I am not a criminal. Just because someone likes their privacy and is maybe a little bit reclusive, it doesn't mean that they are criminals. Tell them that I said I am not a criminal."

"I'm not telling them anything. Sounds like we are making you nervous. Did we strike a chord? Good. I want to be there when we nail you to the wall."

"The information will be sent to your laptop whether you look at it or not is up to you. It will cost you your job if someone discovers that you had the information and didn't make it available. That is all I am going to say about it. I will talk to you soon."

Just as William parked at the airport Larry called him.

"Boss, everything is loaded and we are ready to go."

"I am pulling up now. Did Samantha get you the list and confirm everything that we needed?"

"Yes, she did."

"How about the rest of the team?"

"This guy Chuck who says he is your team leader is standing beside me. Do you want to talk to him?"

"Yes, put him on the phone."

"Hello Mr. Stradom. It has been awhile, but it is good to hear your voice. I assume that this is not a drill, but live."

"You don't have to assume. Yes, this is not a drill, this one is for real."

"I am surprised to hear that you are coming with us. I'm looking forward to it though. I have completed the equipment and personnel checks. Everything and everyone is accounted for. Is this going to be a regular occurrence for you?"

"This is our first intervention. All of the years of training you guys for this has been well worth it. You remember, no one and nothing left behind. There can be nothing that can trace back to us or to any individual or manufacturer. While we will have superior technology, it means nothing if we start by losing our anonymity."

"Yes sir. I have to be honest; I did not expect all of the gear would make it. Some of this stuff is really impressive. I also didn't expect the team to be so large."

"The team is so large because we have a time crunch. We have about forty-eight hours to get this done so that hopefully we can keep other people from dying."

"What are you talking about? Are there people already dead?"

"Yes, Chuck, some people have died."

"I understand then. Let's load up we need to get in the air."

Larry walked up to William and shook his hand. "Sir, everything worked out with the flight plan. We've been cleared for takeoff."

"What's our ETA?"

"We should arrive in about a little over an hour sir."

As everyone was seated, the flight attendant informed the captain that they were ready to takeoff. After takeoff William told Chuck to open up the packet and pass out the mission parameters.

"Sir, we do not have enough manpower to cover a square mile in forty-eight hours," said Chuck.

"Yes we do, there is a team already on the ground that will join us." We have enough equipment with us for both teams. Chuck you will take the lead. You all know that we could never do what we are going to do without the technology that we have. What we are doing is necessary and has never been done before. The most difficult part of this job will start after we complete our first mission."

"Why is that?" Chuck asked.

Because after completing it you will be all excited and you are going to want to share your accomplishment with friends and love ones. Then you are going to realize that you can't share it with anyone. It will be tough. The other side of this coin is you have trained for many years for this day. Once we do this today, you will be in demand for the rest of your lives. None of you have had the opportunity to see the results of your training in a composite form. Once you experience a completed mission you will begin to understand how important your work is. We take no shortcuts when it comes to this work. Every detail is significant. We have taken something that has been around forever with no practical use and turned it into a useful tool. What we have done is the same thing that the world is going to do. You know your stories. As we have grown up in our environments, people have often looked at us and written us off with no expectations. People won't see us, and the credit will go to others, but those who get credit are going to look at all of us and have great expectations. Our power will be in our anonymity. If we lose that, we and our families will be at risk. Now, our home base for this trip will be in the rear of this plane. The complete system is setup similar to a wireless application and will gather all of the information in the next two days. Are there any questions?"

"Hello, I'm James, since we have an area of a square mile, where do we start?"

"Chuck I believe that question is for you. Chuck will set all of the mission parameters."

"Thank you Mr. Stradom. James as well as everyone else, we will have a print out in about two minutes that will show each person exactly the areas they will cover. The schedules and timelines will be synchronized to the overall mission timelines. Let's wait until we receive the printouts then we will review where we are at. Remember no one and nothing is left behind. I know that we have all been looking forward to this day. We have trained hard. This is our first mission. Make us all proud. Be conscious of your environment, what should be there and when something or someone is out of place. We don't know who we are up against. They could be watching for the same things that we are. Cameras are easy they are mechanical and repetitive, but humans are not. We will use protocol #2 in the event that we suspect that someone has been compromised."

"Thank you Marge. Please pass the printouts out by name. We've got about twenty minutes to landing. Take some time and review the printouts. We will have a meeting upon landing to make sure everyone has received all of their equipment and supplies. The other team is already there. The teams will split up into two sections both covering a half mile. Once this is done, we will immediately deploy. All alternates need to remain on alert. If you are contacted the window is extremely short with our time lines. We can't afford for you to lose any time deploying. IT team, remember while you are tasked with monitoring everything from a distance, you too are to be on the lookout for anything that seems out of order as well. This is as real as it gets guys. Let's go get this done."

"Chuck walked back up to Mr. Stradom's private area. Sir, I do have one question. Is this mission sanctioned by anyone?"

"No, it is not. We will never be sanctioned as you have been in the past. Because of the nature of our work, we will be funded but unsanctioned. The whole world is about commerce. Anything that is worth anything is for sale. Do you know anything about sports Chuck?"

"A little."

"What about some guy named Michael Jordan?"

"There is probably no one alive that has not heard of him."

"Good. Then you know that because of him Chicago had a decided advantage over the other teams in the NBA as long as he was on the team. Chicago took full advantage of that edge. Can you imagine the NBA going to Chicago and saying you either are going to have to allow Michael to play for some other team, or we are going to have to handicap him somehow, because you having him gives your team an unfair advantage? Well, that didn't happen. During his time, they reaped the benefits of his uniqueness, until it ran its course. Now, what you don't think about is how contractually they protected themselves to ensure that they could maximize the benefits of his unique ability. They of course had the options of retaining him or selling him to the highest bidder, but they chose to keep him. What we are doing Chuck is simply keeping our advantage. Can money be made? Absolutely. Keeping our advantage just like Chicago did outweighs any monetary benefits that we could receive not only for us but the world as well. The whole league benefited from him using his abilities to the fullest even though his primary services were limited to one team. Any successful business will always be trying to acquire and maintain a competitive advantage in the market place. What we do will have the same effect."

"Thank you sir, I honestly don't have any other place that I would rather be. What you are doing I personally believe is very important. I know I said what you are doing, not what we are doing, but the opportunity that you have given me means so much to me. I won't let you down."

"I know Chuck. Just remember even with the best laid plans things can go wrong. If you go to war you know that it consists of many battles. You can lose some battles but still win the war."

"Yes sir."

Chuck stood and turned to leave as Larry told everyone to prepare for landing in five minutes.

William gazed out the window and marveled at the view as they were approaching the city. What an incredible site he thought. He only wished that Theodore Wexell somehow could be here to see the fruits of what he had began.

As the plane landed Larry taxied to a small secluded hanger where the plane was rolled inside. The rest of the team already on the ground converged on the plane as everyone began to exit. Chuck stepped out and greeted everyone and directed them to meet in the large open area of the hanger. There were over 200 team members present.

"We have over 200 members of which 50 are alternates. 10 of the 50 are cross trained for both IT and field. The 150 primary members will deploy immediately. 10 will be remaining at the hanger to deploy the computer programs and the other 140 will be split up into 4 teams. Each team will have a primary lead and 2 backups. The printouts that you were given all have a number and a letter to denote your number on a team. The letters denote what area of town that you will be working and the number represents your position on the team. The leaders are designated in numerical order. S1, S2 or S3 are the members on team south with one being the lead. I1 through I10 will be the tech team. We have some additional team members that are in charge of equipment inventory who are not cross trained for any of the other duties. The IT team is now released to begin their work. We will expect to be deployed completely in about 30 minutes. Does anyone have any questions, asked Chuck?"

"Yes, sir. If our cover is blown, we do not come back here but we still get home?"

"Yes James. You will receive instructions at the time you indicate your cover is blown, which will lead you away from here, to protect our mission and anonymity. Now the aerosol spray will rise. Remember to allow the dispenser to auto adjust to accommodate any outdoor or indoor square footage computations. While we calibrate the many variances, the time lapse between the event and our recovery is key. The time lapses determine the velocity and angle of application, while the vertical and horizontal read times are based on the impacted settlement ratios. Since we are covering such a vast area, the computer will be able to establish sink lines by means of reverse dissipation which it will then be able to overlay the full square mile and establish the directional flow of everyone extracted from our composite model. We are using P.A.W.L. 4.0 which means that we have a diagram which outlines exactly where each P.A.W.L. will need to be placed in order to maximize data recovery and provide accurate coverage of the designated area. Our work is all about precision. If we are done with the questions, then everyone line up to receive your equipment and supplies. It's time that we earn our paychecks. Group leaders use your list to account for both your team and their equipment. When your teams are ready I will let you know when to deploy."

Chuck began to walk toward the plane, just as the tech team leader Tracy Duncan stepped off the plane and hurried toward him.

"Chuck we have a slight problem."

"What's wrong?"

"Although the system is on the plane, it was designed to rely on its power source outside of the plane because of the amperage needed to run it."

"So, what are you saying?"

"We currently do not have enough power to run our system."

"Tracy, we don't have time for this. You probably have at the max about twenty minutes. You have about five minutes to come to me with a viable solution."

"Sir, can we use the alternate team tech guys? One of the guys, Dan is really good with thinking outside the box."

"Go, ahead."

Tracy turned and called for Dan to come with him. As they were walking he explained the situation to him.

Dan immediately said to Tracy. "I am going to grab a couple of the alternates to go with me really quick. I'll be right back." He grabbed them and they headed to the door that lead outside of the building.

Tracy watched as they exited the building, turned and walked back into the plane with Chuck. As he entered the plan he said, "Guys we've got about 14 minutes to get this done. Did anybody come up with anything?"

"Is it possible to get the floor plans for the building?" asked Terri.

"I'm sure we can but not in the allotted time," said Chuck.

"Is there another hanger that we can use?"

"I don't know. I can definitely check. However, more than likely the amperage will probably be pretty close to the same. Let me check."

"Okay, thank you."

"The alternate site appears to not be an option."

Greg asked, "since we have four teams can we reduce the power requirements by only powering up the bare essentials for one quarter at a time?"

"No, we will barely be able to complete the mission with everyone going full force for forty-eight hours. It would extend our stay six more days. That is not an option that we have. We have to complete everything and be out of here within the allotted time."

"Okay then is there a percentage that we can live with?"

"I know that the current amperage allows us to operate at about sixty-five percent capacity, but nothing less than one hundred percent will work for us."

"Can't we just run with the sixty-five percent and live with it?"

Just as Tracy started to answer, his phone rang. "Hello."

"Tracy, I understand you have a problem."

"Yes sir Mr. Stradom. We are working on it."

"What have you got."

"Sir, we are working on a, hold on for a minute please."

The door swung wide open and in walked Dan. "We got it. We need a couple of things to happen really quickly."

"What is it?"

"We can use the backup generator as a second power source. We have already disconnected it and hooked it up to a line. It is unable to reach the plane where it is. We need the pilot to reposition the plane between the two power sources. Once that is done we will be able to hook up both power sources to a converter that we robbed from the utility room. The computer system will not know that there are two power sources. This should double the power that we have. Will that be enough?"

"Yes, that will be enough," said Tracy.

"Sir, we have figured it out. Can I get back to you?"

"Yes, you can."

"Thank you."

"Dan, great job."

"I'm just thankful I got an opportunity to help sir."

"Tracy picked up the phone and called Chuck. We've got it sir; we just need one thing from the pilot."

"He's standing right beside me; I will hand him the phone."

"Project leader Chuck, Team S is ready to go."

"Was your equipment check good?"

"Yes, sir we have everything. We remember why we need to complete the first phase under the cover of darkness. Go team S1. He picked up the megaphone and announced the first team to deploy is S1."

Immediately team S1 headed out the door. Chuck walked over behind them and watched as they jumped into their vehicles and slowly disappeared into the night.

Team N1 was next followed by E1 and W1. As he watched the last team depart, he noticed that one of the teams was having vehicle trouble. He looked over and saw Mark and said to him that one of the vehicles was having some trouble.

"I got it sir."

Mark ran over to pick up some keys before he disappeared out the door. A few minutes later Chuck saw the team leaving with Mark looking under the hood of the stalled vehicle.

Chuck turned and looked at the hanger and then walked into the plane. "Tracy where are we at?"

"We are up and running sir, thanks to Dan. He came up with a great idea to boost the power and it worked."

"Good job team," said Chuck. "The first phase will take about eight hours, which means that everyone will have just a few minutes to transform so we can immediately move to phase two. Remember to schedule your regeneration periods. This is not a sprint."

"S1 reporting grid application started sir. Every location was available."

"Thank you S1."

Chuck turned and walked back into the hanger to address the alternates. "I know it is going to be hard because everyone is excited, but remember you are here to back up anyone if they get in trouble. That could be simply someone getting too tired. Every time a phase is complete, you need to immediately change for the next phase. You should all be prepared to go at a moment's notice. In the meantime it is regeneration time for some of you."

Chuck walked back to the front of the plane to talk to William. He walked to the door way only to find that he was not there. He dialed his number. "William, we had a few adjustments to make but everything is going fine."

"Good. I'm not in the plane, but keep in touch with me to let me know how everything is going."

"I'm curious, but I'm not going to ask."

"We've got a long way to go, get some rest." said William.

"Albert, here are the geo coordinates that I will need to have time lapses on in addition to the others. You did get yesterdays as well?" asked William.

"Yes sir. We began capturing the images about thirty minutes after you hired us. Of course the scope was much broader at first. We have narrowed the scope since we spoke to you then based on the new coordinates you gave us. We will continue to record the images for the two months that you requested. By the way, this may be, no this is our largest project so for. I really appreciate the business. Just remember Mr. Cotton, we also have the capabilities to analyze and overlay the images."

"Thank you for the pitch. Just remember our agreement."

"I do. We ship all images to your designated contact and we are not allowed to store or keep any of them. We have no longer than forty-eight hours to prepare and send the images from a completed day's work. No questions asked, no questions answered."

"Let me know when we get to the coordinates that I gave you."

"Yes sir. We will be there in about three minutes. I don't know how to talk to you, based on your restrictions you gave me."

"I am an independent business man. I've been in business for a while."

"You obviously have achieved some kind of success to be able to spend the kind of money you are spending on this project. Honestly, it was hard for me to even imagine that you were actually sincere about the project."

"I'm going to say something to you now, success has nothing to do with how much you accumulate in life, but how well you recognize and seek to fulfill the purpose of the time and resources that are entrusted to you. Too often we think that resources reveal our purpose, but actually purpose reveals resources."

"That's a little deep for me right now. I'm going to have to think about that one for awhile. Anyhow, we are at your destination."

"Here is the authorization to land. Please put down over there and wait for me. It might be a little while."

"Will do."

"Stay alert. If anyone approaches you leave. I tell you what, why don't you go ahead and leave. I will call you to come and pick me up when I'm ready. Stay by the chopper, I will continue to pay your regular hourly rate."

"Yes sir."

After landing on the rooftop; William rode the elevator down to the 32nd floor.

CHAPTER TWENTY-NINE

When he stepped off the elevator and walked to the meeting room, he could see that everyone else had arrived.

"Good evening everyone. Let's take advantage of this time. I know that the FBI has been all over this thing. Leroy you want to give us a briefing."

"Basically, Mr. Cotton the scenes are still roped off, and yes they are all over it. We have seen a slight build up in the agency. Now I don't think these guys are regular FBI agents. They don't seem to look are dress like typical agents. Based upon our observations they are not following agency protocols."

"Hold on for a minute. You are correct. Let's just say that they have revised their methods of operations until this is over with." said Mr. Cotton.

David asked, "Why are we here? What does this have to do with what we are doing?"

Both are good questions David. "We are here because what we do can be adversely affected by what happens to the FBI."

"I don't understand sir."

"Sir we've been on the ground since it happened yesterday, because of local law enforcement and the FBI, we have not been able to make heads or tails of anything," said Leroy.

"Leroy, do you have anymore to add," asked Mr. Cotton.

"I have a written report but we have made little headway. The report identifies who is in charge here and some of the people that they have questioned."

"What I am saying is that we have entered a time where it is going to be a benefit to us to embrace public policy. Thank you, Leroy."

"Frankly sir, I don't see how what I presented here is helpful at all."

"Leroy and all of you, tonight isn't about what we have been doing. It is about where we are going. Things are changing partly by necessity and partly by destiny. In the past we have benefited greatly from the businesses that we run. We have developed and participated in some business trends that have yielded a lot of money over the years. Things are changing and part of the evolution is to prepare and forecast for the future. Our size is causing an adverse effect on our ability to remain anonymous. We knew it was going to happen. Our growth will eventually exceed our ability to protect what we do. We are fortunate that it has happened in our lifetime. We have to evolve. I would have chosen a different way to present this to you, but things are moving rather quickly. I will be introducing you to Thayor, he is our company representative. He will be the face of our companies. While before it has never been necessary to have a public face. It has become necessary now. I have a map here that I need you all to look at. The map is of a square mile in Baltimore. Now this is important. We need to know if any of your associates were in the area yesterday, and if not, they need to stay out of it for the next forty-eight hours. There is an audit being performed of every single person that has been or will be in the area during this time. The audit will actually record everywhere you go and everything you do at a DNA level. We need you to quietly give your employees leave. No one is to go anywhere near the area. I have maps for all of you. We need to man the phones and contact everyone."

"There is no so such technology like that and even if there were would it be legal?" asked Arthur.

"This is happening as we speak. That is why we are meeting in this building. We worked too hard to let something like this expose us and ruin what we have. We need to know everyone that was in the area, their name, ethnicity, and any pictures that you may have of them. We are going to have to find a way to remove them from the audit. There are going to be many more of these, which mean that we are going to be busy. We don't have much time so let's get started. Today is Tuesday you need to shut down the offices until Friday morning. Make sure that this is a paid leave. It can be a mandatory team building event as long as it is away from the area."

"I can see how this could be a problem," said Don. "If this is going to happen, perhaps we need to meet on a regular basis, to help us understand all of this. We would not be where we are without you. We will do what you consider necessary."

"Thayor will be contacting you. He will be the one that will orientate us on how to do business in this new market. His job will be to map out the landscape for us. I will make it to the first couple of meetings to help with the transition."

"What would have happened if you were not here?" asked David

"The FBI would have retrieved your information and your ID's and would have been crawling all over every employee in your divisions. When they couldn't get enough information, they would turn their focus on you thinking that you were the cause of their problems. We do not need that."

"You seem to know a lot about all of this," said Art.

"It's my job as the protector to always be looking out for all of you. You know this, much too well. We have been together for a long time. We know that the responsibilities that were given to us were passed on through great tribulation and loss. It is imperative that we do everything within our powers to grow and continue this legacy no matter what the cost to us."

Meanwhile, Chuck had to replace two team members on the West team because of sickness. W1 had gotten caught up with a security guard and was compromised, so he had to be replaced as well. The data had begun to flow into the servers. Everything was working as planned with the exception of some minor glitches with some equipment. E1's team was a little behind schedule but they assured Chuck that they would make it. They all knew that N1's team would be the most at risk because the area they were covering would include the crime scene. They would be the most likely to run into FBI agents and local law enforcement.

"Chuck, we are behind as we expected, the additional equipment did slow us down, but what really slowed us down more was the fact that there are so many different law enforcement personnel around. We are not getting out of here without losing some of the team. I have a plan but I am going to have to sacrifice four team members. I need four additional team members to start in sector N40 on the North corner in about 20 minutes. We will not lose them completely, but they will be detained for a while, then we will get them out. They are going to have to be locked in until a shift change takes place, and then they will be free to go. We will treat them as compromised once they get out. This will also allow me to get back on schedule because for a few hours they will be working simultaneously." said Barry the team leader.

"N1, will this get everything deployed at the crime scene that we need?"

"Yes sir. By the way, compliments to the engineers. They really made the deployment seamless. When we started out with the testing it was way too complicated and heavy to be able to do this mission. You almost had to have a PHD to read the instructions. They actually listened to us and now I would say that the design is perfect, at least from operational and setup purposes. I will have the affected team members call in once they are free."

"The additional team members will be sent out immediately."

"Thank you, sir."

Chuck turned and walked down the corridor to where the IT team was feverishly working. "Tracy, how is everything going? Is the data segregation accounting for everyone and all the defined parameters?"

"Yes. The crime scene data is really fascinating. When you can acquire and compile that much data at a microscopic level in these quantities and still map it at an individual level you really are turning the data recovery world upside down. This is exciting stuff. Sorry sir I get a little excited. We are capturing the data from all four teams. Two of the teams are running behind. I know your plan said that team N1 would run behind but not necessarily team E1."

"E1 had some slight equipment problems, but you should see a slight acceleration in their upload. For N1 you are going to need to expand their field. They will be adding four additional team members for the next four hours to get them back on track. Has there been anything notable on Sky View?"

"No, the teams have done a great job of not disrupting the community. They have for the most part, gone unnoticed. Since the last time we tested Sky View, we put in an alert system. Even if we don't necessarily find anything in our target area visually, the system is now designed to auto detect things that may change in the target area that we may not see with the naked eye. Anyway, nothing is visible there either."

"Okay, I will follow up later."

Chuck's phone rang so he stood up and walked away. "This is Chuck, who's speaking."

"Chuck this is Randy, the hanger manager. Sorry to bother you, but I have a bit of a problem. I need to put another plane in the hanger. We have a situation with the owner."

"Sorry Randy, it sounds like you are in a tight situation. I can't help you with that right now. No one will be allowed in the hanger except our team. You are going to have to find another way to resolve your problem."

"I wouldn't be calling if I had another alternative. This is my last resort call."

"Hold on a minute. Okay, maybe I can help but you are going to have to fill me in on what is going on. I don't need all the details but I do need to know if it just simply a plane storage or do you need security or something. Where is the plane now and when will it arrive?"

"Just the plane. The guy makes up 60% of my business. He's the type that you don't say no to or make excuses with. This obviously was unexpected. It should be here in about an hour."

"Does he have to be in the hanger, or does he just have to land and have his plane stored?"

"He just has to land and have his plane stored."

"Good, have him land here, when he leaves I have another place across the field where you can store the plane. Does that work for you?"

"Sorry, what is that going to cost me?"

"Don't worry about the cost I'll cover the cost. If the plane is still stored when we leave, we will move it back over here. I know that it is not customary for you to rent out your hanger short term, so really don't worry about it. Just remember our agreement with you. We were never here."

"That will work. Thanks man you saved my life. Are you going to be able to put the plane in the hanger tonight?"

"If he arrives on time it will be in the hangar before daylight."

"Thanks again. I will call you when he arrives."

E1 called Chuck. "I think we are back on schedule now. Thanks for the reducers. They didn't waste any time getting the replacements to us."

"Team S1, report," said Chuck.

"We had a little bit of mist over here but I don't think it was enough to affect anything. Deploying at night really makes things a lot simpler for the first phase. The team although a little tired has really been on task. Even miss personality has really been productive. Obviously, this is a major project that we are doing, but I don't get it yet. I don't necessarily have to; but it would be nice to get it someday."

"In time, S1, in time. team W1, report."

"Sir, I think we are slightly ahead of schedule. We had a little tension upon startup, but everything is fine now. These clothes are a little itchy, and it was a pain to unwrap all of the equipment. It would be nice if all that was done so all we had to do was blow and go next time. Perhaps maybe laundering the clothes before we wear them might help. I also wouldn't mind the communication equipment being voice activated, so we don't have to be pushing all these buttons, or dialing numbers."

"How about the mission? Are you having any problems with the mission?"

"No, sir. You know my team is not going to have any problems with any mission that you send me on. Once they understand what I expect of them, they deliver."

Meanwhile,

"Mr. Cotton, we didn't expect to be here all night. Can't this wait until tomorrow?" asked Fred the COO of Baltimore Marketing.

"No, it can't. Whether you realize this or not, our original plan was to be prepared to move at a moment's notice. Part of being able to be that nimble as an organization is being organized. I need to know that we operate our businesses with that understanding. Now we could make some assumptions about where everybody was, but that is too great of a risk now. Our IT team will be able to cross match the list that we compiled tonight with our human resources files tomorrow. The human resources files will have the pictures to match up to, so that we can complete this project. By the end of the night we will have everything we need. On Thursday we need to present this information so that they can be excluded from the audit. My guess is if we have about thirty more minutes of compiling and we will be done. Let's just get it done."

Mr. Cotton dialed Albert's number. "Albert I need you to come pick me up in forty minutes."

"I will be there sir."

After they finished compiling the list Mr. Cotton told everyone thank you and then headed back to the hanger. He called Chuck to check in on the mission.

Chuck answered the phone. "We are on schedule sir. A few adjustments but we are moving forward."

"Good. I am going to head to the hotel to get some rest. Call me if you need anything."

CHAPTER THIRTY

Agent Plaiedeaux woke up to a very quiet apartment. As he rolled over to get out of bed, his phone rang. When he answered, to his surprise it was Angie.

"How did you get this number?"

"I don't have your number, but the office got tired of me bugging them so they patched me through to you. Can you believe they are the FBI? I get them to do whatever I want."

"I can't have this anymore, Angie. We are not anything anymore. I don't want you calling me anymore. I don't want to have anything to do with you. Can't you get that through your thick skull?"

"You don't talk to me like that. I know that we are not married are anything like that, but we are supposed to be together. That junk you just said is not you talking. It's all of your little buddies at the agency that you let run your life. I am never going to stop until you realized the truth."

"The truth is that you need help. I have tried every way I know how to get through to you that I am done with you. Does it even matter to you that you have made me a laughing stock at my job?"

"No, you have made yourself a laughing stock by disrespecting me. All you have to do is apologize to me and to the people at your office for keeping up this façade and everything will be okay."

"This conversation has gone on way to too long. I can't get through to you. This is the last call I'm going to take from you. After I hang up, I am going to do everything within my power to make sure that I never take a call from you again. I am done with this."

"Yeah, I've heard that before. Some big threat. I am trying to tell you that I love you and this is the thanks I get. I will keep my end of the deal; I am never giving up on you."

"Good bye crazy." Tom hung up the phone and dialed SSA Smithren. "Chief, sorry to call so early."

"Is something going on? Did you find out something?"

"No, no. It's the other problem. Angie, I can't do it anymore. Thank you for letting me try. You do whatever you have to do. I will support it even if you have to press charges. I just need it to end."

"You know this might get ugly."

"What do you mean ugly?"

"While she is psychotic, she is not stupid. We can block her calls, put a restraining order on her and even arrest her, but none of those will keep her quiet. I'm just saying someone will probably listen."

"I don't care, as long as it's not me."

"Okay, consider it done. Anything else?"

"No, I just hung up on her. My guess is she giving the people in the office hell right now. I didn't want to be tortured today, or anymore. You might want to call as soon as I hang up. Thanks chief."

He turned to see that it was 6:30 AM. Great, he thought. I can now go back to having a quiet day. He decided to get up and have some breakfast, maybe then he could come up with something to do. After getting cleaned up, he remembered that his old supervisor who brought him into the agency had retired. I need to talk to someone I can trust. This thing has gotten way out of hand. He picked up the phone and called him. When he dialed the number, Harold Clark answered immediately.

"Harold speaking, who's there?"

"It's me sir, Tom. Tom Plaiedeaux."

"Well now, it has been awhile, what are you up to?"

"I'm still with the agency, sort of."

"What does sort of mean?"

"I'd like to explain. I hope I didn't call too early. I have some free time on my hands for a few days. I was wondering if I could possible catch up with you today. Sorry for the short notice."

"I seem to have some free time on my hands since I am retired and all. I could use the company of an old friend. You want to stop by my house. My wife is on some kind of retreat with a few of her girl friends, if that's what you call it these days."

"You still live in the same place?"

"Yes, I do."

"If you don't mind I'll head over now."

"I'll be here."

Tom looked around to see if there was anything he needed to do before he left, and then headed out the door.

Thirty minutes later he arrived at Harold's house and knocked on the door.

"Come on in", said Harold. "I gather you are suspended."

"Yes I am. How do you know that?"

"Did you do whatever they suspended you for?"

"No, but it's not that simple."

"It never is. I know it's early, but do you want a cup of coffee, or maybe a beer."

"I could go for some OJ if you have some."

"Good, still a boy scout. That's remarkable for the time you have put in. So, how long are you suspended?"

"They gave me a week with pay."

"Let me help you. I know you can't talk about any specifics. They create an environment where this stuff is your whole life and then they cast you outside of it and expect you to function as if nothing is wrong."

"That sounds like a voice of experience."

"You really can't call yourself an agent until you have been suspended."

"You sure I'm not imposing?"

"We're good."

"So, you were suspended before?"

"Three times."

"Wow. I didn't expect to hear that."

"Listen kid, I will be happy to tell you about them, but you are in the middle of this thing, so let's focus on you."

"Well, I didn't really do anything. I started investigating this case. There were a lot of things that happened that I was advised to not put in the original file. So I kept a second file. It is by no means your typical case. The things were kind of unexplainable."

"Are we talking about crimes or criminal acts by agents or something like that?"

"No, no, that would have been easy. It was more like things I know I saw happened, but as far as I could tell, it was not possible for them to happen. The only way that I can describe it is like this. You go to sci-fi movie and sit and watch the hero and the villain do all these crazy things with all of these cool weapons, but you get up and leave knowing after the movie is over that none of it is real, only this time I saw the stuff for real, but if I told anybody I would be put in an insane asylum."

"Was this like some government agency that had this stuff?"

"That's kind of the problem. It was a suspect that I am investigating that had all of this stuff."

"You're the FBI."

"That's kind of my point. I'm an agent for the FBI and he has and uses technology that I have not heard of before and at the time was incapable of dealing with when we encountered him."

"So, can't you give the case to someone else?"

"Believe me; I'd love to do that. However, there is this catch."

"So, what is that?"

"He lives like a king, but nobody seems to know who he is. He wants something, but I don't know what it is. He allowed me to meet with him face to face. After pressing the issue, he agreed to controlled communication whereby he will only speak to me."

"Why didn't you arrest him?"

"This going to sound funny, but he won't let me. He had his computer disable my gun.

"Did it take it from you?"

"No, it just flew in the air around me and then went back into the wall.

"Were you awake when all of this was going on?"

"Yes, I was and no I did not imagine this."

"So, why can't you let this case go?"

"Basically, he won't let me go. We are trying to bust him and he uses that by telling the FBI that he will only talk to me. So now I'm stuck in this stupid game of his. I can't drop the case because he and the agency won't let me. They think he is behind all of the killings."

"Now I get it. He has taken control of your life. Still you're the FBI. How does he communicate with you?"

"Mostly by phone now."

"Don't tell me. He has some kind of phone that the "FBI" can't trace?"

"You got it. I've even been to his house one week it was a one story home, two weeks later it was a two story home, and then it didn't exist at all."

"You kids today do have fun."

"He calls it fun. I do not. Any way, supposedly I got busted for having two different case files, only to find out that the agency was setting me up to try to get to this guy."

"First of all your suspension doesn't count. You are going to have to really get suspended before you can say you are in our club. This mambe pambe stuff doesn't count. What do you have on him?"

"Failure to comply with a federal officer, and paying income tax without disclosure of income."

"Now what?"

"We have no evidence."

"This guy is pretty smart?"

"Smart and Gutsy. I get to have dinner with him anytime I want, of course nothing but fine dining. He will look me in the eye and meet with me all day long while he is conducting business. I have never met a criminal like this in all my life. Yes, he is smart. He is so smart; it makes me think I'm in the wrong business. I want to go back to school, but I know that there is not enough school in the world for me to outsmart him."

"It's called a C-Snare."

"What's a C-Snare?"

"That's what we called it in our day. A C-Snare. Short for Criminal Fixation Snare. For some reason you have been picked as the one he wants to catch him. The criminals usually end up being compulsive and even serial killers. They just decide that they only want you to do the dance of death with them."

"So, how do they normally catch them?"

"Do you want the good or the bad news first?"

"Let's try the bad first."

"You need to know why he chose you. Since you don't even know who he is, you are probably not going to get that answer. The problem is that the answer is normally locked up somewhere in the deep recesses of his mind. Without it you are forced to follow his lead and complete the dance. In that case family, friends, co-workers, anybody you associate with end up at risk. Your natural tendency will be to withdraw from everyone to protect them. The problem is, if he is this close already, if you withdraw now it doesn't protect any of them and it makes you more vulnerable. In most cases, you withdrawing actually accelerates harm to them, because they think that maybe you are starting to figure them out. That's when they start upping the ante. Picture how a team plays to win in the final few minutes of the fourth quarter."

"Before you give me the good news I have a statistical question. How many of these have the guy turned out to be a good guy?"

"As far as I know. Zero."

"Now the good news; if you decide to call it that. It appears that you are in the fourth quarter of this game; which means that the clock is ticking and time is running out. There have been a few cases where the crimes have just stopped and the perpetrator has just disappeared."

"So, that's the good news. Are you telling me they got away with their crimes?"

"I wouldn't give them that kind of credit. I would say that the law just hasn't caught up to them yet. The majority of these cases end with some kind of confrontation that leads to death including suicides. You know more than when you came here. Be careful however, at the end of the day you want to catch the bad guy and get your life back. If you follow through; the bloodshed will stop and agents will stop dying."

"Do you think this is somehow all of my fault, and these deaths are somehow on me?"

"This world is messed up. There are so many crazies out there. You shouldn't feel responsible for any of their actions. That is exactly what they want. They want to get inside your head and mess you up. You wouldn't be human if you were not impacted somehow. It will force you to make some hard decisions. No one can make promises to you about the outcome. You need to be careful and take care of yourself. Unfortunately, your trust circle is going to be very small until this is over."

"When it has been over for others, did any of them get to know the reason why they were chosen?"

"Yes, a few. While it seemed clear to the perpetrator, it often times didn't mean the same things to them. You have to know that logic goes out the window for the answer to that question."

"You know he doesn't say he is innocent, and he doesn't say that he is guilty; he just keeps saying that there is more to things than I know."

"I imagine there is a lot more to the story than you are telling me."

"Yes, there is."

"Just the few things that you shared with me help me to say this next thing. Some of the things you told me I can honestly say maybe unique to your case. There is a rational explanation for most things, new technology is not magic, but it often borders on it when you are trying to figure things out. In time things will become clearer to you. I hope that I have been helpful to you. Good luck. Let me know how all of this turns out for you."

"Thank you Harold. I will keep in touch."

CHAPTER THIRTY-ONE

William awoke to see that his clock was flashing. He looked around to acclimate himself to his unfamiliar surroundings. "Man I was tired," he said. He stumbled as he walked toward the window. He reached over to check his phone and saw that he had not had any calls. Maybe I'll take a few minutes. He grabbed something to drink out of the refrigerator and then reached into his briefcase and pulled out the book about Theodore Wexell. He turned to the middle of the book where Johnny was getting ready to graduate from Law School.

Two days before graduation, Johnny was walking toward his dorm, with Theodore beside him. "You know I can't have you at the graduation looking like that," he said.

"What do you mean massa Johnny. I ain't suppose to be at no grageation."

"Who's going to carry my books?"

"They be habin books at grageations?"

"No, no stupid. They give you this graduation book to show that you are graduated."

"I don't know anythin bout dat."

"Like I said, I can't have you looking like that. We started this thing together. You carried my books for fourteen years. We are going to finish it as well. Now, I need you to get cleaned up and some new clothes."

"I don't got money to get no new clothes'."

"I'll give you the money, we just have to figure out how to get you cleaned up and in new clothes'."

"You can't go into our stow."

"I know that. I can stand outside and you can tell them to come outside so that I can tell them that I will pay."

"Massa Johnny, I got clean clothes."

"Yes, you do. I need you to have new clothes."

"Okay massa, it be down here."

"Let's go then."

After completing the process, Johnny made sure that Theodore understood to be cleaned up and dressed in the new clothes for his graduation. Once they both arrived, Theodore was not allowed to sit with Johnny during the ceremony, but when Johnny's turn came to walk the stage, he had arranged for president of the school to hand his diploma to Theodore rather than himself while they both walked across the stage.

Theodore smiled inside at the thought of receiving his diploma from a school that doesn't allow Negros to attend. All of the pictures that Johnny had taken included Theodore with the diploma in hand, with no one thinking anything about it.

After reading this, William closed the book and smiled. "What time is it anyway," he wondered. He walked over and picked up his watch. One o'clock. What?

"He picked up the phone; Chuck, I didn't hear from you. What's going on?"

"Sir, everything is going well. All four teams are on schedule. We are five hours into phase two. We expect to finish the phase about two hours earlier than expected. The IT teams modified some overlays which accounts for our increased efficiency. We had to compromise a few members to get it done. We have not had to compromise any of the team because of exposure from outside."

"Good Job Chuck. Let me know if you need anything."

"Sir, I did have an extra expense that I approved last night. We had to store someone's plane at another hanger, rather than here. It was the only choice we had with timing and everything."

"Don't worry about that Chuck. You did well. You protected our home base. It was necessary. Do you need anything else?"

"No sir. We are good."

"I need to run. I'll talk to you later today."

He hung up the phone and called Daniel.

"Daniel, I'm uploading the data that we discussed about the businesses. You will need to cross match the data to human resources to complete the package so that on Friday morning we can run the Separator."

"Yes sir I will be ready."

"Let me know if you need anything else."

William called Samantha. "Samantha, I plan to be back a little early. I should get back in town around lunch on Thursday afternoon. I expect to arrive at the office around 1:30. I need you to set up that conference call with the Cyber security company and invite Daniel and Thayor to attend."

"Sir did you get to watch the media event this morning with Thayor. He really did a nice job. They tried to trap him again."

"No I actually missed it. Tell Daniel to send me a link so I can see the whole thing. Is anything else going on?"

"Well I wanted to wait until you got back. There has been some guy poking around the perimeter trying to get in. He's pretty stupid, you ask me. He seems to think that no one can see him."

"That's what he wants us to think. Don't worry about him. Have someone take him something to eat when he shows up tonight. He will be back. I'll see you tomorrow."

"Okay sir. Bye."

William decided to head over to meet Albert. "Sorry for the late arrival Albert. My time just got away from me today."

"We're good Mr. Cotton, I am just thankful for your business."

"Let's get started then. Where do you want me to go?"

"See the machine to your left over in the corner. Let's head that direction. Forgive me for how the place looks. I'm trying to do better."

"Don't worry. How are you going to show me the images?"

"They are going be in chronological order and time stamped. Is there some place you want to start?"

"I think I would like to start around 11:30 PM and go forward. How fast can I view the images?"

"The high setting is thirty-two. That's pretty fast. Let's just start out on about eight and see how that works. We can always speed it up. You ready?"

"Yes I am."

Here we go. Albert pushed the button that allowed them to start reviewing the images.

"Are you at 11:30 already?"

"No, give me a couple of minutes."

"The images are pretty clear and a good quality."

"Okay, now we are approaching it. 5, 4, 3, 2, 1. We are here. Check the speed to see if you are able to see what you want to. Remember we can speed it up or slow it down."

"The current speed is good. It looks like it is live rather than on film."

"It is a combination of both."

"Are we near twelve o'clock?"

"Yes sir."

"I need you to rewind to eleven thirty and let it run until two o'clock. Switch with me and tell me what you see over that time frame."

"You really want me to go first? I don't know what I should be looking for, if you told me that maybe."

"Yes you first. That's the point. I need you to look at it with no bias."

"Okay, let's switch then."

"You don't have to narrate. I'll be quite."

After about 15 minutes Albert put the machine on pause and then turned and said, "I don't really see anything. It did seem to get a little foggy, but other than that I didn't really see anything out of the ordinary."

"Now if you don't mind let me look at the same time frame."

Albert started the machine again.

"This looks perfect. I see what you mean about some areas getting a little cloudy. Thank you, this was very helpful. I won't keep you long; I have a team that is going to review it in more detail when I get back. You guys did a good job though. You really did."

"I'm always glad to know that we have a satisfied customer. Thank you."

"I saw what I wanted to see. You can go ahead and package this up. I will be in touch."

Albert flew William back to the hanger and dropped him off.

Chuck came to meet William as he stepped off of the helicopter. "Good evening sir. Welcome back."

"Good evening Chuck. How are you doing?"

"I am well sir."

"Good. I have some information that I would like to discuss with you. Let's head into the plane." As they entered the office in the plane, Chuck shut the door behind them and sat down.

"Chuck when we have missions like this we have other concerns that I have not discussed with you. We have to know as much as possible about the environment so that we can take the necessary steps to protect ourselves. By ourselves I am talking about our anonymity. We did that here which is good. Part of the protection is how we are perceived by everyone in the environment and those that are watching it as well."

"I really don't have a clue about what you just said."

"You know that now there are satellites, planes, helicopters, night vision goggles, google earth, and even tall buildings. They all present an opportunity for someone to view us from a distance. It will allow there to be a possibility that someone can see something from a distance and think that something is going on or something is out of place. We have to be sure that when we run our missions that we review our missions from that perspective and learn how to do them in such a way that even from a distance it looks like nothing is going on."

"How do we do that?"

"That's what I have been doing. First of all, our mission specific training was designed with that in mind. We have a team that has been assembled to provide us with views of all our missions from this perspective. Now that we are active I am going to turn this portion of the projects over to you. I just viewed some of the images from this job and they are fantastic. You and I will get together when we get back to complete the transition."

"Wow. I didn't expect that. Is this absolutely necessary?"

"Yes, absolutely. Our current delivery system for P.A.W.L. is evolving as we speak. It has to, we have to remain invisible as long as we can. If the knowledge of this technology ever gets out, we will become hunted in a life and death battle for as long as we live. Everyone will want it, and will stop at nothing to get it. We are dealing with people, so I do not live under the illusion that this will be hidden forever, but I will work toward it being hidden for as long as possible."

"Sir, I don't even know where P.A.W.L. comes from. I know that we have it in our hands, but no one would believe it exist anyway."

"Everything has a reason. It is for our own protection that no one knows. How do you feel about that?"

"You know all about where I came from sir. All the training and experiences in my life I count as preparation for today. I don't have to know everything. I know this is a big deal sir. I am very happy that you wanted me to be a part of it. I know that there were others more qualified, and yet you chose me."

"I'm going to head back tomorrow morning. This office becomes yours when I leave. You are going to be very busy from now on. I will have Samantha compile the project cost for the imaging and get it to you.

Make sure you get her the complete cost of the project from deployment to mission end ASAP. It may not seem that way, but you and your team will simply be providing a service that will be in high demand."

"Yes sir. I will get with Samantha and accounting for the project cost."

"One other thing. If we all do our parts we can accomplish our goals and objectives. One key part of leadership is respecting people outside and directly under your command. Devin has the huge responsibility of accounting for every single piece of equipment. We can't have one piece come up missing. He is a peer not a clerk. It's your job to foster a high level of respect for him and others like him so that every team and every job is made easier by not having internal friction deriving from disrespect. We are all people and things will come up, so if we do our jobs we can at least minimize some of the causes of friction between us."

"Sorry about the problems before. I have addressed the issues and taken corrective action to insure that there are no misunderstandings like that again. I will continue to work toward making sure that I and everyone on my team understand that we are all part of a team."

"Now on Friday we will go live at 2:30 with the second member or members of the conversation. I will be in the meeting at that time which means this will be the reveal time to all of the attendees. Friday I am going to have a really tight schedule and a lot of unhappy, frustrated, and confused people. It is a big day for us. We have made the permanent acquisitions which led to the discoveries that we anticipated. With them thinking that they have gotten away with this, they will resume thinking that it is business as usual. There is nothing at this time that tells me that they will change the time or their meeting place. If they change their meeting place but not their time we are still good for 2:30."

"What time do your meetings start on Friday?"

"The first one is 8:00AM."

"I will contact you at 7:00 to let you know that everything is set. If anything changes I will give you a heads up tomorrow. When we are done tomorrow night I will give you a call as well. Does this work for you?"

"Yes. Is there anything you need from me?"

"No sir. We are all good here."

"I'll talk to you tomorrow then."

Chuck turned and walked out the door.

William wanted to take time to prepare the agenda for Friday so he could get it over to agent Plaiedeaux. He knew that he would need to go over it a few times and run it by Thayor to get it right. After getting everything written down, he decided not to critique it until the morning.

CHAPTER THIRTY-TWO

William walked into the office expecting to head into his office with no fanfare only to be swamped as soon as he walked in the door. "What is going on?"

"Didn't you hear that there was an attempted shooting in Baltimore this morning. According to news reports they missed. The shot was an attempt to kill another FBI agent," said Samantha.

"Samantha is everything set up for the meeting?"

"Yes, Thayor has already joined the video conference and Daniel is in the conference room. As soon as you are ready I will patch the other callers in."

"Patch them through in about three minutes. Get me some video of the news about the shooting. I would like to view it when I get out of this meeting." William walked into the conference room and closed the door.

"Good morning Thayor. No, I haven't got a chance to review your interview yet. I will do that later this afternoon. This meeting is mostly about you. We are adding our Cyber Security team to monitor your profile. We don't want the public demand for information to go unfed. We will create a hybrid blog for you. It will not necessarily be a daily forum like most of them, but it will be a way to give them some information about you. I also need to talk to you after the meeting regarding my agenda for tomorrow."

"Good morning George and John, next to me is Daniel, he is the head of our IT department for this division and Thayor is our company representative. Thayor is the one that you will be working with to establish his online presence. As I told you, he will be the totality of your work. His online presence will have no connectivity to any company, but his brand of disconnectedness if that is a word, will allow him to become exactly what we want. Your job is to establish his brand and market him. He will not be selling anything or buying anything, but people will need to become curious about him. They will need to begin their days by wanting to know what is going on with him. He will not be running for any public office, nor will he become a political figure as the current world knows political figures. We will cultivate all of his profiles to reflect this. Some will get frustrated with him because of questions that will go unanswered about him. Some will hate him. He will not go away. The analysts will weigh in and classify him as some kind of weird trend, prophesying that his time will pass quickly, but they will be wrong."

"Sorry our boss was not able to attend this. This in no way implies that the work that we are doing for you is not important. Now, what are your timelines for his profiles to be ready to go? You have to know that this is a unique request. Is someone going to be available to collaborate with us and sign off on the work?"

"I know why he is not here. I am comfortable with his assurances that you guys are more than capable of doing the job to my standards. However, you might want to sit down for this one. Tomorrow, there is going to be a huge event that will start the demand for information on him. It will only build from there. You are going to have to play catch up. Daniel will be available to help you expedite things, he already has some templates ready which will help you get up and running by tomorrow. Yes, you will have enough access to us to get the job done."

"What kind of event and where will we need to be to capture this event?"

"While things are going to be happening all around us, you will never be in a position to know what is going to happen. Your job is to always provide the right commentary and or reaction to solidify his branding."

"Since this is so different than other marketing projects. How will we know if we are successful?"

"Daniel has developed a statistical model that we will use to accurately establish a rating system for the site. He will work with you to help you understand it. I know you might not completely understand things right now, but as we move forward you will. Daniel will work through the rest of the details with you."

"What if we fail?"

"It may seem like it is totally different but it is not. We will figure it out. You will not fail. George and John it was good to talk to you again. I will get with Daniel to see how things are going. Thayor I will transfer you to my office."

"Okay, Mr. Stradom," said Daniel.

William walked out of the conference room and into his office.

As he walked over to the video screen, Thayor spoke up. "That was quite an announcement."

"Before you begin check your email. I sent you the agenda for tomorrow. Why don't you print it out and take a few minutes to read through it? You might want to sit down for this.

"Wow. You're going to do this to the FBI and they are going to go along with it."

"We are not doing anything to the FBI, we are simply helping them."

"Now I get it. I am going to be on the "hot seat", I mean wow."

"We have two things we need to accomplish right now. Edit the agenda if necessary, and then discuss your online profile. Does it matter what agency we work with? Is there anything in our discussion previously that gave you any indication how serious this was going to get?"

"No, it doesn't matter and yes you told me it was going to be real. I knew it was coming, but forgive me if I am a little surprised anyway."

With a smile William said, "I forgive you." Then they both laughed.

"You are giving them just enough for them to have to stay engaged for the whole day in addition to item number 4. You really expect this to happen in a two-and-a-half-hour span. You really are optimistic. You must have some really significant information that you are going to share with them for them to agree to this."

"Yes we do and tomorrow you join the big leagues. When everything's said and done, I will bring you in and introduce you to them. Actually I will introduce you to one of them and he will introduce you to the rest of them. This will probably happen sometime around 3:30 PM. I will video conference you in for the introduction."

"May I ask a straight up question about my introduction?"

"Sure, go ahead."

"Why am I only meeting the one guy and not all of them at the same time?"

"The guy you are going to meet is the person I chose to be my liaison with the FBI. He is the only one that has talked to me and met me. I may have to talk to someone else for the purpose of strategic planning, but I do not meet them. Also, the voice they hear will be computer generated. The conversations we will be having tomorrow will be the first time that anyone else will be involved from the FBI in having a conversation with me. This is why I had to set the parameters so rigidly in the agenda. Of course they will try to breach the parameters. Remember that you will never be put in a situation where you will know enough about what we do for them to trick or rely on you as a source of information regarding our companies. They have never seen me or even heard my voice."

"Why would you have needed a liaison prior to tomorrow? Have there been other things going on that cause you to deal with the FBI?"

"When you are a small business most of the time no one is concerned about you dominating a market, or you making too much money. When you grow and become a big business most of the world is concerned because in their minds you are making too much money."

"You know the training I have had over these years doesn't just shut off when I'm talking to you?"

"We didn't train you to have you turn it off. However, your training was supposed to help you look at both sides of everything, not just your objective."

"Okay, I get it. So what you are saying is sometimes an evasive response is all the answer that I am going to get."

"Exactly. Sometimes an evasive response is all you have to give as well."

"William, I'm still learning."

"It will take a while for you to get all of this. It would be the same for anyone. Since your training was so specific, you are well ahead of anyone else that would have taken the job. None of us is perfect. What we are responsible for is to do the best that we can. If you do that then everything will work out fine. Thayor, most people grow up in an environment which helps to establish their views and perspectives. To the average person, living a life based on those perspectives is okay. They can live, love, and enjoy life. A few of us are called to not just have a local perspective but a global one as well. You can't have global perspective if you are not exposed to global events. You are one that because of your calling are not able to remain with only the perspective you started out with. You will grow into your new environment and it will fit you well."

"So, what do I do now?"

"Now, we get something to drink and finish out our preparation for tomorrow."

"You have so much going on. You are so confident that everything will work. I hope someday I will be like that."

"You will have to be. Despite what it looks like, this is a project that has been planned for years. Don't get me wrong, it would be nice to say that I was able to plan every aspect of this project to a "T", but that is not true. When I started in this direction a lot of things happened that were not planned but assisted us to complete the project. If those things had not happened, we would not be here today. Like I said what you are responsible for, is to do the best that you can. That is all that I have done."

"I know this is huge, but why is this so important to you?"

"I was handed this responsibility. When I accepted it, I accepted everything that goes with it. Did I know what all of that meant? No. Could the person, who passed the responsibilities on to me, tell me all that it would mean to me? No. They could have told me what the responsibility meant to them. I was put here for a specific reason. I had to figure out what all of these responsibilities meant to me. Once I did that, everything became easier. I initially thought of replicating what had been done before, but I soon learned that was the worst thing that I could do. I had to allow who I am and why I am here to come to life. Once you do that, there is no stopping you. We are going to take our time and walk through this. I figure we have about two hours."

"Can I ask one more question before we get started?"

"You have the floor."

"As sensitive as all of this appears to be, why would you entrust my profile to an outside company? Wouldn't that put everything at risk?"

"Good question. Under normal circumstances you would be right. What you do, needs to be held in the highest confidence. However, what George and John don't know is who they were talking to. That is one of the companies that I own. It is important to me to see how they handle high profile clients so that this company can grow. Their track record was excellent when I acquired them, but where we are going the profile of the company needed to be raised. What better way than for me to become a customer. In Cyber work there are huge growth opportunities and we have positioned ourselves to occupy a significant share of the market."

"You are full of surprises. I have never known or heard of anyone like you before. Somehow you can do anything you want, whenever you want to."

"I am not unique in that capacity. There are others that have similar resources available to them who you have not had the privilege to meet yet. For some reason your first exposure happens to be me. There are no accidents."

"Okay. Thank you for this time. I know I need it so that I can get ready for tomorrow. Let's do this."

William called and asked Samantha to bring in some tea and water and some snacks. His phone had been vibrating so he checked some of his messages before continuing. The afternoon seemed to move quickly as they hashed out the profile, agenda, and his introduction. Thayor suggested some modifications to the agenda which William liked and adopted. Just as they were about to finish his phone rang, when he looked and saw that it was Chuck, he told Thayor to give him a minute. He stepped into the conference room to talk to him.

"Okay Chuck, I was in a meeting. Is everything okay?"

"Yes sir. We will be finishing up in about thirty minutes? The FBI and police have been everywhere today. We caught the news clip about the attempted shooting this morning. We will probably be delayed from departing tonight. They are grounding all planes from taking off."

"Talk to Larry the pilot; he will have instructions for you on how you guys will leave tonight. Dan, the tech guy that helped with the electrical problem, will be in charge of getting everyone home tonight. I have been in meetings so I haven't had a chance to see the news yet. Was the attempted shooting within the square mile that we worked in?"

"As a matter of fact, yes it was. We didn't attempt to do the thorough analysis at the other site, but yes it was."

"You know if it is recorded live there is no need for the thorough analysis. The information we have from the attempted shooting is as good as we can possibly get. Since the complete project has been real time, our data analysis is now only running about an hour behind your extraction times. Tracy and Larry will be in charge of staying behind with the equipment to bring it home when they can."

"Good job Chuck. Is there anything else?"

"Nothing that can't wait until we get home."

"Tell everyone to get some rest tonight you are going to have a really busy next few days."

"Will do sir. I will talk to you later."

William returned to his office to finish up with Thayor.

"William, the agenda we are working on is only an outline, but not the agenda that you will have tomorrow am I right?"

"Yes, the agenda tomorrow will go by this outline, but with all the details filled in."

"Without knowing the details, how can I be sure that the suggestions that I make are any good."

"The more you and I communicate the better your suggestions will be. In this job, for the most part, you will not be in the detail business. I won't have to keep reminding you of this once you get your feet wet. You will be thanking me for not sharing the details with you."

"If you present this situation to anyone reasonable, I can see how what you do can be misunderstood."

"Don't be afraid, go ahead and say what you were going to say."

"It is hard not to think that something illegal is going on here. Drugs, guns, or something worse. Obviously, there is something you are protecting as you said. It strains the imagination, but nothing comes to mind short of that. I do believe that it is short of that."

"You need to arrive there on your own, because there will be every attempt made to separate you from that belief. You are going to experience lies, intimidation, deceit, manipulation, even witchcraft, if there is still such a thing, to get between me and you. They will think that the organization is vulnerable and you are an asset that can give them or get them details. They are going to be shocked when they test you, have you take lie detector tests, truth serum, hypnosis, and so on only to find out that you do not have any details and you do not have access to any."

"Have we covered everything that we need to for tomorrow?"

"Yes, I think we have. They will play it safe tomorrow with our introduction. Always let them know that every conversation with them is recorded."

"I missed one thing on the agenda. Who or what are alternates?"

"They are two other divisions of the government that are very interested in working with us if the FBI is not willing to. The rest of the government will have to permanently pay a penalty rate if the FBI does not agree to our terms."

"How much is the penalty?"

"They will have to pay double the rate if the FBI doesn't come on board."

"Will the other departments know that they are paying double because the FBI refused?"

"Yes, they are all expecting proposals tomorrow."

"Will you only work with the FBI exclusively if they agree?"

"Any department can use us as long as they agree to our contract terms and adhere to them. The one catch is they will always have to work through the FBI. If a department attempts to get around our contract or tries to replicate any of our equipment, then all departments will serve a suspension but still be required to pay us. Once the general suspension period is over with them the department that broke faith will have to pay us double for one year plus reimburse us for all of the salaries of our employees that work under the contracts for a year. By the way, the penalties and salary reimbursement will be considered a legal court award of damages and therefore legally excluded from declaration as income. There is much more, but you get the gist."

"Who will be in the conference tomorrow?"

"All three departments. However, the other two departments can only have a maximum of three people in on the conference call. They will get to introduce themselves and tell what department they are in and listen only with no questions. The FBI is the only department that will be allowed to talk and ask questions. You will only be meeting with the department that makes the final decision. If for some reason the FBI doesn't choose to work with us, we will be having another meeting excluding the FBI, with the other departments."

"While one FBI agent will be with me, the rest will be participating in a voice conference call. I will not meet the other groups either. My voice will sound natural to them, but it will be a computer generated voice over the phone."

"Why tell me these details?"

"Think about what you are being told and then try to answer that question yourself."

"Okay. They are not going to like the terms, so when I get in a conversation with them, that is one of the first things that they are going to want to confront me with."

"What will be your response?"

"I'm sorry guys I have not read the contract and I have too much on my plate to even think about trying to. We have some things to discuss, why don't we get to why we are here today."

"Good answer. I told you just enough so that when they confront you, you won't be shocked. At the same time, I have told you nothing. What services are we contracting? If asked your answer will be I don't know. Is it food, furniture, cleaning, or cyber work? I don't know. How long are the contracts? I don't know. How many contracts? I don't know. What company are the contracts with? I don't know. Who owns all of these companies? I don't know. And so on."

"Thank you for being so open with me. I can see that I am still in need of lots of help."

"We've run a little longer than expected, but we are good. You get some sleep. Big day tomorrow."

"Yes sir. Talk to you tomorrow."

"If you think of something else, feel free to call me."

"Yes sir."

William shut down the video conference and reached over to his computer to see if Samantha had sent the link to the FBI story. She had. He clicked on it to listen to the story.

There was another attempted shooting of an FBI agent in the city of Baltimore today. It happened about 9:20AM. According to witnesses who were near the area where the shooting occurred, they heard at least three separate shots fired in the general vicinity of the agent's car. This appears to be a continued trend of some type of war that has been declared on the FBI. In the last three months, there have been multiple shootings involving FBI agents most of which have been fatal. The agent's car appeared to take two direct hits in the driver's side door. No one was available for comment including the agent who possibly was the target. The last statement we had is that there is an ongoing investigation.

After he listened to the report William opened his door to see if Samantha was still there. She had left for the day. He walked over and picked up a bottle of juice and walked back into his office and closed the door.

It's time to call agent Tom Plaiedeaux. William speed dialed his number.

"Good evening, who is calling?"

"Tom, it's me William."

"I figured you would be calling. You've had a busy couple of days."

"Yes, but not the way you are thinking. Some of us actually have jobs and work for a living, rather than having our paychecks handed to us while we sit around and do nothing."

"That's a good one. So where were you today?"

"I was working as usual."

"That's not an answer to my question."

"Yes it is. Perhaps if you asked me if I was in Baltimore and if I attempted to shoot an FBI agent while I was there, you would get a more specific answer."

"You would be too smart to do it yourself. So my question would be more like. Did you have any involvement in the attempted shooting of an FBI agent in Baltimore today at approximately 9:20 this morning?"

"Good, because the answer is still no I did not attempt to shoot, nor was I involved in any way in an attempted shooting of an FBI agent at 9:20 AM this morning in Baltimore, Maryland. At some point you are going to get tired of this. I know I am. But on with the game for now."

"Again, somehow people getting killed are described as a game by you."

"That is not the game that I am talking about. You won't just be honest with me. You go and have your little strategy session and then you come back to me to try something else. You actually insult yourselves."

"What are you talking about now?"

"I know that you are now the bait. You are supposed to continue to show a little bit of hostility while you gain my trust and lure me in. Well guess what it is working. I needed you to become the bait, because with you being the bait both sides are fishing. Here's the thing about bait. It has to stay bait as long as required by the fisherman to catch what the fisherman wants to catch. I was waiting for you to become the bait so that we can move forward."

"You think you are so clever?"

"Tom, I am clever and I am smart. I don't apologize for that, I never will. I didn't get here by allowing you guys to push me around, trick me, or deceive me. I don't plan to start now. You are suspended because of duplicate files you have on me."

"You can't just tap the FBI's phones or bug their offices and think that you are going to get away with it. That is illegal."

"Tom, you are a broken record. I didn't tap their phones or do anything illegal."

"Then you must be bribing someone then."

"No, that is not what is happening either."

"Okay then, what are you doing?"

"Nice try, are you forgetting something?"

"What am I forgetting?"

"You are supposed to get me to talk rather than you listening to the sound of your own voice. I am ready to talk. That is why I called you. Am I going to have to do your job for you?"

"Talk then."

"You are not going to like what I have to say."

"I said talk didn't I?"

"Okay, here goes nothing. Tomorrow morning at 8:00 I will send you an email. The email will contain an agenda for the day, and some highly sensitive information along with 21 additional attachments grouped in pdf files. The agenda will detail several high level collaborative meetings. The timelines will be critical and absolute. Missing a time line will terminate the agenda for the day and the topic for the meetings will not be discussed with the FBI ever again. Some of the subjects and actions that will need to be taken will create some highly intense internal discussions. Every moment will be critical; there will be no time for you to waste. Your computer which is not capable of handling the size of the files at all will receive the files. You can send them where you want to. It normally will take you quite a while to print out the pdf files, but the main color printer on the 14th floor of your office building is set to print tomorrow morning only 500 pages per minute. The total pages for the files are right at 2000. The system will separate each of the 21 packets. In order to save time, I am going to suggest that you are going to need 21 lawyers that deal with contracts for the government. Each package has a summary and cover page on top of the detail pages for each package. You are going to probably need to sequester a team of high level decision makers in order to get things done tomorrow. Did you get that?"

"No, I didn't get all of that."

"Remember you are just the bait. The bait doesn't interpret what is going on around them; they simply lay there in hopes of someone taking a bite of them. I am taking a bite. You will be able to be with them early in the morning, but after that you will spend about 6 hours with me alone at my house. About three hours of the time will be recorded because we will be in conference, and three hours will be off the record. By the way, I sent you an email while we are talking now, that includes all of the information that I said before. It was sent to your phone, but not to your computer. The information tomorrow morning will be just the opposite."

"What are the packages?"

"I am not going to answer that question, again bait don't ask questions."

"I think this is some sort of plea bargain. You really think you are smart enough to somehow kill FBI agents and then plea bargain your way out of the death penalty. I don't plan on being at your house for one minute. The house that doesn't exist. I will spend six hours with you in an interrogation room."

"You don't have to worry about breakfast; we will have a pretty nice spread. Lunch will be a nice spread as well. By the way you want to hear some good news?"

"From you, the only good news would be if you turned yourself in and we stopped the senseless killings."

"You want it to be over with don't you? That's your good news."

"Now what are you talking about?"

"If what you believe is true, and the FBI decides to stop the agenda tomorrow, then this could be our last conversation. I am saying if they stop the agenda tomorrow, you will no longer have access to me. I will shut everything down. I will be out of your life. You will be able to go back to whatever it was that you were doing before you "found me". The house will be gone as well."

"Just like that?"

"There is no reason for me to turn myself in. I have not done anything wrong. Half of your wish will be granted in that case."

"You think you can order us to drop this case? We are not your subjects. That's not the way the law or law enforcement works in the United States. We will find you again. We found you once."

"I believe you have some calls to make. My guess is that you have a long night ahead of you. I will send the recording of this conversation to your laptop as well, see you in the morning. By the way you are going to have to do something that you swore you would never do tomorrow. Remember that I can be contacted by you only on your phone. The system partly works on voice recognition, you can't even dial the phone and give it to someone else, and so, you will have to call me."

"It's not going to come to that."

"Good night, Tom."

William called Daniel to follow up with him.

"Good evening Daniel."

"Good evening Mr. Stradom."

"How are you doing with our project for tomorrow?"

"The front end design has been very successful. Chuck let me know about thirty minutes ago that they were done. I expect that it will take another couple of hours or so to complete the downloads. Everything has come off without a hitch at this time. I can send you some of the modeling so that you can see them before tomorrow."

"I have had my system monitor up and have been reviewing the modeling from the beginning. I have sent you a couple of things to check on. Nothing major. How has the data encryption keys gone for the emails?"

"We got that solved yesterday sir. I sent you a bullet sheet on the steps you need to take in order for you to send them in the morning."

"Does it matter that I have the emails saved and ready to go?"

"Yes sir it does. You won't simply be able to press send tomorrow. You will have to open the saved email and then run through some of the steps before pressing send. I assume that you saved the email with all of the attachments."

"Yes I did save it with all of the attachments. The timing of the email is critical. Come by my office about 7:30 tomorrow just to make sure we are all good."

"Yes, sir. I will be there."

"Good night Daniel. Oh, by the way. How did the meeting with the Cyber guys finish up?"

"Once they received what we had they seemed to get over the initial shock and got down to business. They brought in the president of the company to help them clarify some things for them. He kind of translated for them, which put them more at ease. They really kind of exploded on the scene from there. They are really good sir. They have a long night ahead of them, but I think they will be ready sir. Obviously it will not be perfect, but we will get through it."

"See you in the morning Daniel."

CHAPTER THIRTY-THREE

As William returned home to get some rest himself; he ended up having a restless night. It took him awhile to finally get to sleep. He was still sleeping when his 7:00 AM call came from Chuck.

"Good morning sir." Chuck said.

"Good morning Chuck. You are calling pretty early; my alarm hasn't gone off yet. What time is it?"

"7:01 sir."

"Great, it appears that I overslept then."

"I don't understand. I thought I was supposed to call you at 7:00."

"No, no it's not you Chuck. I had planned to be up at 5:00 to get prepared for today."

"Oh, I'm sorry. Do you want me to call back later?"

"No, let's just keep it brief. If we need more time we can always circle back around on Monday, unless we need to do it sooner than that."

"Yes sir. Well, while the trip home was an event itself, everyone was able get back except Tracy and Larry. I checked with them this morning, the travel ban should be lifted sometime this afternoon. As soon as it is lifted they will be on their way."

"Okay Chuck, remember we discussed that we may need to cover some dead sites. The sites where crimes have taken place but more than seventy-two hours have passed. We can still piece together information, but it will be using P.A.W.L. F. which will take a little longer than the project that we just completed. You know how it works. You may get a call today to deploy immediately to do some more sites."

"How many?"

"We don't know for sure yet how big this thing is, however my guess is seven maybe eight. Before the day is over we will definitely have a better handle on the scaling."

"Can we stack them or will they need to be done simultaneously. I know we have planned for large scale deployment, so it really doesn't matter, either way we are ready?"

"If I had to guess, this next project will be multiples and simultaneous."

"You weren't kidding about us being busy. I know how much this cost just for this one. Seven is going to be crazy. Honestly, it has been costing us a fortune these last couple of years, training so many people. I did what you ask me to do, but I couldn't see how there was going to be such a need. Is this already a go?"

"No, not yet. But it should be before the day is out."

"Is Devin ready for this? I mean, is the equipment in place?"

"Yes, he is ready."

"You are talking about a little over 250 P.A.W. L. F's not to mention everything else."

"I have to run now. Yes, he is ready. You will get a call from Thayor to let you know."

"Who's Thayor?"

"He works for me; we will talk later." William had turned on the shower as he was talking to Chuck. He jumped in the shower and got dressed quickly and headed out the door grabbing a juice on the way. He arrived at 7:35 about five minutes later than he had told Daniel he would meet him. As he turned the corner in the hallway he saw Daniel sitting in the hall waiting on him.

"Good morning Daniel."

"Morning sir," Daniel replied. "I'm ready if you are."

"Let me boot up my computer and we will get started. By the way, I get focused sometimes and forget to say some things. I appreciate all of your hard work. You have been doing a really good job."

"Thank you sir. I appreciate you saying that."

"You have received a great deal of additional responsibility in the last few months. You have handled everything well. If you need some additional help or anything, just let me know. Now, I have your notes."

"Sir I know you have a lot going on. I will be happy to set everything up and then all you would have to do is press send. We can always go over how all this works later. Per your requirements the email will not be traceable and we will still have a read receipt."

"Okay, Daniel. Go ahead. Just let me know when it's ready. I need the email to arrive in their inbox at exactly 8:00. Does the file size hurt? Forget that. What time do I need to send it so that it arrives at that time?"

"Give me a second to look at your file sizes. Okay, you should send at 7:56. I'm just about ready sir. We will have about five minutes to spare."

"Five minutes. You know I overslept this morning."

"Can I say something and not get fired?"

"Go ahead."

"It's no secret that Samantha is crazy about you, she hasn't said anything to anyone, but you can read her body language when you are around. She lights up."

"Is that so?"

"You don't have to say anything back. I just think you guys should take a shot."

"Wow, you really don't like your job. Just kidding. How about I say I will take that under advisement."

"Okay then. sir, you've been putting in a lot of hours. You know that it will eventually catch up to you."

"You are probably right. Hopefully after today, I might get some time to rest."

"I'm done sir. Let's switch places. You have about two minutes. Are you ready for this?"

"To be forced or permitted to evolve means that you are involved in something much greater than yourself and something much greater than your own abilities. Yes, I am ready and I submit to the change voluntarily. Here we go. William grabbed the mouse and clicked send. Have you got everything in place for 10:30?"

"I'm sure you were just talking out loud, because I do not have a clue about what you just stated. Also, no I'm not ready yet sir, I have a few loose ends, but nothing major. Once I get that done I will contact Thayor. We have already discussed his patching in. It will only take a couple of minutes. Based on the agenda, he is scheduled to be patched in at 3:30. If anything changes regarding the time, we can move his time. You will just have to let me know."

CHAPTER THIRTY-FOUR

Agent Plaiedeaux had met with SAC Johnson and SSA Smithren. He was adamant about not wanting to be any part of any of the meetings. Johnson ordered him to be at the office at 7:30. Agent Plaiedeaux let him know that he would be there. He said he couldn't believe that they were doing what Stradom wanted. The next morning Tom walked in a few minutes before 7:30.

"Chief Smithren sir."

"Tom, what if he is confessing, wouldn't you want to be here for that?"

"Yes, but based upon my conversation with him last night, he is nowhere near confessing."

"We have to see where this is going."

"By the way, where is SAC Johnson?"

"I talked to him a few minutes ago. He said that he has been up all night."

"He's that worried about this meeting today?"

"No, he said he has been on all kinds of calls from the Chief of Staff, a Commander from the Navy and a Colonel from the Air Force."

"What does that have to do with us and William this morning?"

"I don't know, but it is time for you to fire up your laptop."

"I am doing that. I guess he is going to miss all of this."

"He did say that something is going on with this meeting."

"I received it, now I am sending it just as I was told. Now I am printing out the five copies of the agenda. Did they really send 21 attorneys?"

"Yes, they are down stairs on the 11 floor. As soon as the print outs are done, they will be given to them. We need to read the agenda."

"Here you go sir. The copies are now in your hand. Do you want me to take one to SAC Johnson?"

"No, Arial please take this into SAC Johnson immediately, he is waiting for it."

"Yes sir, I will do it right now."

"This is crazy. This looks like he is trying to negotiate a contract or something."

"Go back up to section three."

"I read all of that. I don't believe any of it. So, that's why he didn't say anything about it."

"You read the part where he said he has collected evidence including dates and times and live conversations in Baltimore which includes the trigger men in the murders and attempted murders. He mentions that the evidence shows the real times that the murders and attempted murder occurred which we withheld from the public."

"Chief, he is like a magician; somehow he comes up with all of this stuff. There is no way that he can prove any of this stuff."

"I think you are compromised. You've let him get in your head. We can hate a suspect, we can dislike him both personally and professionally, but we can't let anything he says or does prohibit us from pursuing justice."

"Are you telling me that you believe all of his crap?"

"No, but I do have a long memory. Explain to me what a living fax is, or how he disabled a gun without touching it. Forget the gun thing. That living fax thing delivered us a criminal within two days of an agent getting shot. We didn't have any evidence that would have led us to an arrest at the time. It's like solving crimes on steroids. I admit, he is definitely a person of interest. There are enough questions about him to make you think of him as a criminal that has not been caught, but there are also some things that make you want to question any circumstantial evidence because of what he has been doing. Who would hang around and create dialogue with the exact person that is trying to destroy them?"

"Just as Tom started to respond SAC Johnson walked in."

"Good morning everyone."

"Is anyone else coming to meet with us?" asked Tom.

"We will be doing a lot of teleconferencing today. Before we get started. Not everyone's agenda is the same. There was something specific to each of us. The schedules are the same but the agendas are a little different. Tom I need to ask you some questions," said SAC Johnson.

"Okay sir."

"I need you to clear your head for a minute. You are the only one who has met Mr. Stradom."

"How am I supposed to know that? I know that his conditions were that I had to meet him alone, but I don't know if I am the only one that has met him. Am I being accused of something?"

"I need you to sit down and listen for a minute."

"Yes sir."

"I need you to confirm some of the technology that you have been introduced to through Mr. Stradom. What is Transightal Security?"

"It is something that he said only he knew about."

"What is it?"

"I don't know how to describe it."

"Did you experience it?"

"Yes, according to him. I experienced it first, and then he told me what the name of it was."

"What was your experience?"

"We were supposed to break into his compound and arrest him. We tried tearing down his metal gate with force using chains and so on. We had no impact on the gate. We had a welder cut the gate down with a torch. It looked like he had cut the hinges on both sides of a section of the gate so that we could get into his compound. The gate even though it looked like it was cut, remained suspended in the air as if it was not cut. We still could not move it even though it appeared to not be attached to anything. A few minutes later the sections where the welder cut kind of filled back in by itself as if it was never cut. We tried dropping some men from a helicopter but there was some sort of invisible barrier over the property, and they could not get in either. The house that we were storming looked like a one story house at the time, but when I went back two weeks later, it was a two story house. A month or so later we went to the house and there was only a vacant lot with no signs of a house ever being there."

"Are there more stories like this?"

"When the first agent was killed he sent us an untraceable living fax."

"What is that and who did he send the fax to?"

"He sent the fax to me."

"Did you give him your fax number?"

"No sir. He also acquired my phone number each time it was changed. He sent us a fax that somehow was tied to a suspect that had shot and killed an agent. The fax which came off of a regular fax machine, had a live real time GPS system embedded that tracked the suspect. Anywhere the suspect moved the GPS would update us in real time to let us know he had moved. It had something like a three-hour window and then it would stop tracking him."

"Are you saying it was tied to his car, or phone or something?"

"I'm not sure, but I think somehow it was tied to him. Because we arrested him before the time expired, we noticed that when we separated him from his phone and his car, the fax still showed exactly where he was. We even took the evidence while maintaining the chain of custody; two miles away from him, and the fax still showed his physical location."

"Are there more stories?"

"Now that you mentioned it there are a few more. Would you like me to tell you about them?"

"No, not at this time. Before you met him, had you ever heard of any of this stuff before?"

"No, sir. It sure sounds like I'm in trouble or something."

"When he used this, did you get to see any of it?"

"There was one piece he called Paul."

"What did it do?"

"I will tell you what happened. I do not know what it actually did. It appeared to be some sort of voice operated, talking, chameleon, security, flying computer."

"That's a mouth full."

"Yes sir. It wasn't visible when I walked into his dining room. He spoke to it and told it to scan me. It came out the wall without leaving a hole and flew over in front of me. It said that it scanned me and found my gun. It asked him if he wanted it to take the gun or deactivate it. He told him to deactivate it. It told him that it did and it was dismissed and it disappeared back into the wall."

"Are you saying that a door opened or something and it came and returned through the door in the wall?"

No sir. It kind of just melted into the wall to the point that you could not identify that it even existed. By the way, my gun was deactivated and wouldn't work after that."

"Have you ever seen anything like that before?"

"No sir. What does this have to do with why we are here today?"

"Do you think William is capable of murder?"

"I think he has a lot of fancy toys and a lot of money. I don't think he is going to let anyone take that away from him without a fight."

"You didn't answer my question."

"No, I don't think he has it in him to do it himself, but I'm just not sure that he wouldn't have someone else do it. Are we done here?"

"No, I've been up all night dealing with this thing. The Air Force and Navy want me to see the examples of real data that he promises to show us. They want us to follow through with the agenda."

"Why would they want that?"

"Apparently they have had an eye on William long before you were introduced to him. None of them have ever met him."

"How do they know if it is him then?"

"That is classified."

"I could be wrong, but since I've been here I don't remember ever collaborating with them on anything. Come to think of it, I have never participated in any discussions like this before either. I am not sure what this is about, but I told William and you both, I don't want any part of whatever this is. I was looking forward to today for different reasons."

"What do you mean?"

"Based on what he said yesterday, I figured he was going to drop off of my caseload for a while. I still believe he is up to no good, but at least I would get to rest for awhile."

"Tom, you have been reinstated as of 8:00 AM this morning and we are giving him his six hours with you today."

"You're kidding me right?"

"No, Tom we are not."

"Chief Smithren, are you going along with this as well."

"Tom, you have worked with the FBI for a long time, you know how fiercely we protect our reputation. We will never do anything to damage that knowingly. Sir what if there are things brought up in those meetings that are above Tom's security clearances?"

"Tom, you will be granted a temporary top security clearance for this meeting as well as being named acting head of a new Special Projects unit and you're being promoted to Supervisory Special Agent."

"There is no such thing as a Special Projects unit."

"We know that. It is the best that we can do for now. Things may change before the day is over."

"There is obviously something that you are not telling me. What is it? Hold on a minute, I haven't said that I was going to accept the promotion or whatever this is."

"Tom, be sensible. Have you ever heard of a C-Snare?"

"Yes I have."

"Then you know that you are trapped in one."

"Yes I do, now!"

"You know how they work. Do you know why?"

"No, I don't."

"You do have a choice, but you don't if you are fighting against it. If you don't let it run its course it will not let go of you and things will only get worse."

"Wait a minute; do you know how long I've been trapped?"

"We think so. It appears to us right now that it started when you joined the agency. But, that's only because there are some things we don't know. It could have started earlier."

"Are you telling me that somehow William is connected and has been in my life for over seven years?"

"We can't jump to conclusions, there is too much that we don't know about them."

"What do you mean them?"

"I meant your case."

"No, you said them."

"C-Snares. C-Snares were designed to work both ways. Although there are no documented cases of them going both ways. Tom, we don't have time for this now. How long does it take for you to get to Williams from here?"

"It takes about 20 minutes on a good day, if the house is there."

"This is not a good day, and we've got 30 minutes. We can't miss that window. Hold on. Get that chopper over here right now. We need you here on top of the roof in 5 minutes."

"Okay, I'll do it, under protest. Will I get any preparation for the meeting?"

"No you won't. That is also one of the conditions for the meetings."

"You're telling me that one man controls whatever this is and the FBI, Air Force, and Navy are powerless to stop it."

"No one is powerless, Tom. There is more at stake than you can possibly imagine."

"Maybe I am a little thick, because I don't get it. I'm headed up to the roof. Is anyone going with me?"

"No, we will teleconference with you."

Tom walked up to the roof and climbed into the chopper and closed the door. "Pilot I assume you know where we are going?"

"Yes sir I do. I was the pilot who attempted the aerial drop of agents when we were trying to get into the property before."

"Of course you are. There's room to land on the road near the gate, drop me there."

"I can do that. We should be there in about 6 minutes."

"I'm ready let's go."

The helicopter took off, flying towards William Stradoms' house.

"Okay sir. We're here."

Tom gave the pilot a look of acknowledgement and climbed out onto the road outside the gate. He gathered himself, looked at his watch and began to walk toward the entry gate. He had fifteen minutes to get to the house. He called William to get the code to open the gate. Tom punched in the code and walked through the gate. As he walked toward the house, he noticed that now it was looking like a three story home. The same elderly man greeted him as before.

"Good morning agent Plaiedeaux, it is good to see you again. I hope you had a nice helicopter ride. I've never been in one before. I'm afraid of heights, so don't look for me to ever try that."

"It's not my favorite mode of transportation, but it will do in a pinch. I assume that you are taking me to William."

"Yes sir. He is in the media room lounge. Breakfast is already served."

After walking through several hall ways filled with expensive furniture and art, the doorway opened where he could see to his right a small seating area like a little breakfast café with seating for about twenty. To the left there were microphones, hanging TV's, a projector screen and a large desk that sat in the center of the room. William was sitting behind the desk. He stood and walked toward Tom.

"Good morning Tom. Good to see that you made it. Why don't we go ahead and grab something to eat, I know I didn't get to eat this morning."

"I didn't get to grab anything either."

They both grabbed plates and made their selections of food while remaining silent.

"You are different this morning, Tom. I guess you have a lot on your mind."

"Yes I do. Looks like we will have time for that today."

"Yes we will. Let's eat I will call as soon as we are finished."

They sat down at a table across from each other. The silence was loud as they both consumed the food that was before them. Both equally determined to force conversation to come from the other. As usual a stalemate turned out to be the result.

After they finished, Tom looked at his watch. "It is 10:40, we are late," he said.

"They will wait for us."

"Do you have respect for anyone at all?"

"I do, but I know that this couldn't be helped. Neither you nor I needed to get locked up in this meeting on an empty stomach. Science has revealed to us that food will allow our brains to fire on all cylinders, especially breakfast, it is imperative that we have all our faculties when we start this meeting. Now, we can sit anywhere in the room and both talk and listen. There will be only audio in this first meeting. There will be two interested parties, representatives from the Air Force and the Navy, however they will be introduced and then be relegated to listening only. The meeting is primarily for the FBI. The Air Force and Navy are interested parties. If any part of the discussion approaches a prohibited subject matter, SAC Johnson will step in and handle it. Do you have any questions regarding the meeting?"

"No, I don't, unless you count why am I here? Of course that's rhetorical."

"Okay, then here we go." William picked up the phone and said, "go ahead and patch everyone in."

"Good morning everyone. I consider it a privilege and am thankful to have this opportunity today. There are many things that we can discuss regarding how we arrived here today, but we don't have five days. Let's just say for now, we are here and that the lengthy discussion can take place at another time. I have chosen to do the introductions in no particular order. I am William Stradom, I will be moderating the meeting. Now I would like the Air Force, Navy, and then the FBI to do their own introductions. Please include your rank and position. Once these are complete the Air Force, and Navy will only be able to listen to the meeting, their microphones will be turned off. Gentleman let's get started."

Slowly one by one everyone introduced themselves until the last person which was agent Plaiedeaux.

"Hello my name is, SSA Tom Plaiedeaux, I am the head of the FBI Special Projects unit."

"Okay Mr. Stradom," said SAC Johnson, "it's time to show your hand."

"I will do this with limited fan fare. I'd like you to listen to something. The names and the location have been redacted for the sake of this meeting. It is going to be tough to here because of the sensitive nature of the topic."

William reached over and pushed a button on his computer.

"I did it guys, I got me an FBI agent. It was like skeet shooting or maybe shooting a sitting duck. I did everything that I was told to do. I didn't make any mistakes. They didn't even know what hit them. They should have never messed with us."

"No, I didn't report it yet. We are not supposed to report it until the job is finished. We are supposed to get two on separate days in Baltimore. You know we're supposed to change things up. They are already running scared. We're ghosts to them; they can't touch us. When _____ get's his tomorrow, then we will report it."

William pushed the button again to stop the playback.

"We thought you were smart. Now we can't use that. You can't use an illegal wiretap in court," said SAC Johnson.

"That's all you have", said agent Plaiedeaux. "This is the way that you present it. This is a waste of our time."

"It is not a wiretap." said William.

"Now you are going to talk semantics. I suppose a bug is not necessary a tap." said SAC Johnson.

"It's not a bug." said Mr. Stradom.

"Do you even know who this guy is? This could be made up." said SSA Smithren.

"Yes, we know who the guy is, yes we have DNA evidence that confirms he was the shooter, yes we have evidence of exactly where the shots came from, yes we know exactly where he parked his car and video of him walking into the crime scene, yes we know exactly who rented the room, where he fired the shots, yes we know exactly where he is right now, and will know where he is for the rest of his life, yes we know where the gun is that fired the shots. Now let's listen to some more."

"Hey _____, I'm on my way to get me one too. I think it is brilliant that we do not use the same shooter for both kills. We will never get caught that way. Any advice for me."

"Yeah man. You always get a little nervous when you do things like this, take your time. If you rush it, you will miss a little high and right. This is a big deal, don't do anything stupid. You should only take one shot."

"Big bro always looking out for me. I will get there and get set up a little before eight, then I will have to wait until the first agent pulls up. Yes, I do have my pictures of the agents that work in the office. I knew you were going to ask that."

"Hold on a second. You got the second shooter on tape as well?" asked SAC Johnson.

"Yes, with the same criteria as the other one. We know almost everything about him."

"So you are telling me that you have this information and you have done nothing illegal to get it?"

"That's what I am telling you. The information that you have heard has been obtained legally."

"We've asked you whether you did a wiretap or bug and you said no. Do you have someone on the inside wearing a wire?" asked SSA Plaiedeaux.

SSA Smithren said, "Maybe we are asking the wrong questions. Will you tell us what we are missing?"

"Yes sir. It took our team 48 hours to gather this information. It was done totally with new technology. It would be ideal to get to a crime scene within 72 hours, but the worst case right now is 90 days, and from it we can extract this type of information."

"It takes several weeks to get DNA results back, it has been just a little under seventy-two hours since the shooting in Baltimore. Are you telling me you already have DNA results and matched them to the shooter as well?" asked SAC Johnson.

"Yes, I am telling you that we have done both. Our DNA system recognizes a sample at the subatomic level within about 30 seconds and matches within in 60 seconds."

"Are you talking about your own database, or any database?" asked SAC Johnson.

"We are getting a little off track, without going into the technical details, pretty much any data base on the planet, as long as our system is allowed to search the database."

"How do we know that this isn't some sort of setup, and that you aren't involved in these killings somehow?" asked Tom.

Agent Johnson, "I believe I will let you handle that one."

"We spent the night validating some work that he has been doing for the Air Force and the Navy for the past fifteen years. He has been volunteering and chairing committees for them all during this time. He has been an asset to them, during this time, even though there was one specific requirement he had. He would never meet anyone face to face."

"So, what did he do, that made them accept his condition?"

"I won't go into everything that he has done, but I will tell you one example. He bought the equipment and designed an engine for an F15 fighter jet. Then he bought a F15 Jet shell and assembled it including adding the new engine. He donated the complete jet and its schematics and blueprints to the air force. He could have made billions of dollars off of his design. It saved billions of dollars in manufacturing cost and they came away with the fastest, most fuel efficient, and nimblest F-15 in their fleet."

"Is that good enough for you Tom?"

"Yes sir. Obviously, there are some things I don't understand."

"Now gentlemen, listen I am going to push play so that you can hear the next excerpt, for this one I'm skipping a lot of information so that you can get the demonstration from a different perspective. Here we go."

"Man Bobby didn't I tell you to take your time. You messed up big time. We have to demonstrate that we can complete our assignments. We can't fail at our assignments."

"Jimmy, give me another chance. I will get it right this time. Let me tell you what happened."

"You missed killing the agent that you were supposed to kill. That is all that matters. You don't get a second chance on this one. We as a team get a second chance, but you don't. Now we have been given thirty-six hours to complete the mission with specific instructions not to include you. You are done for now. We've got work to do. Brady will be taking care of this."

William reached over to his computer and pressed stop.

"Hold on, are you telling me that was a live conversation and they are going to try and kill an FBI agent within the next thirty-six hours in Baltimore?" asked SAC Johnson.

"Yes, according to what we just heard."

"The shootings in Baltimore just happened, one three days ago, and one yesterday. How is it possible to capture live conversations but there not be a wiretap, a mike, or a recording?" asked SSA Smithren.

"SAC Johnson, will you tell them the rest," asked William.

"From talking to both the Navy and the Air Force last night, they explained that William has always reminded them of his main concern for his technology. He will not be selling any of his technology. With the help of the FBI, Navy, and Air Force he will develop a collaborative that everyone can agree with that allows him to manufacturing and supply the technology at the levels and quantities that we need, if we choose to utilize his technology. With today's markets to be able to experience a quantum leap in technology giving you a decided advantage in the marketplace would be incredible."

Mr. Stradom said, "Right now we are only discussing this one piece of technology. Obviously, the software will be named once we get through this phase. Either there is a high level of interest or curiosity is getting the best of us, either way we need to move beyond this quickly. There are a number of applications and scenarios that you haven't considered. Let's take a look at President Lincoln's assassination. If we were deployed twenty-four hours before his speech, every gun and its location is detected, all DNA is registered within a designated area, and all conversations will be captured."

"You're telling me that you will be able to capture conversations that are not linked to some cellular device, telephone, or satellite?" ask SSA Smithren.

"What I'm telling you is if two thousand people were in the designated area when President Lincoln was assassinated and if the same people were in the designated area today, there would still be two thousand conversations that we could listen to today," said Mr. Stradom. "Before we get too far ahead of ourselves, we can demonstrate that our technology works because this is how we got the information in Baltimore. There were a lot more than 2000 people there. I think our first priority is to find a way to catch these guys. The more time we waste; the more lives are lost. Why don't we concentrate on getting this done so that we can move on?"

"Don't you even feel bad trying to blackmail the US government into this in the middle of this crisis?" asked Tom.

"Agent Plaiedeaux," said SAC Johnson, "apparently they had this scheduled for a year, this situation just came up. He doubles his money if the FBI doesn't participate. The collaboration comes into effect if we choose to be a part of it. Literally the FBI saves the government fifty percent if we participate. The other part of that is our special projects division will be the liaison between all departments. There will be no direct contact except through your department."

Tom stood up and looked at William. "So if I decide I don't want to do this what will it cost?"

SAC Johnson started to answer and Tom interrupted him. "Excuse me sir, if you don't mind, I want to hear it from Mr. Stradom, if that's okay with you."

"It will cost the government about forty billion dollars two times over per year," said William.

"That's all."

"That's eighty billion dollars a year for the next forty years."

"So you are telling me that this deal is done either way. The government is willing to pay a guy that they don't even know his name, eighty billion dollars a year for 40 years?"

"Agent Plaiedeaux, we haven't told you everything. He has saved us more than that in the last fifteen years. His involvement was understated to you. Many projects that he chaired, he also funded we can't even discuss here. Yes, this is highly unusual, but it is also highly beneficial. He now has a proven track record of providing useful, innovative software and hardware, equipment, and inventions while being a pivotal solutions partner to the government. No one in their right mind would turn this down. I hope you are getting the picture," said SAC Johnson.

"Obviously the most important thing right now is to stop these killings. Can you actually do that?"

"We have enough information that will allow the FBI to reverse engineer the network or organization to bring the whole thing down and yes stop the senseless killings," said William.

"I do not like the way this is being done, however I also do not want any blood to be on my hands. So what now?"

"Take a step back and look at where you are at right now. You and Mr. Stradom are in a meeting room face to face having a teleconference with us. Do you get it now?"

Agent Plaiedeaux was silent for a few minutes. "I've done everything I know how to get away from him, and now it appears that I'm to be married to him. So this whole thing was somehow about getting me on board?"

"It was more like finding a way to work with Mr. Stradom and his requirements to form the collaboration that he requested and that we could agree to."

"So if I say yes, it's like I am making a decision to spend forty billion dollars a year."

"There are enough ties to the money that the statement wouldn't be too far out of bounds. However, if you say yes, you would more accurately put it as saving the government forty billion dollars," said SAC Johnson.

"So I'm saying yes, so can we get out of here and stop them from killing more agents?"

"No, we will get busy, you have some time to spend with William, off the record."

"At your word, just remember the time lines, and we I will provide the information you need to get started while agent Plaiedeaux and I have a discussion." said Mr. Stradom

"Agent Plaiedeaux, what's your decision?" asked SAC Johnson

"What if I agree today and then change my mind later on?"

"Tom, you will always have a choice. You are one man, it may seem like everything is up to you, but it's not. There is some good work to be done that will help this country as a whole. All any of us is ever responsible for is doing the best that we can with what has been put in front of us," said Mr. Stradom.

"You know I don't like making fast decisions. This is rather abrupt. However, I'm in."

"Thank you gentlemen for your time today. In about five minutes you will receive an email from agent Johnson that will put you in contact with my representative. The email will contain the contact information and directions to proceed. It will also contain directions on where to send the signed contracts. The batch of fourteen goes one place and the seven goes to another. For the sake of time the emails will be sent to SSA Plaiedeaux and you will be CC'd. Once we get past today, you will be dropped from the emails. Is everyone good?"

"Yes, I think so. Let's move forward," said SAC Johnson. "Goodbye."

Silence filled the room as the conference call ended.

Tom turned and looked William in the eye. "Why me? Am I going to get straight answers now?"

"You took a test right before you entered college and your results fit the profile of someone that I was looking for."

"What are you talking about? Wait, Wait. Are you telling me that you have been following and or monitoring me since college?"

"Yes. Since a week after you took that test."

"Why?"

"For what I do, I have a very specific profile that I needed to find to work within the FBI, and you fit the bill."

"I didn't know that I was going to end up at the FBI."

"At first I didn't know either. Once the Navy and the Air force came on board the FBI was the only one that was missing."

"Are you telling me that you chose for me to end up in this career path?"

No, we followed you and helped open doors for you. With your personality you are predisposed to working in law enforcement. Now, do you really think that you would have got in on the first time you tried without help?"

"SAC Johnson told me that they didn't know who recommended me, but that the recommendation was accepted. Enough of that for now. Answer my question. Why me?"

"You demonstrated in the meeting today why you. You have very strong ethics that you do not compromise and no one intimidates you. Do you know that they had to consult with the president himself regarding all of this? You took your time and made your own decision in the face of all of this. That's why you. You're unflappable. You are hard wired that way. They only told you part of your job. On the table over there is a package that contains the rest of it."

"What, am I going to work for you now?"

"Not exactly. My name is not important, I will be here awhile and someday someone else will take my place. The work I do here must continue."

"Are you dying?

"No, but you are going to be my protector."

"What does that mean?"

"How about you let me talk for awhile. What I do impacts hundreds of thousands of lives. If it becomes known what I do in our country even today it would be disastrous. I'm not going to share all that I am involved in because it would be too big of a burden for you, and also an unnecessary burden. I am going to have to share some things with you that you can't share with anyone."

"Hold on I'm not going to get tied up in anything illegal with anyone."

"Not quite. Nothing that I share with you and nothing that I'm doing is illegal. At some point laws may be written that will deem what we do as illegal, but as of now what we do is not illegal. I am an Acoustological Historian and we found and are able to retrieve sound from an Acoustological Reservoir."

"That doesn't mean anything to me. Am I supposed to be impressed?"

"By the way, this is one of the secrets that you are going to have to keep. No it doesn't mean a whole lot to you yet but it is going to as soon as I explain it to you. You see we have the ability to capture your voice DNA similarly to how we can capture your physical DNA. Not yet? How about this, from the time that you came into my house, I have been able to capture every single word that you have said audibly. No matter where you go no matter what you do from now until the day you die, I will be able to capture every word spoken out of your mouth."

"You used me. I guess you expect me to believe you."

"I am ready to demonstrate every little secret. I apologize for this but I need you to know that this is real. Here are the words you spoke from five nights ago starting at 11:35 PM. Do you remember where you were at then?" William turned on the machine and after a few minutes Tom told him to turn it off. "This is when you were told that you were suspended." Tom listened for a few minutes and then asked him to turn it off.

"Don't turn it back on again."

"Okay, but I want you to know that you are caught in a C-Snare, but this is the other side. I am not a criminal, because the problem with that term is that C stands for criminal. They have not yet defined a term that describes someone that is not a criminal. By the way, in the next few days I am going to be exonerated as a murder suspect after all of these years. We finally have proof that I was set up. I won't go into that now."

"So you are saying that I have been the "leak" in my office and you can capture every word that I say?"

"Everything, forever."

"Can you turn it off so that you are not capturing what I say?"

"Yes."

"Can you turn it off and later turn it back on?"

"Yes."

"How is that not illegal?"

"There are no laws written yet to regulate the capture of voice DNA from an accoustiological reservoir. They would first have to know that one exists."

"Until today, I would not have believed that there could ever be such a thing. If all of this proves to be true, do you know how dangerous this could be?"

"Yes I do. That is why control of these tools is so important. This is one of things that you will be protecting. Now if you want me to, I will turn yours off."

"Turn it off."

"It's done. Just one thought before we go any farther. Imagine that you are undercover and we have the combination of your voice and physical DNA in which we can track you. We turn it back on, they don't stand a chance. Because we know where you are, we can capture not only everyone in the room, but right now everyone in a mile radius. If you can, now think about other uses and how many people would want to get their hands on this technology. Your demonstration just showed how valuable it could be to someone. I knew everything that you knew and you had no clue that I was listening. This quasi homegrown terrorist like group that is killing agents have no clue, and will not have a clue when they are taken down. They are going to try to figure out how they got caught but are not going to be able to. Now think about if one of them had their hands on this technology and the police and the FBI didn't know. You would never catch them. This is a very powerful tool that has a first line of defense of anonymity. You are going to have immense pressure on you. The access and value that you will add to the country with the tools that we are providing are going to be immeasurable. What you don't understand yet is how the partnership works. We are not going to sell any of this technology. The government when they requisition the use of it will be leasing my operators as well. We will control its uses. We understand that with something this significant, the demand plus having people involved, it will eventually get out. You do not have the resources to stop it from getting out. You also will not have the ability to take the necessary steps to do the damage control once it does. No one in our organization knows how the systems are manufactured. They only know how to operate them. The security level we operate at is like nothing you would ever expect to see. Today, we know that humans and machines alike are vulnerable. The goal is to protect the secrets as long as possible."

"Thank you for answering plainly. I guess I might have been mistaken regarding you. Everything points to you being the opposite of what the evidence led me to believe."

"Do you remember Greg Bolden, the electrician?"

"Yes, I do."

"I sent him to you. You did not discover him."

"So, this was a setup from the beginning?"

"In a good way. You tell me how I could have approached you and told you my story and arrived where we are today."

"You couldn't have."

"Exactly. Thank you for being honest about that."

"The problem is the average evidence would have been right. There is nothing that prepares you for when the evidence is wrong. The percentages are always against the evidence being wrong. Changing the subject. Let's talk about stratum corneum. Do you know what that is?"

"No, I can't say that I do."

"Every single person in the world deals with it, the problem is medical science has only scratched the surface on its uses. For the most part it is something that is useless to the world. Every day our outer skin called the epidermis sheds roughly one million cells. Everywhere you go you are shedding skin. The dead cells are microscopic. They can't be seen by the naked eye. Our systems make the cells seem as large as donuts. So, what does that mean? We are able to capture and extract DNA Samples from those cells. We are also able to capture and retrace where you have been. It's like following a trail of bread crumbs. These things I will share with you but nobody else."

"So, you are trying to help everyone."

"I'm tasked with protecting what I do for future generations and strengthening and expanding the services we provide to become more helpful to our country."

"So you made this move so that you won't have to protect yourself from the government anymore. Now the government will protect you from themselves."

"Basically yes, as well a number of people who would not like where our resources come from to be able to do all of this, as I said, I will tell you that only. Realize, there are serious consequences if any of this gets out."

"So you are telling me that what you do is legal, but who you make your money from will cause problems, if you are found out? Why the FBI, Air Force, and Navy?"

"A threefold cord is not easily broken and it gave me coverage (Land, Air, and Water). None of you are overly political but all are very effective in what you do. In my opinion, the FBI is the most tactile in what they do. This is why I chose the FBI as the lead agency. The next step was to choose the right person in the agency. I chose you. You are the right person in the agency. Revealing our income sources would be a huge detriment to the US economy."

"Since we are off the record, what is the big secret? Why can't anyone know your real name? Why do you file your tax returns with no information? I am supposed to trust you, but you tell me there are things that you are not going to tell me. What would you do in my situation?"

"I probably would have responded the same way you did. One thing we have in common, we both do not trust easily. I won't say that I could get to the point to trust the situation and circumstances around all of this, but I would simply measure what I could by the known end results of each decision. I would take these decisions one day at a time. This would help me to build the trust that is needed. You have already started this process."

"How did I do that?"

"You realized that agents were being killed. You decided the greater good would be to embrace the situation today to stop that. That's called a "small step approach." I too would take the small step approach knowing that I have a choice each and every time."

"How can I manage something like this when I know so little about anything that is going on?"

"So, what you are telling me is that you consider yourself the smartest person in the FBI. You also know exactly everything that is going on in every department."

"No, I would say that I am one person in a large organization that has perhaps learned most of what he is supposed to in the small area that he is assigned to."

"You just said that you came to understand what role you play in the agency, and you really do not concern yourself with how the whole agency functions, because your job is simply to do your job well. I imagine that means that somehow you always seem to keep busy doing what you were hired to do. That's no different than what you are being asked to do now. You have a role to play. Get familiar and comfortable with your role and simply do your job well."

"The role makes it seem like I am being asked to be a double agent. I work both for the FBI and you or rather this mysterious organization you run."

"Your job is to oversee and protect the interest of the FBI regarding some equipment and personnel that they have under a lease contract. By doing that you will be protecting both my interest and the FBI's as well. This is not in any way similar to the requirements of being a double agent."

"That helps some. So, every time a request comes in whether it is the Navy, Air Force, or FBI, it has to come through me?"

"Yes, you and your department."

"I then have to turn around and contact you?"

"Not exactly. We have to design a system that allows us to move very quickly. Today we will video conference with Thayor Marcus. He will be the one that will be answering the calls when you want to deploy our assets. Between you, he, and I, we will work out the communication piece so that it is as smooth and painless as possible."

"You said video conference. Who is this guy and what is he to you? You are actually going to introduce me to someone else in your organization?"

"Yes, he is our company representative and he will be the liaison between you and the assets that you want to be employed."

"What is his official title for your company?"

"Company Representative."

"Will there be a specific company that he will represent?"

"No, he will represent all of my interest that are known to him and he will be contacted exclusively by you."

"Will anyone know what those interests are?"

"No."

"This is getting to be like a broken record. I get it. Let's move on. Where will you and I stand once he comes on board?"

"We will continue to cultivate our working relationship."

"What if I get into trouble with one of the government agencies regarding the lease contract?"

"You won't."

"That doesn't help me."

"The contracts have stipulations and or penalties to protect the interest of the FBI and the government even from itself. Let's say that the Air Force decides that they want access to the equipment so that they can manufacture their own. If they attempt this through legal channels or some sort of covert operation the use of the equipment for Air Force purposes will be suspended and they will have to pay several billion dollars per year until they are reinstated."

"Wow. Who would notify them of their suspension?"

"You would. You would be in charge of all enforcement proceedings."

"What if it were the FBI rather than another agency?"

"That is where it will get interesting. In that case, Thayor would be in charge of all enforcement. However, every department that has had access to the equipment will be suspended along with the FBI and every department will have to pay several billion dollars per year in penalties until the suspension is lifted."

"For how long?"

"Until the 40-year contract is up."

"If any of that happens, what happens to me?"

"Nothing. The requirement is that there has to be an approved administrator of the contracts in place at all times whether everyone is suspended are not. If there is not an approved administrator in place at any time, then the penalties are doubled at a minimum of 12 months and could exceed 12 months if no administrator has been assigned upon completion of the 12 months. Having no administrator triggers suspension of all services as well."

"So, they would have to be willing to pay billions of dollars if they chose to get rid of me."

"Yes."

"What if I died in a car accident?"

"Then there would be no administrator."

"Why should it cost the government billions of dollars because I died in a car accident?"

"You just became the most valuable employee in the government from a cash perspective, it is their responsibility to take that in consideration when you are driving."

"Wait a minute. I guess I'm done with field work. Do I even get to drive anymore?"

"If it wasn't you, what would you recommend to the company that had an employee that was required and posed such a financial risk at the same time?"

"I would do whatever I could to minimize the risk. How is the government going to explain me living like this? There are no SSA's that can live like that. I will have to live in a secure compound or something."

"They are not going to have to explain it. You have been investing in a publicly traded software company for years, next week your common stock shares will complete an unprecedented conversion to preferred stock which will be bought out and the shares bought out. The net result is you will make approximately thirty-eight million dollars after taxes. This is not insider trading. The transaction has already been complete. The stocks are frozen right now because of the transaction. By next week you will have the money in hand."

"I'm going to have thirty-eight million dollars next week?"

"Yes, your broker will be contacting you so that you can tell him what to do with the money."

"What am I going to do with that kind of money?"

"You are going to need it. You've had a few small financial issues in the past. Nothing that will cause you to get in trouble on your job, of course. You are going to be secretly investigated, but proved to be innocent. Here is a business card of a financial advisor that can help you. His name is Jonathan Mays. He will know exactly how to set up everything so that you are financially protected. No one has to know how you manage your money once you receive it. What matters is that you will have the ability to hire your own driver, buy your own secured car, and your own security. You will not have to put that on the agency. This is a decision that you need to make to protect your public image. Also, you will get a significant pay increase to compensate you for your new responsibilities as an SSA. Be aware that just because you choose your driver and security personnel, and pay for them, it doesn't mean that they aren't going to want to train them and sign off on them. That's okay. They have to be sure that you are protected."

"What if I said no? Would all of this still have happened?"

"You would have been fine. Based on your personality profile, you will need to immediately enroll in some management training courses that are job specific. Due to the nature of the courses you will be attending classes that are only one to one teacher student ratio. The classes are paid for by the contractor as a part of the agreement with the FBI."

"You want me trained specifically to handle things the way that you want them to be handled."

"I hope by now you see that we too have a significant investment in you along with the government. Not everyone is going to be happy to see you transition into your new position. Many will feel like something illegal is going on. You are going to encounter some of the same resistance that I encountered with you. In most cases you are not going to have the luxury of solving their issues. They are going to want to ask you questions that you cannot answer. This will be difficult for you. No one in your command structure will be allowed to order you to do anything that violates our contracts or the spirit of our contracts. Someone that is in a similar position that you are in is Thayor. He can be a resource for you and he has been trained specifically for the position that he serves in. Your "Angie" situation is over now. She will not be bothering you anymore."

"Did you have her killed?"

"You really didn't want the FBI having to handle a delicate situation like that. You are too close to them. It would have never worked out. No, we did not kill her. That's all you need to know."

"Okay! I really don't want to know. So, when do I get to meet Thayor?"

"In about two minutes. Remember that SAC Johnson is setting up everything but it is you that has to lead them to close out things starting today. They can only go so far."

"Okay."

"We can continue eating our late lunch while we talk to Thayor." William reached over and pushed a button on the keyboard of his computer. The video screen turned on revealing Thayor sitting at his desk.

"Good afternoon William and Tom, I'm sorry Tom I don't know how to pronounce your last name."

"That's okay, most people don't know how to pronounce it. That's not necessarily a bad thing. Thayor is not that common either."

"That's a long story also. I gather that since I'm getting to meet you that you are in as well?"

"Yes. It was a hard sale, but I am in."

"We both came that way. I imagine there was a huge information dump followed by a short fuse on a required decision."

"Something like that."

"For what we are going to be doing, it is more than likely the best way to do it. If it was done any other way, we would probably just mess it up."

"I imagine one of your fields of study was psychology?"

"Yes, it was required."

"Forgive me if I try to cut this short. You are going to be my primary contact and liaison. William can we pick this up after we close out this project?"

"Yes, Tom we can pick this up later. Thayor, why don't you give him your number so that he can call you. You guys don't need me to get to know each other. However, Tom you will need to conference and introduce Thayor to your team before we conference to set up the final strategy. They have already spoken to Thayor, however for the sake of convenience they did so without knowing his name."

"It was good to meet you Thayor, I look forward to us getting together soon. I imagine you know that we have some pressing matters to resolve."

"Yes, I do. I'm available as soon as you are ready to move forward."

"William if it is okay with you I'm going to head to the office."

"Sure, I think you probably forgot something, though."

"What's that?"

"How did you get here?"

"Oh yeah. I got here by helicopter. I need to call them."

"That's okay, I took the liberty of ordering you a car and driver, and the driver doubles as security. This can be temporary or you can buy the car and hire the driver if you approve of them."

"You never stop do you?"

"There is nothing gained by delaying what is necessary."

"Tom paused for a minute, looked around and then looked at William, shook his head and walked out the door."

Chapter Thirty-Five

As Tom stepped into the car he called SSA Smithren. "Chief I am on my way to the office, where are we at with the information that we were given?"

"Tom, you are going to have to talk to SAC Johnson about that. I can tell you a little bit but there is so much to this. I was assigned the task of securing warrants in the different states. This is the largest operation that I have ever been a part of. The data that they have given us is so specific and detailed that it is almost as if a militia has written an autobiography of everything and every person that is involved and handed it to us. We are going to need you to do your part so that we can finish this. By the way where are you?"

"I'm on my way back to the office."

"Did you call for the chopper?"

"No, I got a ride. I will explain it later. Why are we calling them a militia?"

"They are a lot more than that; it is an organized crime group, with a slight twist. They seem to have their own system of government, some system of taxation, and they have their own military. They are into, drugs, prostitution, gambling, murder, gun running, and many other things. It is a monster."

"Can you transfer me to SAC Johnson?"

"Sure. But before I do; how did it go between you and William?"

"I don't know how to answer that. Let's just say for now it appears that I have been his puppet. There is too much going on right now, but when I get a chance I will have to decide whether that is good or bad. Sorry, we will talk but I need to talk to Johnson right now."

"Okay, let me transfer you."

"Good afternoon SAC Johnson."

"Hello agent Plaiedeaux. Are you done with William?"

"I'm not sure about that but I am on the way to the office."

"How quickly will you get here?"

"I should be there in about fifteen minutes."

"Is the chopper flying that slow?"

"No sir. I caught a ride. I will explain later."

"Okay, we have a plan; we just need you to sign off on it."

"I will be there quickly. Sir I need to tell you something. I will have someone with me when I arrive at the office. It's going to seem strange."

"Just say it agent Plaiedeaux.

"My security will be there with me."

"Security. You have security of your own?"

"Yes sir."

"We are all going to have to do whatever it takes."

"I'm also going to need a place for my car when I get there."

"It will be taken care of."

"Do you know the number of locations we are talking about hitting?"

"We should know by the time you get here."

"I assume that you already have someone requisitioning personnel."

"Yes, it is going to be all hands on deck."

"What conference room are you in?"

"We are in 13B."

"Good I will see you in a few of minutes. How quickly do you expect to be able to move?"

"We will be pulling an all nighter. So we are hoping to be able to move by tomorrow afternoon. The only unknown is how quickly your team can deploy."

"Let's talk strategy when I get to the office."

Tom called Thayor. "Hello, Thayor, this is Tom. Sorry for the abrupt change of direction, I just thought we didn't have a lot of time."

"No problem. I assumed that you are using a sectional transitional phone?"

"Yes I am. It is standard issue for us."

"I may need to have several hundred of the team deployed by tomorrow afternoon. How long of a lead time do you normally need for these things?"

"We know that most of our responses particularly at first will be done in crisis. So we are prepared for whatever you can throw at us. Though we are responding in crisis, we will still have to keep in mind our long range objectives."

"So, you will be a resource to help solve an immediate problem, but ever conscious of how it impacts our ability to solve other problems tomorrow. So it will probably be more efficient if you guys were a part of the strategic planning in each event."

"Since we know more about the equipment that we are deploying and its capabilities, us being a part of the strategic planning will certainly make our collaboration more fluid."

"Are you going to make that simple?"

"It will be simple for us, maybe difficult in concept for you."

"What's the catch?"

"Our team leader will need to be unnamed and have a non-speaking role."

"He will basically listen in, and if he has suggestions give them to you and you speak them?"

"Technically, he will speak, but it will not be his voice that you are hearing. It will not sound like a computer generated voice either. He will never be introduced not even with an alias. No one will meet him. For today, he, William and I will be a part of the strategy session. They can video conference me and voice conference William and he in."

"Will they ever meet you in person?"

"Yes, but it may be in your best interest not to."

"What do you mean by that?"

"When you decide you want to meet me, there are contractual protocols that come into play. The consequences for violating the protocols are very costly. The temptation or opportunity to be put in the position of violation is minimized by us avoiding face to face meetings. You are the FBI. At some point someone is going to look at the protocols and think that they have figured out how to beat them. They will make the recommendation to the leadership that it can be done, and leadership will go along with it. We do expect that every protocol will be tested. It is in your nature. Those violations will be costly. We will not be swayed by public opinion. When there is a violation, there are punitive damages that will go into effect. Each penalty will be exercised to its fullest."

"I just pulled up to the office. I will get back to you in a few minutes. I will video conference with you to make introductions. I will introduce everyone else who will attend as well. I'll talk to you in a minute or two Thayor."

When Tom hung up the phone, his driver began to speak to him. "Sir, I will remind you that my name is Reginald, but everyone calls me Reggie. I will need you to remain in the car until they show us to secure parking."

"Okay Reggie. I think that's them coming toward us."

Reggie pulled into the location that was designated for them. He locked the car and proceeded to walk with Tom into the building.

"Reggie I'm headed to a conference room on the 13th floor. There will be several senior management people and some other agents in the room. What do you need to do for the meeting?"

"I will go in the room with you just to take a look around, once I see that it is safe then I will leave the room and stand outside the door. Take this sir. It looks like a pen, but it is an alarm. You need to keep it near you at all times. Just push it and it will alert me that something is wrong and let me know exactly where you are at."

"We will work on all of this at a later time. I am good with that for now."

"Good afternoon SAC Johnson, and everyone else. Please excuse Reggie he will be in here just for a moment. Sir, you want to bring me up to speed."

"This one is going to be a little different. Normally, when we close these big cases, we get a couple of leaders and mostly foot soldiers. What we actually have is an entire leadership structure with evidence of them participating in the conspiracy to commit murder. Every murder has to be sanctioned by their board, when the board makes the decision; it is passed down through the organization to the foot soldiers that will carry out the order to kill. We have names and addresses of where they are right now and where they will be for their next planned murder. We also have confessions of some of the past murders and DNA records tying them to the crime scene. There's so much data that we may need some help on understanding how it ties to the crimes. I've never been involved in a case where there is so much data. I'm curious about how this works."

"So what resources have been requisitioned for deployment?"

"We have 67 sites like warehouses, buildings, restaurants, etc. We have another 138 homes. Through collaboration we can hit all of them over the next two weeks."

"So based on your plan, how many do you expect us to collar in the next two weeks?"

"The percentages are usually a lot lower than this. But we expect something like 25%. Once you start all the others scatter. We will eventually get some of the rest. It will take some time. Back to resources, we should have our warrants in the morning, we have the permission for wire taps, we have temporary holding set up in all of the towns. For a few we had to resolve some placement issues because of family, relatives, friends, or VIP status in the communities. We have booked flights and hotels. We just don't know how many will be on your team."

"Thank you, sir. Let's go ahead and conference with my team. I think their perspective may help some. Now the man that you spoke to today who sent you all of this information is Thayor Marcus. He is the company representative. He will be the primary liaison for us. His job is to coordinate any and all deployments and to be our resource in the case of any media events. We will video conference him in while William and one other person will phone conference in. I have approved this way of communicating, so let's get through this and we will have time later to discuss policy and philosophies about who we communicate with."

"We will talk later," said SAC Johnson.

"I look forward to it."

"Now let's make the calls."

"Hello, everyone," said Thayor. "It is okay if we don't go through with all of the introductions, it will be too many names to remember. I also have one other person with me. William, are you here yet?"

"Yes, I am here."

"William this is Tom. I just had a briefing and we would like to deploy in about 205 different locations. What we need to determine is how many locations and how quickly can we deploy. It may not be all at once but over the next two weeks, we plan to carry everything out."

"What is your expected percentage of capture?" asked William.

"Initially about 25%."

"With our resources you can increase that number to 100%."

"That's ridiculous, I would say more like impossible," said SAC Johnson.

"I stand by what I said, 100%. We also expect to do it without incident."

"How do you plan to pull that off?"

"We will deploy P.A.W.L. and he will take care of everything. He will be able to do a couple of things. One disable all guns within the area, two recognize every person in each building and give us the exact location in each facility."

"How is he going to do that in all the locations? Won't it take forever?" asked SAC Johnson.

"P.A.W.L. (Preemptive Anti Weapons Limiter) is not a he, it is a piece of equipment. We are ready with your permission to deploy it at every site. It is a chameleon robotic computer like organism. Its job is to interface with the environment in a way that is totally undetectable. While there it will capture all measurements of the environment and detect every weapon on the premises and every living thing. Not only will you know the location of every living thing, but also you will have video of it all. This includes environments with electricity and environments without it. One other thing. While the functions I just described happen automatically upon deployment, there are countless actions that can be taken with a simple command. One example is, it can deactivate every weapon within the specific radius that it is empowered to affect. How much time we have can greatly affect the radius of the environment it is able to limit."

"I have never heard of this. I am on the forefront of technology and I have never heard of anything remotely like this," said Deputy Director Jones. "That's like something straight out of science fiction."

"I knew that this was going to be difficult for you. So we arranged a little demonstration for you," said William. "P.A.W.L. move over to just above the conference table and set your projection system to the south wall from there."

P.A.W.L. moved slowly out of the door and hovered about two feet above the conference table. He turned his projector toward the south wall.

"Display the location of every person in the building and reveal the count of people and the number of weapons on every floor. Skip the thirteenth floor with that command and I will have different orders for the thirteenth floor."

P.A.W.L. did as he was commanded. When he completed his instructions he asked if there were further instructions.

"William told him to only count the people and weapons in this room, but to list the weapons by the individual who is carrying them and the serial number on each of the weapons.

P.A.W.L. completed the task as well.

"Are you telling me that you can actually deactivate a gun so it doesn't fire?"

"Agent Smithren, and or agent Plaiedeaux I will let you answer that question."

"Yes it can," said SSA Plaiedeaux. "I actually experienced it firsthand. I believe that one of my guns is actually still inactivated. SSA Smithren would you confirm that?"

"We still have not been able to use the gun since it was deactivated".

"So when you pull the trigger what happens?" asked deputy director Jones.

"Nothing"

"Did you change out the bullets and try?"

"Yes, and nothing."

"Can the gun be reactivated?"

"Yes it can," said William.

"P.A.W.L. stay where you are for now." said deputy director Jones.

"P.A.W.L. has a subatomic voice recognition system. It's pretty complex, but basically you are not going to be able to give it orders without the security clearance to do so."

"Can he pick up everything that we say?"

"Yes if the command is given to him to do that. He can not only pick up everything you say, but he can pick up who is saying it in video real time."

"Are you saying if people are having conversations throughout the building, he can pick them up all simultaneously and recognize every person who is speaking as well?"

"Yes, provided we deploy the right P.A.W.L."

"With the right radial coverage?" asked deputy director Jones.

"How do you suppose we achieve 100%?" asked SSA Smithren.

"We made some assumptions and even as we speak our teams have already been deployed. All of our equipment has been strategically placed. Correct me if I am wrong, but we are set to be able to limit all of the sites simultaneously tomorrow, while putting all the assailants to sleep" said Thayor.

"That is correct," said William.

"We don't have the resources yet to move on all of the sites tomorrow," said SAC Johnson.

"What is missing?" asked Tom.

"Manpower. In order to do this, we would have to shut down quite a lot of activities that are going on," said SAC Johnson.

"Anybody have any suggestions."

"I think we are missing the point of the collaboration. What if I asked you the question in another way? I don't know how much manpower you have projected to allocate so far, but we are using the term militia to describe what we are dealing with. If that is the case, then shouldn't your resources be greater than just what you can scrounge from the FBI?" asked Thayor?

"This does call for some thinking outside of the box. I think Thayor is right. Let me make a call," said William.

"Hold on a minute, if you are talking about the Air Force or Navy, they are outside of our command structure," said SAC Johnson.

"Yes they are. Perhaps even different philosophies as well. They also have a centralized command structure which is strictly adhered to. That is enough to get us more than half the way there. There is no time like the present to kick this collaboration off. I just need to know how many people we need."

"We would need at least a hundred and fifty," said SAC Thompson.

"Will any of them need to be lead onsite?"

"We would deploy them two by two to the houses. There would need to be 75 leads."

"This is crazy why can't we consider the first plan?" asked deputy director Jones.

"They have struck at the foundation of law enforcement in our country; this is a necessary and appropriate response to their actions. They need to know that they have awakened the giant."

"Sir, all you will need to do is call Commander Stallings and he will set up a briefing for his team so that they will be ready to go tomorrow. This will need to get a lot of press so that everyone will know of the collaboration. We will not be mentioned and none of the technology will be mentioned either," said William. "Tom, you can coordinate with

Thayor and Commander Stallings to prepare for your media event. While we want to give credit to each agency, what we don't want is to give them access to anybody other than a representative. You should have a speech supplemented by a few answers to some questions that makes it look like the representative is very knowledgeable. You do this and you take away from them the ability to retaliate. You are basically taking their stealthy mode of operation and using it against them. The last recommendation is not to address that they were all asleep. Just say that all of the arrests were without incident."

"This is to be classified top secret and nothing discussed in this room can be mentioned outside of this room," said SAC Johnson.

"Now we have some other issues to discuss," said Thayor. "We need to think about our future collaboration. If the militia is able to communicate after their arrest, they will know that all of their weapons malfunctioned at the same time. They will know that something is up. They may not know what, but they will know something is up. This will put the criminal world on the path to looking for answers about what happened. We need to do this with a twofold process. We should do it while they are asleep and the weapons are limited. If we do it in that order, they will never know that their weapons were limited. They will wonder why they were all asleep at the same time, but they will not be able to establish a cause. They will only be looking for why they were asleep. This will allow us to complete the arrests without incident," said Thayor.

"How will we get them to sleep all at once?" asked deputy director Jones.

"This is considered an act of terror right?" asked Thayor.

"Yes, it is," said SAC Johnson.

"Then P.A.W.L. will convince them to go to sleep."

"Are you saying that "PAWL" will be able to convince the ones inside and outside of the perimeter to sleep?"

"Yes," said Thayor. "Now you see why there shouldn't be complications with the arrests."

"P.A.W.L. you can retire now by joining the conference table," said William.

P.A.W.L. turned off the projector and then assimilated into the conference table. He disappeared right before their eyes.

Deputy director Jones, reached over to touch the table where PAWL had landed. "You can't even tell that it is there."

"That was only the point of entry. It is not there anymore," said William.

"That's crazy."

"Do we have a plan?" asked William.

"I will call Commander Stallings," said SSA Plaiedeaux, "since my department is supposed to be the liaison between divisions."

Chapter Thirty-Six

Tom gave everyone instructions and let them know that they would reconvene in two hours. He went back to his office to review all of the recordings. He recognized that there was something missing and called Thayor. "On any of the voice recordings has there been any mention of what this group calls themselves?"

"No one has mentioned anything about a name of the organization."

"I know the board members are on your list. Can you isolate their conversations and run through them to see if we can pick up anything that will let us know what they call themselves?"

"Let me get back to you. I believe that we can."

"Good, let me know."

During his call to Commander Stallings he let the Commander know that he would like him to participate in the conference call that they would be having in a couple of hours. Commander Stallings agreed.

As he sat down at his desk, SSA Smithren knocked at the door.

"Come on in chief."

"Well, Tom, quite a change for you. Are you okay with all of this?"

"I'm not sure if okay is the right word. I just became someone completely different than I ever expected to be. In a matter of days everything about my life changed. It appears that even though I had a choice to do the right thing, it felt like I didn't have a choice."

"You can do this Tom."

"How will I be perceived by the other agents?"

"I'm a bit of a historian and I have never seen anyone in the position that you are in. You are a first of your kind in the agency, for that matter probably in any agency. Let's set that aside for now. Whatever this is that is causing agents to be killed needs to be stopped. We now appear to have the upper hand because of your willingness to do this. If this is what it takes to get there it is worth it. I imagine that if you had chosen not to do this it would have come about some other way. If this works, think of how many lives will be saved. You have been a good agent. Can I stand here right now and say that you deserve this? Nobody can actually say that with enough knowledge to know it to be true."

"Yesterday, I was an average agent living the life of an average agent. Today, I am a guy who will live his life in limousines, with security, and millions of dollars. I will have no real peers. I will no longer be able to be just one of the boys."

"This may not seem like it to you, but all of us know that we have to make sacrifices in order to serve our country. Many of the ones that have gone before us have even sacrificed their lives. We may have a definition of sacrificing our lives that is to narrowly defined; especially if the only way that we are willing to sacrifice our lives is through our physical deaths. You would gladly sacrifice your life if it meant that someone else lived because of your physical death. When we chose our paths, our choice meant that we were choosing not to do many things as well. You are unique in the fact that you are the only person I know that I can say that the life of prominence is truly sacrificial living for you. I just talked myself into understanding why they chose you. There will be many envious of you with no clue of the burden that you will carry. By the way, someday, if you don't mind, maybe you can explain the millionaire piece to me."

"Someday, maybe I will. Thank you chief."

"Don't get me wrong, I don't think it is going to be easy for you."

"I'm getting that. I need to have some time before the meeting."

"You take care of yourself. I will be here for you as long as you want me to be."

"I know that chief. I'm not going anywhere."

"You can't help it. You already have, whether you can admit it or not. Listen, I'll see you in a few minutes."

"Tom closed the door behind SSA Smithren as he walked out the door. He walked back and forth in his office as he had done many times before so he could acquire the familiar calming effect of his alone time. This time it failed him. No matter what he did, he was not able to get to that place where he was comfortable. He didn't know what to think of that. After looking through some files on his computer, he looked over at his watch to see that he had about fifteen minutes, until the meeting. He picked up the phone and called William.

"Good evening agent Plaiedeaux, are you ready for your meeting?"

"As ready as I will ever be. Are you ready?"

"This is your show now, Tom. I am just along for the ride."

"How many friends do you have?"

"I really don't have the luxury of gathering friends. It has been a necessary sacrifice because of what I do. Now, did I know that from the beginning? No. I'm not sure exactly when I figured it out, but I can tell you that at some point I made a conscious decision to accept it for the greater good. You didn't ask me all of that, but I guessed at where you were heading."

"Did you ever get married?"

"I can't answer that question for you or anybody."

"Can P.A.W. L. be hacked?"

"Yes and no. He can be hacked from inside our network right now."

"Are there more things that it is capable of?"

"Yes, much more."

"Do you have any suggestions?"

"No, but you can always talk to Thayor, he will be a true strategic asset for you."

"You're having nothing to add because you are pushing Thayor and me out front?"

"Yes. These first meetings are going to establish the foundation of your relationships with the teams. I made some suggestions to Thayor that will help with your request. It is important that everyone involved view you and Thayor as a key component of the mission, not me."

"Let's head into the meeting."

"Good afternoon everyone. For now, for the sake of time, let's move ahead Thayor."

"Yes sir, I found what you asked me to find."

"I'm sorry, everyone, I've asked Commander Stallings to attend this meeting. He has joined us and supplied some needed help we asked for to complete the mission in its entirety."

"Sir they call themselves the "Black Light.""

"Would you repeat what you said?" asked Commander Stallings

"SSA Plaiedeaux asked me to check and see if anyone in their organization had mentioned what their organization was called. In one of their meetings, they were called the "Black light." Does that mean something to you?"

"Yes, said Commander Stallings. Yes, it does. There was a Navy Seal named "Gregory Plankton" that used to go by, "Black Light". He was nicknamed that because he seemed to operate like one of those crime scene infrared cameras. You put him in the dark and there was almost nothing that he couldn't do or see. He was highly intelligent and deadly. He became increasingly hard to manage. He is a highly decorated ex-Naval Officer. We counseled him on many occasions. When it came time for him to re-enlist, he dropped out of sight. The last I heard he had made an attempt to join the FBI."

"What was the big deal about him," asked SAC Johnson.

"He was very confident in everything he did. Honestly, he probably had good reason to be. He flat out got things done. The problems arose when you said no to his ideas. Toward the end of his enlistment, he must have been written up three times for insubordination in his last six months. He just would not accept no from any commanding officer. If it is him, his work required him to be very brutal. He would die before he accepted no from someone he thought was inferior to him. He also would not start a fight that he didn't think he could win. He may have some other Seals on his team that were fans of his work."

"Can we get a photo of this guy? His name hasn't come up, but he could be using an alias," said Thayor.

"How long has it been since he separated from the Navy,' asked SSA Plaiedeaux.

"Probably, fifteen years ago."

"Do you think he would plan this long to retaliate?"

"I think he would. He was the type that never would give up. Like I said earlier, he wouldn't be doing this if he didn't think somehow he was going to win. Something must have happened recently that made him think that he could win now."

"All the more reason for us to move now," said Tom. "Let's name this mission "Operation Light's On", said Tom. "We've got Washington DC, Maryland, New York, Ohio, Illinois, Arizona, Utah, Wyoming, West Virginia, Oklahoma, Texas, New Jersey, and Tennessee to cover. Thayor are your people in place?"

"Yes, they are."

"How will the rest of the team be able to identify them?"

"They won't have to they will never see them."

"Just in case."

"Sir, they will never see them. Command will be their point of contact only. Since I am command to them, I will be with you during this time."

"SAC Johnson."

"Most of the teams will be in place by 4:30 PM central time. I expect all of them to be in place by 6:30."

"SSA Smithren."

"All of the warrants should be completed by 2:00 PM central time. I will just need to coordinate with the teams, so that I know who to get the warrants to."

"Get in touch with deputy director Jones. He will coordinate the distribution of warrants," said SAC Johnson.

"Commander Stallings."

"Our team should be in place by no later than 8:00 PM."

"Are there any problems with any local authorities?" asked SSA Smithren.

"We have solved all of the conflicts that we are aware of."

"Since this is considered an act of terror, we will be able to sidestep local politics through our rapid transfer process. We will have to deal with local politics after we transfer the prisoners," said deputy director Jones.

"Since we have three different time zones we are dealing with we will strike at 1:30 AM central time," said SSA Plaiedeaux.

"You need to make the call before we finalize the time," said Commander Stallings. "SAC Johnson, give him the number."

"What number? What call?"

"You need to call the President."

"The President of the United States?"

"Yes, you need to make the call."

Tom looked around the room and slowly walked over to SAC Johnson.

"I will be back in a minute."

"Tom stepped out the conference room into the hall to make the call."

Within a few minutes, he walked back in the room. "It's a go."

"One question," said Thayor. "How are we handling the actual media event in case of any inquiries?"

"Any calls will be routed through agent Smithren's secretary, and we have assembled a team of representatives from each agency for any media events. The president will call SAC Johnson if he feels like anything else needs to be done. If we get flooded with calls, then we have an automatic response message," said SSA Smithren. "Any media people that tries to circumvent this system will be routed back through this call system. Is there any other questions or comments?"

"We haven't discussed the courts in dealing with the legal battles that we will face," said SAC Johnson

"I will deliver them to you SAC Johnson," said SSA Plaiedeaux. "I will make sure that you have the evidence that you need to convict them. You will deal with the court systems, the lawyers and whatever else goes with convicting them. Once we get them, the ball will be in your court. I will be available if you need me."

"I've already talked to a federal judge. We will be ready," said SAC Johnson.

"Sir the handheld communication systems are being delivered as we speak. Everyone should have them prior to departure except for your team," said deputy director Jones.

"You do not need to get any to our team. The system that they have is compatible with your system," replied Thayor.

"Anything else," asked SSA Plaiedeaux.

"Agent Plaiedeaux, your new office will be ready for you on Monday and your secretary will be in place by then as well. Also, your parking issue will be resolved by then as well. Sorry, I'm not sure if I will see you before then," said SAC Johnson.

"Thank you sir," said SSA Plaiedeaux.

"Agent Plaiedeaux, are we also good with the situation in Baltimore?" asked SSA Johnson.

"If you are talking about the timing of their next planned attack, Thayor do you know where we are with that?"

"Yes sir, they got an extension on time until Monday morning outside of the federal building. We are good with that. By getting the extension, they are now required to kill two agents instead of one. We are monitoring every conversation. We will hand off the information to whoever you designate so that they can be apprehended prior to completing their required goal. This may not happen considering the timing. During our initial sweep tomorrow night, we should pick them up."

"Okay. I will need the teams to let me know when they are in place. You can do it by department. Once this is confirmed, then we will require radio silence until about thirty minutes before go time for "Operation Lights On". This conference room will continue to serve as the command center for the length of this mission until capture. Because of the timing, we have targeted suspects that have become visible to us. There are probably many more of them that will come after this."

"Agent Plaiedeaux, we are still reviewing the large quantity of data that we are receiving, however based on the data I received this afternoon, all of the shooters of the FBI agents seem to be accounted for in this first raid," said Thayor.

"I know this was done in a hurry. It was both necessary and prudent that we move this way. I know that there are lots of moving parts, people out of their comfort zones, all of this is where we are right now, but it is not where we are going to remain. In the next couple of days, we are going to make history. All of our training has prepared us for this and will get us through this, now let's go and make our country proud," said Tom.

"Give Thayor and I the room for a few minutes." Everyone quickly dispersed.

"Thayor, you seem rather comfortable with your role."

"It's my training sir. However, you do realize that this is my first meeting of this kind."

"So, how did you do it?"

"If you are talking about all of the information I was disseminating, an earpiece goes a long way sir."

"Thank you for your honesty."

"By the way sir, you seem to be fairly comfortable yourself."

"You do not serve in any military capacity, call me Tom not sir."

"What has changed?"

"We are going to need each other. In the middle of all of this I couldn't help but notice the comparable positions that we are in. I have to admit that PAWL's demonstration was like watching a science fiction movie come to life. Even though it wasn't my first time seeing it work, it was no less impressive. I still can't wrap my mind around it."

"That was my first time to see PAWL at work."

"Do you go by another name besides Thayor?"

"No, not really. I think the name was so different that people couldn't relate to it well enough to give me a nickname. So, are you okay, or rather do you need anything Tom?"

"Yes and no. I need this to work. We are going to go through this process of getting to know each other. I wanted to reassure you that I wasn't disrespecting you earlier. I can get very focused sometimes. From my understanding, you won't necessarily be in future meetings."

"We will play that by ear. I think both of us will do what we can to ensure that this partnership is a success. I do have confidence that we will be successful in Operations Lights On."

"Let's call William," said Tom.

"William, I still have Thayor on video. It is just the three of us. Do you have anything to say?"

"Tom, how did it go with the President?" asked William.

"I will admit that was surreal. Everything was okay until that point. I kind of understood how important this operation was, but not really. When he answered the phone, it all just sat on me. I'm now reporting directly to the most powerful man in the world. It seemed crazy but I got over it."

"The thing you said just sat on you is called a Destiny Jacket. It will be uncomfortable at first, but you need to get use to it. I hope both of you now know how necessary you are to our country and the world. You were both put here on purpose. Now, be clear on this. You both need to grasp hold of the distinction between you and the people you will be working with. They understand being elected and appointed to a position because they are both temporary positions. You two have been chosen. Most people who are elected or appointed don't understand people who are chosen. I'm not going to explain everything to you right now, but you will come to understand it. Over the next few years of your lives you will come to understand the distinction and embrace it."

Over the following two days the joint task force arrested 272 Black Light members including Gregory Plankton their leader, without incident. They were all transported to temporary holding cells overnight and then transferred within 24 hours to undisclosed locations to await trial. 100% of the targeted suspects were arrested and incarcerated. Never before had the FBI or any government agency or agencies ever been so successful. The media became extremely frustrated with the fact that they were told of the joint task force, but could not report on any details other than the fact that there were 272 arrests and that they were all without incident. The rest of the Black Light group scattered because they didn't know how their leaders were captured and who could be trusted that remained in their organization.

Made in the USA
San Bernardino, CA
21 March 2017